# Murder at the Asylum

by

Richard Alumbaugh

**Murder at the Asylum**

Cover Art by *The Wild Rose Press, Inc.*

The Wild Rose Press, Inc.
PO Box 708
Adams Basin, NY 14410-0708
Visit us at www.thewildrosepress.com

Publishing History
First Edition, 2023
Trade Paperback ISBN 978-1-5092-5101-8
Digital ISBN 978-1-5092-5102-5


Published in the United States of America

"Let me be clear. We will use every legal means to gain access to witnesses. Make no mistake the public will demand this. That means witnesses will be subpoenaed if that's what it takes," Turpin added.

"I cannot and will not force Nurse Best to violate her confidentiality oath to patients. I will not break that trust. And there is one other consideration. I will protect our patients' privacy. Most of our patients have been adjudicated by Cook County courts as incompetent due to mental disease or defect. Ask your prosecutor. How do you subpoena an incompetent witness?"

"Here you sit in this beautiful office with a nice view and an attractive secretary with the full blessing of the administration. Tell me. Do you ever get involved with the outside world? You know—townsfolks? If you did, you would see how this murder has affected many. People are frightened. They want answers. Rumors are circulating that a nutcase is running loose somewhere in this hospital," Turpin said.

# Dedication

To Mental Health Reformers

Chapter 1

*Halloween 1970*

"Did you ever wonder how we caught such a disease as 'mental illness?'" Shannon Audrey asked.

Maggie Nilsson, a fellow patient at the Illinois asylum, shrugged. "It's simple. We're too trusting of others."

"You've got that right." Shannon rolled her eyes. "I trusted the court would see through the lies of my ex. He convinced our doctor and a judge to put me away so he could take up with his secretary."

"Yes. Nobody believes me that people are stealing my thoughts to make sure I don't interfere with my son's total control of the estate."

Shannon lagged behind Maggie as Linda Best, a psychiatric nurse, directed patients to the new aquarium, remodeled from a former hydrotherapy clinic. Audrey stared at the building unable to crowd out the memories of the tubs or Fred Hepp's office. Shannon rehearsed how she might enter Hepp's office if she could avoid detection. It was very risky.

Shannon wondered if the evidence was still there to prove Hepp aka 'Hippo' raped Vesta Diaz in his office? Vesta told her a week before her psychosurgery of how Hippo had forced her to his office and slammed her over his desk. Vesta told me her screams were muted by his

1

large hand with a distinctive alcohol scent. Her head was forced backward with such force she feared he would break her neck. Hippo weighed over 300 pounds and had no problem forcing Vesta to submit to repeated assaults.

Shannon recalled her own run-ins with Hippo. Patients showing any reluctance to enter the baths, particularly the very cold tubs, were targets of his attacks with a knotted wet towel. The blows left no lasting mark other than a reddened area that were regarded by ward staff as a byproduct of the therapy. Patients screamed from the pain of the blow, yet ignored by staff at the baths. All ultimately yielded. The shock of the cold water was preferable to enduring any further painful strikes.

Patients resisting his blows to the head or butt were escorted to his office and threatened with harsher forms of treatment if they continued their resistance. Most patients realized their very survival was dependent on avoiding Hippo at all costs.

Since the staff refused to take serious reports of his brutality, Hippo took on the role of an enforcer at the Cook County Center.

Linda Best made her way forward. The heavy steel door had a small reinforced window. The mix of young and old, men and women, some shuffling, others with uncontrollable tics, and some with blank looks with their heads turned down, remained silent as the nurse paused at the entrance and turned toward them with the blinding morning sun in the background.

"Let's check if anyone is missing." Reviewing her list, Nurse Best did a quick count and confirmed, "Everyone is here. Now, how many of you have been to an aquarium?"

No one answered.

Best broke the silence. "An aquarium as you may know is a display of organisms that live in the water. Thanks to volunteers and the administration, this exhibit is a special treat for everyone. You are special. You are the first from our Cook County wards to visit our exhibit displaying rare aquatic specimens from waters around the world."

Best continued, "This is a new day. Take advantage. You can experience life outside our treatment center. We hope your curiosity will be kindled by the view of these rare species. We will have the opportunity after this visit to tour six other sites which are labeled as the 'Seven Lively Arts' exhibits. The other six exhibits include tropical plants, an arboretum, a rose garden, sculptures in motion, desert plants, and an introduction to trotter horses—their care and training."

Shannon wondered if this was a cruel joke to hide staff abuse? Surely whoever dreamed up these sideshows knew these exhibits would not make patients sane or improve prospects of ever being discharged.

"The whole point of this and the other off-ward activities is to help you make the transition to the outside world."

Shannon whispered to Maggie, "What transition? Why would I want to leave our locked ward? How could I turn down watching rotating weather dials on our TVs in the dayroom while Martha yells that she is the Virgin Mary and Ruth laughs nonstop while peeing and shitting her pants?"

Nurse Best looked beyond the entrance to the building to the bright oranges, greens, reds, and browns of maples and took a large breath. "Smell the fresh air and take in the bright sunshine and fall colors. Look at the positives rather than despair. All of us are working toward your recovery so you can get on with your life to appreciate such scenes."

Best moved towards Shannon on her way to the door.

"Don't get near me," Shannon yelled.

"I will respect your space if you agree not to have a meltdown, honey," Best said.

Shannon could not ignore the smokey smell of Best's tobacco-scented dress and hair. Her low-range voice enhanced by her heavy smoking habit was the same voice used to force me into isolation she thought. Shannon fought hard to restrain her hostility. She recalled how Nurse Best had ignored her complaints of Hippo's abuse numerous times. This was no time to challenge her authority.

Shannon wondered if anyone else saw Best's appearance this morning in the same light, as a phony? Best was attractively dressed in a summer outfit dotted with large sunflowers fitted to a size-eight figure. The dress was cinched with a straw belt drawn tight at the waist with a keyring attachment. Her keys left no doubt who was in control. Best's attractive facial features framed by soft blonde curly hair and the perpetual smile left the impression she was different from staff dressed in traditional white. She was their friend. *It's her reference to me as 'Honey' especially when I'm upset that offends me.*

Nurse Best moved toward Shannon.

"Keep your distance."

"Honey, I can assure you those bath units have been shut down months ago and replaced with large aquarium exhibits."

"How can I trust anything you say? Remember when you said 'Trust me. Hydrotherapy will speed your recovery.'" Not waiting for a reply, Shannon shouted, "Recover from what?"

"We have a different approach now. We will listen to you and help you find your adjustment path. Let's save this discussion for later."

"You don't want to hear what happened in those tubs. Well, I will not be gagged. We had no choice. We were forced into the tubs. The treatments were so painful—especially the ice bath. The only way out for me was suicide, and I even screwed that up," Shannon said.

"Shannon, please calm down. Those days are over. You will see all the equipment for hydrotherapy has been converted to displays for aquarium tanks."

"Let me be the judge of that."

Nurse Best made her way to the unlocked door. Shannon lagged patients as they approached the entrance. As she entered the large room with the tiled-lined tubs evident, her pace quickened. She surveyed the large room inside the the1940s brick-covered building looking for the white-uniformed therapists.

Just past the entrance hallway, she quickly recognized a former bath the size of a small backyard swimming pool. It had been converted to a display with a forty-gallon aquarium placed on a reinforced table. Shannon entered the room maintaining a safe distance from all the tubs.

Best greeted Stan Wentz who was waiting inside for the touring patients. Best addressed the patients. "Let me introduce you to Professor Wentz. He is a volunteer who has curated the fish collection we will see today.

Professor Wentz will talk today about his efforts to establish what he hopes someday will be a world-class exhibition of seahorses."

"Thank you for the kind words though I can assure you this is only a small sampling of what is exhibited in other aquariums in the world. We are simply small fish in a big pond of exhibits. That said, I want to acknowledge none of this would have happened without the support and cooperation of your hospital administration. They were very involved in the infrastructure modifications of plumbing and air-conditioning which makes a variety of fish happy."

As Shannon edged her way from the displays, she spotted a door ajar that once had been the hydrotherapists' passageway to their offices. Shannon moved toward the passageway gazing back at the fish tanks. The mentor had directed everyone's attention including Nurse Best to a seahorse exhibit.

Shannon quickly entered the hall. She recognized Hippo's office door. God what a monster she thought. He had an enormous chest with huge arms covered with forests of hair except the top of his head. Memories of Hippo and the smell of a musty chlorine/mildew scent omnipresent brought on a flush of her face and a tremor of her right hand.

She slowly opened the door. A large aquarium was on top of Hepp's metal desk. Shannon turned her eyes to the murky red liquid in the tank.

"My God, My God, My God," Shannon shrieked. "That's a human head in the tank. That's Hippo."

Best ran toward the passageway and could see the open office door. She yelled at Shannon, "Get ahold of yourself!" Shannon moved back to allow Best to focus on a glass wall of a red liquid. Inside the aquarium tank, Best focused on a hazy shape of a human head.

"This is no Halloween prank." Nurse Best bolted toward the door. She shoved Shannon and curious patients back into the hall. "Everyone exit the building immediately." With considerable urging, patients complied. No explanation was given. She notified campus police and secured patients in their locked ward.

Chapter 2

*Crime Scene*
*Saturday Morning, October 31*

Detective Carl Turpin of the Jacksonville Police Department made a call to Sergeant Michael Dyson, his Marine service buddy and ride along in the department.

"What the hell are you callin' me at 7:30 in the mornin' when y'all know this is my day ta' go fishin' and fire up the barbecue?"

Turpin briefed Dyson. "A man's head was found in a fish tank at the local asylum, Jacksonville State Hospital."

"Why do you need me? You're the detective."

"When the shit hits the fan, no question this will turn out to be a high-profile case. Make it a first for me. I need your help on the investigation and to cover my ass when I screw up."

Michael thought it over. "I'll do it as long as we play it by the book."

"What the hell does that mean?"

"We stay in our own lanes. You are the detective. I am the cop."

"Pick you up in fifteen minutes."

Turpin raced the Ford Torino squad car to the mental hospital. Michael tightened his seat belt as Turpin sped through stop lights with his emergency lights flashing.

"Sounds like a weird Halloween nut job to me," Michael said while looking for negligent drivers crossing the intersections ignoring the warnings.

"Who knows? Doubt if we are investigating a suicide." Turpin smiled as the officers approached the hospital entrance.

Beyond the entrance, a campus roadblock was just ahead. Tom Riley, Chief of Campus Security, signaled Turpin to roll down his window. "Wards are in a lockdown. A crime scene has been sealed off. The fish guy gave us a lot of guff about keeping his fish alive. But he agreed to meet us at the building. He's at the entrance."

Turpin was directed through a quarter-mile of a variety of trees planted at the turn of the century to the aquarium. "What weird trees."

"Yeah. I hear they from all over the world. Guess they were tryin' to create a peaceful setting for the crazies," Dyson said.

Turpin pulled into the parking lot. Security Chief Riley parked nearby. Riley exited his car and tucked his .38 Smith and Wesson in his belt.

"So, you think the killer might be in the building?" Turpin asked.

"Who knows? The administration put out an edict that guns were not to be worn by security. The one exception was being engaged in a hostile situation. This qualifies as a hostile situation," Riley said.

"How so?"

"There could be a patient-suspect still in the building," Riley said. "Stan Wentz the biology professor is waiting for us."

"Who is this?" Turpin asked.

"Wentz is a biology professor from some large midwestern university. He made a deal with Sam Scott, hospital superintendent, that he could acquire the fish and equipment for an aquarium from researchers and grant funds, but a special facility was needed such as the abandoned hydrotherapy building. Scott sold the proposal to the politicians as a win-win for fish researchers and everybody else including patients."

"Why here?"

"As I heard from the grapevine, the hospital grounds provided an ideal spot for the construction of an aquarium. There's plenty of space in the abandoned hydrotherapy building to set up the displays and convenient outside parking for visitors."

Michael spotted a gray-bearded individual maybe in his fifties walking toward Turpin and the chief.

"This is Professor Wentz," Riley said.

"Good to meet you. I'm Detective Turpin, and this is Sergeant Dyson," Turpin said.

Turpin asked Wentz, "Is this your full-time assignment?"

"Yes and no. I'm on a sabbatical to study the feasibility of creating artificial aquatic environments for species normally requiring exposure to seawater."

"And do you go by Dr. Wentz?" Michael Dyson asked.

"No, Stan is fine. It's pretty informal around here."

Riley led Turpin, Michael, and the professor through the hallway back to Fred Hepp's office.

"I want to do a complete forensic examination of the victim's office," Turpin said. "Before we open that door, let's set some ground rules. This is a crime scene and access to the office is limited to our investigative team until forensics is finished."

"Ok. I'll notify the administration that the entire fish exhibit is off-limits," Riley said. Turpin took out a handkerchief and turned the doorknob. On a desk, the aquarium about the size of a large hope chest was filled with murky water and the eerie sight of a human head. Turpin reflexively pushed his hanky to his face. Michael could see Turpin struggle to take in the grisly sight.

Turpin quickly scanned the desk for blood. No apparent stains were present. He walked around the desk inspecting the large desk chair and the surrounding floor.

Turpin rushed for the door. "I feel light-headed."

"I'll get a key and lock the door if you need a break," Michael offered.

"I just need some air. In the meantime, have forensics check all other doors, entrances, and exits. Check the office floor and any other floor space for blood traces. We need photos of the scene and also get ahold of the coroner," Turpin said.

Michael was right all along. Rank mattered. "Know the routine."

"I want to set up an interview with the witness who discovered the head—excuse me, decapitation. Today, if possible," Turpin said.

"Not sure we can pull that off," Riley said. "It's a holiday and the weekend for the administration. And one more roadblock. I was just notified by Dr. Gomez, the clinical director, has placed the Cook County ward on lockdown. He told me the female patient on the ward who discovered the head in the tank was not to be interviewed without the approval of Dr. Koeppen."

"Well, at least tell me her name, dammit. The patient who saw the freak show," Turpin said.

"If I get fired for givin' her name, I expect you to cover my ass," Riley said.

"No problem."

"It's Shannon Audrey."

"Look, I can't believe this is a problem. It is a homicide investigation, not a couch session. Witnesses need to be examined early if we are to get an accurate account, especially when dealing with mental patients," Turpin said. "I'll get our prosecutor on this question to make our case. In the meantime, I'd like to see the nurse who was on duty. What's her name?"

"Linda Best you mean. She's on duty now, but I'm guessing you'll have to go through Dr. Koeppen," Riley said.

"Are you telling me that after one of the most heinous homicides I have ever seen, we can't interview a single witness?"

"Let me give you some background. When the new superintendent Scott took over, he turned everything upside down. Patients are no longer called 'patients,' they're 'residents,'" Riley said. "There's a battle goin' on between the old timers and new staff who kiss the superintendent's ass. They are given fancy titles and higher pay grade but have no care responsibilities. Believe me, the former Sup' Dr. Tinsley never would have tolerated these gold-brickers. Patients and staff knew where they stood as to who was running this madhouse."

"So, bottom-line, forget it. This administration is not gonna allow us to question witnesses? Is that what you're saying?" Turpin asked.

"Not exactly. You need some outside help to break through the bullshit," Riley said.

"Okay. Let's start at the top. We want to see the superintendent today and I mean today, okay? Let him know we'll be at his office in ten minutes."

" Let me patch into the office and see if he is even there."

A call was made to the office of Superintendent Scott. There was no answer. An off-campus call was patched into Scott's secretary, Belinda Fast.

"Sorry, I nearly missed your call. I was putting out Halloween pumpkins to decorate our front yard," Fast said.

"You need to get ahold of Superintendent Scott immediately. Detective Turpin is demanding access to witnesses who were present at the murder scene of Fred Hepp."

"This is not the best time given this is a holiday," the secretary said. "How about Monday?"

"That's not gonna cut it," Riley said. "Before you hang up, here's Detective Turpin."

Riley handed the mike to Turpin. "Hello. This is Detective Turpin of the Jacksonville Police Department. We are investigating a homicide at the aquarium site. We need to see Superintendent Scott immediately to clear up questioning witnesses."

"I'll put out the word to the administrative staff they need to make themselves available. Does that include the superintendent?"

"Yes."

"I'll have him call you directly."

The secretary made a call to Scott's residence alerting him of Detective Turpin's request for an emergency meeting. Scott called security and was patched into Riley's radio phone. "Hi. This is Sam Scott.

What can I do for you?"

"I'm Detective Turpin of the Jacksonville Police Department. I need to set ground rules for the investigation of a murder that occurred at your hospital."

"I just want you to know that many staff still have no knowledge of this barbaric murder that was just reported to me an hour ago. So, let's talk about what you see as a priority in your investigation given this is a holiday and staff access is very limited."

"Our investigation cannot be delayed. We need fresh memories and early leads."

"I get it. So, let's get together and see if we can resolve your concerns. Meet me at my office in fifteen minutes, if that's convenient?"

"We'll be there in ten minutes." The detective handed back the mike and motioned for Michael to come closer. "Can we get a check on who has keys to the aquarium?"

"Sure." Michael thought more about his role. Whiteys like controllin' everybody. He thought of popular TV show Perry Mason that did the step 'n fetch routine. Della Street was there ta' light Perry's cigarettes and Paul Drake was always there ta' do his biddin' for a follow-up investigation.

Riley offered to drive Turpin and Michael to the superintendent's office. "Think I can get ya' through the red tape."

Riley parked near the entrance of a brick building with a limestone landing and gothic façade features. The 1847 building was designated as a historic site. Michael read the historic marker on the large five-story building before entering. "Jacksonville State Hospital was established by the iconic reform efforts of Dorothea Dix, an early 19<sup>th</sup>-century advocate for the mentally ill."

Riley told the officers the administration office was located on the fifth floor with wards on the first three floors. The old stairs creaked as Turpin, Michael, and Riley made their way to Scott's office.

"How many acres were set aside for the hospital?" Turpin asked.

"Over 130 acres. This is prime farm soil—will grow anything. Great place to take a walk in the fall," Riley said.

Entering the office, Michael paused to take in abstract paintings and office décor. It seemed out of whack with the old varnished hardwood Wainscot paneling, steam radiators, and reconditioned oak floors. Some version of an abstract styled rug with bright reds and yellows covered the front of the large secretary's desk. The desk really stood out. Michael guessed it was a chrome-steel frame. A glass top was atop it.

"Are you Detective Turpin?" the secretary asked.

"Yes."

"Craig Sweeney, the assistant superintendent, is in his office. Mr. Sweeney would like to brief you before you meet with Dr. Scott."

A tall confident man in his late thirties appeared and invited the officers into his office adjacent to the superintendent's office. "Good to see you, Chief Riley. I want to introduce myself to your sidekicks. I'm Assistant Superintendent Sweeney."

"Look, not to be rude, I would rather not speak to you. It's your boss who has final authority. Sorry, I should've introduced myself. I'm Detective Turpin. This is Sergeant Michael Dyson. We are here to investigate a homicide. I must talk with Dr. Scott."

Sweeney adjusted his skinny-silk-brown tie that matched his English tweed jacket. "Of course, you can talk with Dr. Scott. But to save time, I want to review hospital policy matters concerning patients and staff. Dr. Scott has instructed me to highlight relevant resident policies that might apply to your investigation. Of course, we want to meet your needs and cooperate fully."

"There could be a psycho killer somewhere within a radius of two miles, and you want me to review the fine print as to who I can interrogate?" Turpin's ears brightened to a deep red.

"Dr. Scott is well aware of the political consequences of fear compromising what witnesses may or may not have witnessed. He would like to see the investigation go forward without sensationalism erupting in local or national accounts. Outbreaks of hysteria will distort your investigation, and at the same time flame stereotypes of our residents. In summary, the superintendent's priority is to protect residents."

"I get it. You are the gatekeeper. You're the guy whose priority is to protect your boss's ass, not so much the patients. You at least got one thing right. All hell will break out if the public finds the hospital refuses to cooperate in a murder investigation."

"Now with all due respect, we have a good relationship with law enforcement. Officers have gone that extra mile to transport residents here safely and humanely. On occasion, they have conducted investigations of assault and suspected suicide on the wards. We have had a very cooperative relationship and there is no reason this should not be the case for this incident," Sweeney said.

"Save your bouquets for your boss. You are wasting

our time. I want to hear from the superintendent what constraints, if any, he has in mind for the investigation."

"Okay, okay. In no way do I want you to get the impression this administration or staff are impeding an ongoing investigation. Would you mind reading the inscription on my desk? This represents where I am at this point."

Sweeney pointed to a wooden holder that had once served to display the name and the position of an official associated with the hospital. In large letters, the sign read "ESCHEW HUBRIS."

"So, is this some kind of psycho test?" Michael asked.

"No. Just tell me what it means?"

"What in the hell does this have to do with meeting your boss?" Turpin asked.

"It's a reminder that individuals should resist getting too hung up with their solutions to problem-solving. By the way, only a handful have defined what it means."

"Your two-bit words remind me of one thing my grandpa warned me about, 'If you never stray off a cow path, you're bound to step in a pile of shit,'" Turpin said. "Now let your boss take it from here or I walk out."

"Okay. No need to make any threats. Let's eschew rigid demands. Oh, here is Dr. Scott."

Scott came forward with an extended hand. "Glad to meet you, Detective Turpin. You have quite a reputation as an investigator. Just talked to Jacksonville Police Chief Brady this morning and he emphasized you have a good record of solving assault crimes in the city. That's what we all agree on. We need to bring whoever is involved to justice. And I'm happy to meet you, officer. Now, what's your name? Your police chief failed to mention you."

"Sergeant Michael Dyson."

Scott led the way in the spacious office to an informal conference area. To Michael, the furniture looked similar to upscale chairs and a table he had seen in a furniture store in Chicago. Chairs were placed in a rectangular pattern with a large coffee table in the middle.

"Would either of you like coffee or water before we get started?"

"Can we forget the small talk and introductions and get down to business? We're here to do an investigation. If we can't interview primary witnesses and other parties of interest, we've got big-time problems going forward. Let's start with the patient who entered the office and discovered a human head in a fish tank. Yes or no. Are you on board to allow interrogation of the witness?"

"I appreciate your candor. Of course, we all want a rigorous investigation of this tragic homicide. Identifying suspects and prosecuting the guilty party or parties is needed to bring closure for everyone—including the victim's family. Our mission here is to maximize treatment opportunities for all our residents by emphasizing their involvement in the treatment process. That carries a heavy responsibility to ensure resident decision-making goes beyond token choices afforded residents in the past. And as a part of our efforts to promote their potential well-being, we have insisted on their right to privacy."

"So, you're okay with some fiend out there to repeat another sadistic murder? How does protecting patient privacy square with your responsibility to provide a safe and secure place for staff and patients? And what about the community?" Turpin grew angrier as he fixed his stare on Scott's squinty eyes and half-smiley lips.

"If you put it that way pitting justice against privacy as a dichotomous choice, that makes it a zero-sum game. Except there is an alternative strategy. Rather than use a jackhammer to investigate, I suggest you sit down with staff and negotiate a settlement."

"Enough double-talk. You either bring forth witnesses or I go to the State Attorney General."

"You need to think this over. Historically, the courts have protected patient rights including privacy. Bottom line, we want to cooperate without sacrificing their rights."

"If that's your bottom line, I'll see you in court. Now as to your staff, let's begin with Nurse Best. How can I contact her?"

"You should start with our clinical director, Dr. Santiago Gomez. Next, you will need to contact the Cook County Center Director, Dr. Dietrich Koeppen."

"I thought you were in charge."

"I am, but only if you reach an impasse. Again, I strongly advise you to negotiate rather than dictate terms so an optimal social contract is reached. This is not the military. Authority is decentralized. Dr. Gomez and Dr. Koeppen and his staff will handle the investigation from this point on."

"Translated, you're washing your hands to make any calls to enforce witnesses to come forth."

"If you reconsider working with us starting at the ward level, we can consider negotiating further on limits of privacy constraints."

Turpin threw up his hands and turned his back and headed for the office entrance. Turpin asked Michael,

"Where do we go from here?"

"You're the man. If it were me, I'd get something set today. You know, in cases like these, leads disappear quickly if you mess around." On the way out, Turpin stopped at the secretary's desk. "Excuse me. Would you mind giving me the clinical director's home phone number?" "Do you mean Clinical Director Santiago Gomez?"

"Yeah, that's the one."

"Why don't I dial him now, okay?"

"Yes. That would be great."

Belinda Fast dialed the phone with her pencil eraser. Dr. Gomez answered, "Hello. This is Dr. Gomez."

"Would you take a call from Detective Turpin?" Fast asked. "He's investigating the murder of one of our staff, Fred Hepp."

"Sure."

Turpin picked up the phone and without any formal exchange launched into a verbal tirade over his frustration over access to witnesses. Turpin insisted all Cook County ward staff who may have background information on the victim or who were at the scene come forward and cooperate with investigators.

Gomez listened without comment. After a brief pause, the physician said, "Yes, we need to discuss your concerns and importantly, the ground rules of your investigation. Let's try it this way. Would you be willing to meet Cook County staff at their center today?"

"That works for me."

"That would include staff and Dr. Dietrich Koeppen, Director of Cook County Center if they're still in town," Gomez said. "How about I call Dr. Koeppen and set up an emergency meeting—today if possible."

"How many will show up given it's Halloween?"

"Not that many. How about next week—Monday morning?"

"This case will quickly fall apart if we don't get to witnesses sooner than later." Turpin paused for a moment. "Okay for Monday if that means we get all relevant staff present."

"That's a deal. We'll meet Monday at 10 a.m. in their conference room. I'll accompany you to the meeting. Drop by my office around 9:30."

Chapter 3

*Journal Update*
*Sunday Morning*

Shannon Audrey nervously paced around the day room. Yesterday's shock of seeing Hippo's head in the tank swirled in her head. Distractions on the ward were hard to ignore. Lucy rocked back and forth as she talked about her demons. Sharon cackled "Good Morning" as Shannon walked past her. Lucy once again insisted in a matter-of-fact way she was a virgin. Raised as a devout Catholic, she was proud of her seven children. When confronted about her proclaimed virginity, Lucy would offer wonder and praise of God's miracles—products of immaculate conception. Tilly was in a wheelchair speaking gibberish. During one lucid moment, she whispered to Shannon her husband had infected her with his nasty sex causing her to go mad.

Shannon reflected on what she faced. The staff would single her out as a possible suspect given her confrontations with Hippo. Complaints of patient abuse had led to staff retaliation. She had to convince Dr. Koeppen to restore her rights. Koeppen had scheduled her for a Sunday assessment at ll:00 a.m. This must be linked to Hippo, Shannon thought. It was urgent she update her journal.

The bathroom had cleared. Shannon forced her

attention away from dreariness. For now, she made sure that no one saw her pull her journal from under her mattress and place it in her underwear. Quickly, she headed for a bathroom stall and dated her entry.

*November 1, 1969*

*Yesterday was hell. I know it looks bad. I hated Hippo and all the staff know this. But no one knows the whole story. If I open up, I will never be released and my ex will find a way to eliminate me and collect on a life policy. I can trust no one on the staff other than Carla Fitzgerald. I need to summarize what I know and get my journal to Carla for safekeeping ASAP.*

*Hippo sexually and physically abused patients, and he and his wife Blaze stole drugs off the ward. He bullied staff and patients to do his bidding and threatened to kill me if I disclosed any of this to anyone. Several times he attempted to grope me as he did to other patients when isolating them. The most outrageous assault occurred in his office where he brutally raped my good friend Vesta Diaz. When she reported this to Nurse Best, the nurse scheduled Vesta for an appointment with Dr. Koeppen. He told Vesta she was quite delusional and she had severely regressed in her psychosis. He emphasized staff investigating the complaint concluded Fred Hepp had ever abused her in any manner.*

*Koeppen advised Vesta she needed treatment beyond psychoanalysis. He told her he had consulted with a specialist in somatic treatments, Dr. Bauer, who did a residency in psychosurgery. Bauer agreed with Dr. Koeppen Vesta suffered from hebephrenia and acutely psychotic.*

*Of course, Koeppen did not tell the consultant of*

23

*what made her "acutely psychotic" on the ward. Koeppen insisted Vesta lie on the couch while he put his hand on her leg and pushed it slowly toward her vagina. He told her this was to free repressed sexual urges that had brought on her psychosis. Vesta said she screamed and Koeppen bolted toward the door and requested Nurse Best have Vesta placed in seclusion. After the surgery, Vesta could barely put two words together.*

*Vesta's surgery and my encounters with Dr. Koeppen have convinced me he is a dangerous enemy. I should have known. My sessions with the doctor led to some of my worst moments, ECT treatments and the seclusion room. Shocks to my brain left memories behind that slowly returned.*

Shannon closed her journal. At all costs, it was critical to maintain her wits—especially at times as in the past when Dr. Koeppen was highly provocative."

Shannon heard footsteps approaching the bathroom.

"Shannon, are you in there?" Nurse Best yelled. "Come out immediately. Dr. Koeppen wants to see you right now."

Shannon quickly hid the journal in her blouse and flushed the toilet. She exited the bathroom and approached Nurse Best. "It was that time of the month. I needed to change my underwear. Will be with you shortly." She rushed to her bed and when sitting on the mattress she managed to stuff the journal under the mattress close to the headboard. She quickly returned to the hallway. Nurse Best told her Dr. Koeppen was busy at the moment with staff. He would be available in a half-hour. While waiting, Shannon recalled her journal entry after her last visit with Koeppen.

*It was a disaster. During one of my mood swings,*

*the doctor asked me into his office. At the time, I had very deep feelings of gloom. I wanted to end my life. After the visit to the doctor, the staff assigned me to clean four flights of stairs with a toothbrush. Cleaning the steps at the beginning was a chance to get away from the cacophony of the ward and my despair. That was short-lived. Nurse Brenda Swan, a large woman who had little tolerance for patient resistance to treatment orders, never left me alone while cleaning the steps. Swan critically inspected each step for any sign of uncleanliness, real or otherwise. A toothbrush and a towel with a pail of soapy water were provided.*

*At the first step where I removed any trace of grim, Swan lashed out.*

*"What is wrong with you? That step is filthy. Now get to work with that toothbrush and make it clean."*

*Each step it seemed was never clean enough. Swan demanded I scrub harder with the toothbrush to clean invisible dirt. At first, it was all a blur. Cleaning those steps seemed right in a way. I reached a point where maybe this was a measure of my unworthiness—cleaning steps seemed appropriate. It was on the second day Nurse Swan became increasingly abusive. "You know better than anyone else you are a worthless piece of crap! What have you ever done right? It's always me, me, me. And it's always at the expense of others like was the case when you assaulted your ex-husband."*

*I could not control my anger. Bringing up ex did it. I picked up the bucket and threw the soapy water at Swan. My momentary outburst was met with her muscular hand placed at my throat. Swan forced me down on the steps. The nurse screamed for backup. Two male attendants joined in the struggle. The weight of their bodies pushing my body against the edges of steps produced back and shoulder pain that was unbearable. I remember yelling "Get off me you assholes." My arms were forcibly placed in the arms of a straight-jacket. The more I resisted, the more force was applied. My arms were cinched tightly with restraining straps. A gurney was wheeled to the scene. I was picked up by the two men and body-slammed on top of the gurney. Restraining straps were cinched tightly around my body. The gurney was wheeled to a seclusion room with the jacket still tied.*

*I nodded off. It must have been the shot. I recalled Nurse Swan removed the straight jacket. Swan scolded me repeatedly for assaulting her—that I had better take responsibility for my selfish lifestyle or else bad things would happen. My hate for Swan was held in check given my fear of another incident could lead to more abuse, more volts to my brain turning it into a lightbulb or worse suffering a fate like Vesta.*

"Good morning, Shannon. You look less despondent. You must have had a good sleep and satisfying breakfast," Dr. Koeppen said. The psychiatrist put a couple of files away in his desk and stood. "Let's go to more comfortable seating." Koeppen took his customary seat next to a couch.

"Do you mind if I sit in a chair?"

"I would prefer you use the couch to help you relax."

"Right now, I would rather sit and talk to you directly."

"I can be of little help if you feel guarded and defensive about your past."

"Is it possible for the two of us to talk like real people do—you drop the psychobabble and I can simply be me?"

"I see nothing wrong with that if we come at such a conversation on an even playing field. But at some level you know that's not true. Your history is blighted with events that point to profound mental issues. It would be malpractice to ignore what I know about you." Koeppen picked up a notepad from his lampstand.

"I could ask you the same question as I see it." Shannon's voice rose. "What happens when harmful treatments to patients do not work or make them worse? Is this not malpractice? I cannot ignore such abuse and cruelty and not speak out."

"I can see you are making progress. Your anger is now directed outwardly."

"With all of those degrees on the wall, you must be aware of the difference between moral anger and destructive rage."

"You believe it is morally right to assault staff?"

"I've had my moments and I'm far from being morally perfect. On the other hand, look at how you direct others to assault patients. All are justified with that magic word, *therapy*. Worst of all, you signed off on having a patient's brain cut up which turned them into a vegetable. This is what happened to Vesta Diaz," Shannon said.

"You are making a false moral equivalence. I am not a psychosurgeon. I'm a psychoanalyst who treats patients psychologically."

"You were the doctor who signed off on her treatment. How do you claim innocence?"

"First you are making incorrect assumptions. As to Vesta Cruz's specific treatment regime and subsequent outcomes, that is spelled out in her confidential medical record. I will simply say you have it all wrong on several counts. Staff and a special consultant reached a consensus on her treatment plan. Secondly, I am not surprised or affected by your remarks. It all fits a pattern,—rejection of authority figures. If you could drop your guard, you might discover those destructive defenses cloud your insight as to who is your target. Can't you see the advantage of discovering your own demons—the ones that affect everything you do now?"

Shannon stiffened her back. "Your idea of real demons. Let's turn the table here and when have you ever looked at your demons? After all, I can't imagine you did not undergo some kind of exploration of your past to qualify as a psychiatrist."

"Can we get to the event you have avoided,—the brutal slaying of Fred Hepp?"

"Speaking of avoidance, look at what you are attempting now," Shannon said. "Have you brought up the murder to avoid disclosure of a secret painful past no one knows about you?"

"I couldn't have said it better. Only it applies to you—a common projective defense."

"I am curious. Your heavy accent sounds like my grandfather Heinz's speech. He left Nuremberg as a child after the Great War. He could always tell where German immigrants were from by their dialect. Is there something in your past you are hiding related to the war?" Shannon asked.

"I'm wasting time. This is not a sanctioned tennis match between us to use a sports metaphor. In that context and the present situation, you are not qualified. You will never reach a match-point. You see we are very different in our club rankings Shannon. There's a simple reason. It all comes down to performance. You lack the skills to hit the ball on the sweet spot of a racquet forcefully and keep it in play. At your level of functioning, you are still looking for that sweet spot and keeping the ball in play."

"I know the sweet spot all right. It is simple. I heard you say earlier, 'I looked less despondent.' I don't quarrel with the fact that after the soapy water assault on Nurse Swan, my mood improved. It was you who ordered Nurse Swan to provoke me to a point where I snapped. You just said something about my anger was directed outward rather than inward. Isn't that a good mark? Your therapy worked. So, you should take credit, right?"

Not waiting for an answer, Shannon continued. "You could write this up as a case study in some professional journal. This could advance your career by showing that even a chronic patient in a state hospital can benefit from achieving this type of insight. Even if I piss you off for being so critical of patient treatment, as a psychoanalyst, at least try to be an objective one. You say I have poor insight. Having just read a couple of psychology books—Isn't this all about transference? If I got it right, I'm not striking out at you but some male figure such as my father. I did have issues with my father's drinking and treatment of Mom. In that light, you should see me as having good insight into my underlying problems. I am a competent individual - psychologically at least as to what the court requires. Please take another look at me. I'm asking you to review my petition to the court that I am legally competent and should have my rights restored."

"You have made progress but your emotional lability is still a concern. I need to see a greater stabilization. We may need to modify our treatment strategy if incidents of harm to others or self-directed are evident. Your lack of cooperativeness in treatment is a serious red flag along with your intellectual defense mechanisms. I would be obliged to say at this point contrary to your assessment, you have poor insight as to the nature of roots of your maladaptive acts."

"Oh, one more thing. Your repression of witnessing such a traumatic murder scene is yet another major concern," the doctor added. "This could trigger yet other pathologies far too many to review. At some point, you must open the unconscious aspects of your personality to come to terms with your past and recent incidents."

"In so many words, you say I'm a dufus about reality. I don't have a clue as to the real world and my role in these so-called incidents. You are completely naïve about who I am. It's your insight that is rigidly out of touch. If you knew me, you would discover I'm more aware of my mood swings than anyone here. I can sense the bad mood shifts coming on and for the most part have managed those bad patches. The lithium pills have helped, but my tremors get worse if I don't take a drug holiday. In a nutshell, you have not addressed the court's concern. Namely, can I understand the legal proceedings of a hearing and effectively communicate with an attorney."

"The court's definition of competency is much too narrow in a psychiatric sense. The more compelling question centers on how you would fare in a community absent accountability and constraints?"

"How will anyone ever know? You could say that about any of the patients here. I know them quite well and they trust me. Most cannot even make a legal argument about their rights.—That is the duty of their guardian—few if any know. Basically, we have an indefinite jail sentence, and again not to show disrespect—but in our center, you are the jailer."

"Your last statement is almost the identical words used by one of our new staff. Have you interacted with any of them recently?"

"Not that much. I see them rarely except for the patient government."

"We both know you are not being candid. You had a run-in with a ward worker."

"Are you referring to René Cohen?"

"Yes. And you made libelous statements about her husband, Toby, right?"

"I only said what I observed. And that's only the tip of the iceberg if patients were ever given the chance to air their complaints."

"You once again project on to others your forbidden desires and accompanying jealousy as you did with your husband."

"I've had enough of your bullshit. Call an aide. What I get from all your fancy words is my real problem—I'm a risk, a risk for having too much insight as to what is going on. Patients like me need to be muzzled whatever it takes."

Chapter 4

*Witnesses*
*Monday Morning, November 2nd*

Dr. Gomez greeted Detective Turpin and Sergeant Dyson with a handshake at his office. Turpin outlined what he needed for the investigation. Gomez emphasized the ultimate hurdle was to bring Dr. Koeppen on board to access witnesses from the Cook County Center. Dr. Gomez said he would make the case all center staff cooperate fully. Turpin, Michael, and Gomez headed for the administrative entrance to the center. "The staff meeting room is just ahead of us," Gomez offered.

Entering the conference room with a few staff present, Michael directed his attention to the 19th-century furnishings. A massive, aged oak table with very large lathe-turned legs was surrounded by highbacked chairs. Extra maple colonial chairs were placed on the periphery of the room. A large chair with leather upholstery showing signs of aging was at the head of the table opposite the entrance door. At the headboard of the chair, a vague image of an angel had been carved in relief. That must be the boss's chair.

Dr. Koeppen entered and took his seat in the large chair. Koeppen greeted the clinical director. "Good to see you again Dr. Gomez."

"Dr. Koeppen, let me introduce you to Detective

Carl Turpin and Sergeant Michael Dyson, Jacksonville Police Department."

Staff drifted in and located a chair at the table based on their medical roles. Those dressed in white surrounded Koeppen, while those in casual wear were seated at a distance.

Michael could see Koeppen's formal behavior and dress left no doubt this dude was in charge. His dress contrasted radically with other staff except for Dr. Gomez. His perfectly manicured nails combined with a Cary Grant-styled haircut and three-pieced suit were more fitting for Wall Street than an asylum Michael thought.

Dr. Koeppen turned to Turpin ignoring Michael and introduced Social Worker Carla Fitzgerald, Psychologist Zeke Cody, Nurse Linda Best, and Mahalia Ross, Licensed Practical Nurse.

Michael scanned the conference room. Male dudes were dressed in turtleneck sweaters and jeans. Most had long hair and beards with the exception of the psychologist Zeke Cody.

Some women wore street clothes with bright colored patterns in contrast with nurses who were dressed in white. To Michael, these people were from different planets.

"Excuse me everyone. I see some staff have not arrived," Dr. Koeppen said. "Toby, René, and Terry are missing." Dr. Koeppen scanned the room one more time and grimaced. "The new staff's accountability under this administration's reform plan seems to be inconsequential. Let me guess—they've had a bad hangover after the weekend." A few staff seated behind the conference table snickered.

"This is not funny, dammit. Their slacker attitudes have to be addressed - at least under my watch. I apologize to Dr. Gomez for their absence. In no way does this reflect on our staff's willingness to honor your request," Koeppen said.

Dr. Gomez rose and addressed the staff, "Let me be clear. Dr. Koeppen is in charge here and ignoring staff obligations will not be overlooked if formal complaints are submitted to my office. Now, let's get started. I've requested this emergency meeting to discuss the investigation of the tragic loss of Fred Hepp," Dr. Gomez said.

Gomez addressed the staff. "As most of you know, Fred Hepp, who had served as part of the Center's clinical staff for three years, was brutally killed. Some of you have lent support to his wife Blaze Hepp over her tragic loss. Mrs. Hepp has asked that I pass on to those who expressed kind thoughts, support, and remembrances, it is greatly appreciated. I think we can all agree it was such a tragic death," Gomez said.

Gomez then bowed his head and remained silent. Staff quieted. After a short period of silence, the clinical director turned to the detective and Michael. "I would like to introduce you to Detective Carl Turpin and Sergeant Michael Dyson who are investigating the incident. They are here today to discuss what is needed to solve who did this barbaric act."

Two staff Michael judged to be in their early twenties entered the staff conference room and rushed to seats at the back of the conference table.

Dr. Koeppen interrupted, "Is there some reason both of you show up late yet again? Let me guess, you just got up? Detective Turpin let me introduce you to our late arrivals, René Cohen and her husband Toby Cohen."

"René and I had an emergency. Our horny cat Thumper got in a fight with a hornier cat and lost. We had to take him to a vet to patch him up," Toby Cohen said.

"We have had a catastrophic event involving a staff member. As a result of this tragedy, some patients have regressed suffering acute psychotic episodes. Staffing needs on the wards are critical now. Yet both of you decided there was a higher priority. Both of you had to drive the cat to the vet, is that right?"

"Yoh." Toby gave a fake salute.

"What if every staff member on this unit took your cavalier attitude about showing up for work? Have you no regard for patient welfare?" Koeppen asked.

"Having less staff, or call them what they are— underpaid maids and ward enforcers—You know, that's not a bad idea. Most of these residents could live a rewarding life if we got out of their world, and let them figure out what's best," Cohen said.

"Hold on, hold on. Let's not waste any more time on what should be handled elsewhere," Gomez shouted.

"No need for anyone to get their skivvies in a bind. I'll admit I forgot to put mine on this morning. Hey Dr. K. It's okay to stand up and pull your boxers outta' your ass," Cohen said with a wide smile.

"Let me be clear to you Toby. I've had it with your insubordination. *Just be aware.* You are on notice," Koeppen said.

"Stop it. Hold on. Let me repeat. I did not come here to settle staffing issues. I came here to ." Gomez said.

René Cohen interrupted, "Why should we listen to Koeppen who doesn't give a shit people on the wards have been locked up for over two decades and forced to take harmful drugs or endure high voltage to their brain. A few initials after your name don't mean shit if you keep them locked for a lifetime offering no hope for a decent life. This has been going on for over a hundred years here. Everybody in this room knows this."

Staff members turned their heads toward René and her husband Toby. Michael saw their stares were anything but friendly. Mockingly, the couple smiled at disapproving staff.

"Is anybody in charge here?" Detective Turpin asked. "I'm not here to referee a food fight. I'm here to investigate a diabolical murder."

"Everybody shut up and listen," Gomez yelled. "Now pay attention to Detective Turpin. He has some significant issues we need to discuss."

"Thank you, Dr. Gomez. Let's get to the chase of why we are here. Our first task is to obtain witness accounts of anyone at the crime scene. Second, we would appreciate any tips as to who may have harbored a beef, grievances, or other motives to harm the victim. And third, nobody can be ruled out. That includes patients," Turpin said.

"Aha," Cohen said. "Let me guess Sherlock. The killer must be some mad patient on our wards. And you need to get wired with cocaine tonight to solve the case."

"Well, you sure as hell ain't no Dr. Watson if a cat rules your world," Turpin said.

Gomez shouted, "No more distractions. Now let's give the detective our attention."

Turpin stood and pushed back his chair. "Let's start with the basics——like do any of you know Fred Hepp's last known encounters, any staff or patient issues, or known hidden interests he had outside his job?" Turpin asked. "Are you aware of any relationships that involved fraud or worse?"

Turpin scanned the room looking for a response. None was forthcoming. "One key witness is critical, the patient who discovered the grotesque display."

"You must be referring to a patient who is on our ward. Currently, the patient is working through their reactions to this traumatic event," Dr. Koeppen said.

"Well, why can't we work out an interview where your staff could be present and intervene if emotions should get out of hand?" Turpin asked.

"I'm afraid that's not possible, even though I understand the urgency of your investigation. This particular patient is a ward of the court and found incompetent. We have no authority to expose the patient to an interrogation absent their guardian and an attorney present to protect their best interests."

"You need to understand the sooner we get to witnesses the fresher their memories and better the chances of narrowing the suspect list. I've already gotten calls from anonymous citizens. Some have offered tips that may pan out. I suspect some of those tips came from the staff here at the hospital. There are all kinds of motives for tips—but you can bet some were based on fear—fear that a killer is out there ready to strike again," Turpin said. "We're not here to play judge and jury over the legal status of a patient. However, I can't imagine courts will not back an investigation of someone who may have witnessed events crucial to identifying a psychopathic killer."

Turpin paused and looked at his pocket notes. "Is the supervising nurse of the aquarium visit here?"

"You must be referring to me," Linda Best said.

"If you don't mind, I'd like to end it here for now. Thank you staff for attending this morning." Turpin and Michael walked around the large table and approached Nurse Best. Turpin uttered in her ear, "Could you meet with us in private?"

"I'd rather not. But if it's a brief meeting, Okay I guess."

"Excuse me Dr. Gomez for cuttin' it short. Thanks again to you and staff for your help," Turpin said.

Linda Best exited and headed down the hallway. Michael and Turpin tried to keep up. Her office was located left of the locked ward steel door entry. The officers entered the small office and took a seat in front of her desk. The desktop contained a few folders, a schedule pad, and framed pictures.

"So, are those pictures of your family?" Turpin asked.

"Yes. Those are my daughters, Martha, age ten, and Marsha, age twelve, to her right."

"Let me guess. Your girls take advantage of their names. When you ask one of them to do help with chores, they claim you asked the other one given their names sound so much alike, right?"

"Yes, on occasion. Look, I appreciate your interest in my family, but I would feel better if we get down to brass tacks. You want to interview all witnesses and you are here to make your case. That means questioning patients as well as staff. Isn't that what you're after?"

"Imagine if you were the widow in this case. It's a sure bet with those two beautiful daughters and other family survivors, you would be beating my door down to clear this case. You must understand we need total cooperation from the staff to get to the bottom of who committed this grotesque murder. Right now, I'm starting with witnesses we know were there. That includes you and the patients visiting the aquarium. It is crucial at this point we interview the patient who found the victim. We need to know why she went to the victim's office? Let me check my notes."

While Turpin searched for her name, Michael offered, "Her name was Shannon Audrey."

"Just curious. Who told you the patient's name?" Best asked.

"We protect our sources," Turpin said.

"Speaking of confidentiality of your source, you should not have been told the patient's name. Someone on our staff violated hospital privacy rights."

"You realize we are starting with the most basic information. It is obvious Shannon Audrey could provide some good leads. So, that brings us to you. When did you and the patients enter the building and when did you hear a scream from Hepp's office? Were you aware of any conflicts Shannon Audrey had with Fred Hepp that led to murder?" Turpin asked.

"No comment."

"If we have to, we will get a subpoena to compel you to testify."

"Look, I want to cooperate. I'm on your side. This case has to be solved for reasons that relate to positive mental health for everyone concerned."

"That was a good soft-shoe routine. But let's get serious. How were you made aware Shannon Audrey had entered Fred Hepps office?"

"I need to consult my attorney."

"Why go through this dance? You know the

answers. If you are serious about wanting to cooperate, why the stonewalling? Are you afraid of your job?"

"I love my job and I can go whenever and wherever to another job if necessary. You seem to be oblivious to the impact of this tragedy on patients and staff. As to staff on the wards who have been here for years and are under-appreciated, you have to understand they have fewer options to get another job. They seek a secure environment where expectancies are spelled out."

"Does that mean the boss–this Dr. Dr.–whoever–is the drill sergeant who keeps everybody in line?" Turpin asked.

"Dr. Koeppen, is that who you mean?" Michael asked.

"Yes. Based on the blowup that just happened, it's clear everything goes through him."

"It's more complicated." Best paused and pulled her wavy blonde hair back. "I've said too much already."

"Oh really! What are we to believe when you say it is complicated? You and staff are one big happy family all about peace and love—especially toward the doc?" Michael asked.

"Don't put too much stock in this flareup this morning. As to treatment strategies, different approaches can be positive if the goal is patient rehabilitation."

"Look, I know next to 'nuthin' about the shrink business," Michael said. "But it was obvious this husband-wife duo, whoever they are, were in a pissin' match with the doc. Can we drop the happy talk about your aims here and get down to what is needed—any leads such as any pissin' matches between staff and patients or between staff that may have gone over the line?"

"You are referring to the Cohens, René, and Toby. You don't understand our obligations to patients. Patients require a secure environment where stress is minimized. That is maintained at the ward level in spite of criticisms expressed today," Best said.

"Again, why do this dance? How does dodgin' these questions help anybody on your unit feel safer?" Michael asked.

"I repeat. Staff needs some authority and protection when treating patients. That means enlightened use of drugs and therapy that allow patients to take on more and more responsibility for their own needs."

"Give me a break! We're not here to settle office politics, you dig me? What about useful leads -say any staff who may have been threatened? Fred Hepp was a large man. Did he man up to patients or staff?" Michael asked.

"First, you have to understand many of our patients have been here longer than someone convicted of first-degree murder. This accounts for the younger staff's impatience with traditional treatments to take effect. If any patient shows progress to care for themselves and deal with emotional challenges, we do all we can to have their lives restored."

"What does this have ta' do with Hepp? I repeat. He's a big guy. How did he deal with patients gettin' out of line?" Michael asked.

"Our staff have been trained on proper restraint methods. No one has been found abusive with patients, and for that matter, staff off the wards."

"Is this how you spend most of your time? Coverin' up for the doctor and staff?" Turpin asked.

"Just like a typical male to make your point." Best

stared at the detective and her facial muscles tightened. "In so many words, I'm a lackey who as a woman has little to bring to the table beyond parroting those in power—In this case, Dr. Koeppen?"

"No intent to insult you–if so, I extend an apology. Realize all I have been told today starting with the superintendent is this extreme view that a patient's privacy is more important than protecting the community. It's frustrating—like a killer who confesses to a priest but the priest cannot reveal their identity," the detective said.

Turpin reached for his notepad. "Let's start over. Who may have gone over the line for any reason—office politics or anything else -anyone who had intended to kill Fred Hepp and make a spectacle of it?"

"No one comes to mind."

"Not to offend you, but y'all ain't that convincing," Michael said.

A knock on the door was too loud to be ignored. Michael tracked Turpin's focus on her body as she moved from her desk to the door. It was hard to ignore Michael thought. Maybe it's the dress. She knew how to tease with that high hemline and tight-fittin' sock-like dress.

Nurse Best approached the door and opened it and stepped outside.

Dr. Koeppen whispered, "Number one, we need to speak as one voice for any alleged crime on this campus, and number two, our approach on all counts stands in jeopardy if this investigation gets out of hand. Now get your sexy butt back in there and direct the police to my office immediately."

"I take it this is not a friendly suggestion?"

"This is no time for smart-ass answers," Dr. Koeppen said.

Best returned to her desk. "That was Dr. Koeppen. He ordered me to direct both of you to his office."

"And not to rub you the wrong way again, but do you bow down to every order he makes?" Turpin asked.

"For ethical and legal reasons, Dr. Koeppen is responsible for every patient and staff member on this center."

"I get it. We'll be back," Turpin said. Michael and Turpin started out the door. Turpin stopped and turned to the nurse. "Again, did Shannon Audrey have any reason to seek out Fred Hepp's office?"

"I refuse to answer any question about patient activity. Ask Dr. Koeppen." Turpin grimaced at the response. Frustrated, Turpin headed for the hallway. Dr. Koeppen's office was not hard to locate. Michael and Turpin entered the office. Michael recognized power when he saw it. The secretary's hardwood desk and large leather-covered chairs in a waiting area with other touches made it clear he was the big dog.

The secretary, Millie Funderburk, greeted the officers. "Good afternoon. How may I help you?"

"I'm Detective Turpin and my co-investigator Sergeant Michael Dyson of the Jacksonville Police Department. I was told Dr. Koeppen wants to see us."

"I'll check to see if he's in." Funderburk lifted the dial-tone phone and pressed an intercom link. "A Detective Turpin and Sergeant Dyson are here. Can you see them now?"

The phone was placed on the cradle. "Dr. Koeppen will see you now."

As Michael and Turpin entered the doctor's office,

Michael looked with wonder at the office décor, the ornate walls surrounding his large desk. A formidable library was interspersed with portrait paintings. Behind his desk, medical certificates of specialization and licensure were displayed. The doc's large mahogany desk was adorned with a large ashtray, a pipe rack, and a fancy pen and pencil desk set.

Dr. Koeppen walked around his desk and greeted the detective and Michael. "Good to see both of you. How can I assist your investigation?"

"Those paintings—Are they the real deal?" Michael asked.

"No. It would take a fortune to own the originals of Monet, Renoir, and a special collection of Max Ernst," Koeppen said.

"Art collection's outta' my league. I wonder if we can skip the formalities. Your nurse...ah... Linda 'Bett' was not very forthcoming She points to you as the reason," Michael said.

"Her last name is Best not Bett."

"Okay, I may not have a perfect memory for names, but you know why we're here. She made it clear every decision goes through you. Let us try one more time. Can you tell me why Shannon Audrey sought out Fred Hepp's office in the aquarium? Your nurse stonewalled us on this and every other question," Michael said.

Koeppen returned to his office chair. With an unflinching look, he asked, "Before we talk about how you go forward, let's explore what you mean by being 'stonewalled?'" Michael noted his hands were folded such that his crossed forefingers pointed at him. An expensive European watch near his wrist stood out. His starched shirt cuffs displayed gold cuff links embedded with stones, maybe Sapphires. A three-button-suit and deep blue silk tie matched his light blue buttoned-down shirt. This was one guy, Michael concluded, who dressed to remind everyone who was the man.

"It's clear to us Nurse Best is covering up what she knows," Turpin said. "She was at the scene, and she knows much about Shannon Audrey's involvement. Given she refers us to you to answer questions about what happened this last weekend, what are we to conclude?"

"Detective Turpin, why are you so certain this homicide involved staff or patients? There are numerous profiles from a psychiatric perspective, if I may suggest, that could fit one who goes to such an extreme. Consider Charles Manson who diabolically orchestrated the murder of six Hollywood victims he did not know personally."

"This ain't Hollywood and so far, no one has complained about a wacko-hippie colony," Michael said.

"Tell me, Sergeant Dyson. What is your role in this investigation?"

"So far, a mobile lie detector. But not to be distractin', we want ta' hear your answer. What psychos fit the profile of a potential killer?"

"Yes. You are the shrink. You tell us who might be the killer," Turpin said.

"First of all, I'm a medical doctor specializing in psychoanalysis. It's 'Dr. Koeppen,' if you don't mind. Disrespect for my position tells me more about both of you than I care to discuss now. I will just add one observation. Placing a head in an aquarium tank offers obvious indicators of the perpetrator's state of mind."

"Sorry I offended you, *Doctor.* And I want you to

know, I think anything you can suggest at this point would be helpful even if I'm a little slow on recognizing rank," Turpin said.

"I'll put it in terms both of you might understand if you agree to keep this confidential. Do you agree?" Koeppen asked.

"Why would we expose such info to a potential suspect? Of course, we agree," Turpin said.

"Anyone decapitating a victim and displaying the head surrounded by water has to be understood at a deeper unconscious level. Whoever did this have an unconscious obsession to return to the womb. At the unconscious level water represents our most secure existence during our fetal development. I would look for a suspect who is quite insecure as to their flawed psychosexual development—to the point of never acquiring a secure sexual identity. Such failure at the unconscious level results in self-deprecation which is countered by a powerful evolutionary instinct of all living organisms - the life force. Such a force at the preconscious level redirects destructive urges from the self to others. In summary, this is an individual who finds it difficult to form attachments to others and at an unconscious level is obsessed with the security of his mother's womb," the psychiatrist explained.

"Could you spell this out in terms of how everyday people could understand?" Turpin asked.

"In a nutshell, humans do things where they have little conscious insight as to why. In this case, the killer had repressed memories that the only secure environment ever experienced was their mother's womb. A decapitated head surrounded by water is a classic example of an individual's desire to witness the victim's return to their mother's womb."

"Okay, so some weirdo out there that gets off seein' a victim's head floatin' in his mother's womb. This may be the psycho motive, but that does not get us to concrete facts as to who had the opportunity and means to carry out this sick act. Witnesses are key to answerin' those kinds of questions," Michael said.

"Let me be clear. We will use every legal means to gain access to witnesses. Make no mistake the public will demand this. That means witnesses will be subpoenaed if that's what it takes," Turpin added.

"I cannot and will not force Nurse Best to violate her confidentiality oath to patients. I will not break that trust. And there is one other consideration. I will protect our patients' privacy. Most of our patients have been adjudicated by Cook County courts as incompetent due to mental disease or defect. Ask your prosecutor. How do you subpoena an incompetent witness?"

"Here you sit in this beautiful office with a nice view and an attractive secretary with the full blessing of the administration. Tell me. Do you ever get involved with the outside world? You know—townsfolks? If you did, you would see how this murder has affected many. People are frightened. They want answers. Rumors are circulating that a nutcase is running loose somewhere in this hospital," Turpin said.

Dr. Koeppen opened the top drawer of his walnut desk and pulled out a pocket-sized scheduler. He avoided direct eye contact with the officers fixed on him. With a confident smile, Koeppen looked up. "Officers, your best course of action is to go through the courts to seek your remedies. For the record, I will not break my ethical or legal obligations unless so ordered by the court. I wish you a good day."

Taking their cue, Michael and Turpin exited the office and headed for the car. While in the hallway, Turpin spotted an office door ajar. He looked around the door. "Hi, I'm Detective Turpin and my partner Sergeant Michael Dyson. Do you have time for a few questions?"

"Sure. I'm Zeke Cody, clinical psychologist, according to human resources. But stick to 'Zeke the fixer' if you want to tag me."

"Sure."

"Why fixer?"

"Cuz I, I, spend most of my time fixing stuff—just like adjustin' the points of my old MG. People in this joint need their points adjusted often. Hey, Detective. I dig your tie."

"Give my wife the credit." Turpin tightened his tie. "She gave me this particular tie because of my Scottish heritage on my mother's side of my family. It's supposedly tied to some clan—something like the Tartan Chattian Clan."

"You both look stressed," Cody said.

"For the record, you're the first to get real today," Turpin said.

"To start just so we understand each other, I'm not a 'psych guy' who asks you questions like, 'Have you often had these feelings?' I don't waste my time with shrink tests or that couch stuff. I go where the action is— on the wards where folks are screwed up too often by social choices made by others. I'm all about getting everybody liberated so they can adjust their own points to deal with the real world out there," Cody said.

This guy reminded Michael of Bob Newhart. He seemed smaller in stature yet had that same laugh when he sensed others were on his wavelength.

"I gather you do not use the same playbook as this…Dr. Consti…no, make that Koeppen?" Michael asked.

"You got it right the first time. He's 'Dr. Constipated'—you know, anally retentive as he would tell his patients." Cody said.

"What in the hell does that mean?" Michael asked.

"It's a myth of shrinks that as a kid if you get whacked every time you shit your pants, you, you grow up to be compulsive, un-messy, and everything is in order. Like you got a broomstick up your ass—say like accountants or even psychiatrists." The psychologist dressed in Beetle boots and a turtleneck directed both toward two chairs. "Take a seat," Cody offered.

Turpin made his way to the oddly shaped chairs. "So how do I sit in these contraptions?"

"Do you mean the moon chairs? Just do a moony and let your ass fly."

Turpin aimed his butt at the middle of a round-overstuffed-half-moon chair and landed off target. With an outreached hand, he righted himself. "Good God. This is supposed ta' replace a couch?"

Michael landed cleanly.

"Yeah, I never thought of it that way but maybe you're right. It's like the moon landing when you sit in my moon chairs. It's one small step forward just like the astronaut said. But that's if you land ass-first. You have ta' maintain the correct attitude to make it happen," Cody said.

"Speaking of attitude, what's your take on having key witnesses open up? We were just shut down by your head nurse and doctor," Turpin said.

"I'm a tweener on that score. I'm going to push back on any wholesale interrogation of our residents. But the staff's another matter. They need to cooperate," Cody said.

"Just for the record, how do you get along with the man, this Dr. Koeppen?" Michael asked.

"We find ways to stay out of each other's hair about how we do business here."

"Sounds stiff. That flareup this morning was interestin'. It indicates not all the natives are happy with their chief on this reservation, right?" Turpin asked.

"Well, it's not a love-in for damn sure. And that's my job as a fixer—to give Koeppen his space but yet work at the ward level to, to, humanize caretakers. At one level, most of these folks see they're doin' the right thing with our residents—tending to the basics like eating and sleeping and making sure they do not kill others or themselves. Over years of this routine, residents lose their mojo. They take on all the downsides of being a 'patient'—You know, accept their limitations as patients–that, that they are sick and helpless and dependent on caretakers for everyday demands," Cody said.

"Excuse me, but some are truly sick or they wouldn't be here," Turpin said.

Cody chuckled. "And next you will tell me anybody labeled 'mentally ill' must be sick. And that means it's up to a doctor to go into his toolbox to diagnose and cure their illness. Say you mooned the police chief as a joke and the chief contacted a doctor and he agreed you're crazy. The police chief and the doctor go to court to have you committed. The court commits you to a place like this and a psychiatrist asks you if you have ever heard voices. And you quip, 'Yah…I heard a voice saying fart, fart, fart.' You laugh. The doc asks a few more questions and you are directed back to a locked ward. He submits his clinical report to the staff that you are hearing voices and diagnoses you as a psychotic—a schizophrenic. You are prescribed Thorazine—a drug prescribed to the old-timers at levels that would kill a horse. You protest you are not crazy. You hide the pills handed out daily in your cheek, maybe even up your arse because you see the reactions of old-timers to the drug—the repeated smacking of their mouth and the shuffling of their feet. A ward nurse rats you out to the doctor. Your doctor requests you see him for a 'clinical assessment.' He asks you again about hearing voices. You explain it never happened—you were just joking. He smiles and tells you it is common for patients with your condition to lack awareness of their illness. He stresses you have to take the meds if you want to get better. You can see where this is going."

"Let me get this right. No one here is sick? Whoever killed Hepp is not sick?" Turpin challenged.

"In a way you are right. If someone pushes the bounds of our views of sanity—we use the disease labels to ascribe mythical reasons for anybody's crazy act—just like Jack Ruby. It wasn't Ruby who pulled the trigger—it was a seizure—his fucked-up brain disease did it. That's pure bullshit," Cody said.

"That's way beyond me too—what little I know about Ruby, he hired one hell of a lawyer or had connections. But getting back to this case, I don't see how you can say any sane Tom, Dick, or Harry carried out such a barbaric act?" Turpin asked.

"First of all, sanity is a legal term. The old guard in

the shrink business likes terms such as 'psychotic' or 'mentally incapacitated' even though they do not fit law definitions of insanity. The courts want to know if the accused could form a criminal intent such as knowing right from wrong. That's not what traditionalists in the shrink business want to address. They want to explore things like whether someone's heard voices or thinks everybody is out to get them and shit like that," Cody said.

"But you would agree if for instance, the killer, in this case, heard voices and a voice told them to kill Fred Hepp, that's an act of a psycho, right?" Michael asked.

"Not necessarily if I understand what you mean by 'psycho.' In many of these high-profile murders, at least from what I have read, the majority have not snapped in a moment, that's true from Hitler to Charles Whitman to Ed Gein who inspired the movie 'Psycho.' They got to their evil deeds by approximations. They rehearsed warped schemes sometimes in private or in the case of guys like Charlie Manson forming a cult of believers to buy into his conspiracy theories and carrying out a plan he believed would lead to a racial war."

Cody reached for a folder. "Sorry but I've got an important ward get-together on resident impressions of their ward and treatment. Let's keep talkin'. Here's an option,—Tonight's our weekly bash at the oldest tavern in the city, the Andrew Jackson Tav, what we call the 'Spit and Shit Bar.' The tavern still has a spittoon running water channel at floor level in front of the bar and even has a bidet to clean your ass," Cody said.

"That's the hippie's joint," Turpin said.

"Yeah, depending on what you call a hippie. Our Friday night gang comes in all shapes and colors and has long hair," Cody said.

"You think I give a shit about hair length?"

"Not really. So can we expect you say after five?"

"I have to be honest. If it's a lovefest to convince cops to ignore hippy attacks on my buddies, thanks but no thanks. What do you think Michael?"

"Based on what little we learned today; I think we party with this gang. I'm in."

"As for trashin' police, I dig where you are coming from, Detective. But you need info, right? I'd suggest you loosen your tie and join Michael and the rest of us. You never know what might come up," Cody said.

"I'll check with my wife." Turpin and Michael exited and returned to the station.

Chapter 5

*Dead Ends*
*Monday Afternoon, November 2nd*

After Michael and Turpin left Cody's office, they returned to the parking lot to briefly review going forward. Michael felt at some point he had to confront Turpin about his role. He agonized over being a water boy. Yes, they had gone through the ranks together and paired up to handle calls of threatened or actual assaults including suicide. Trust was not the question. Both of us knew the other would cover the other's ass if de-escalation attempts failed and the situation required intervention. Even the chief had told us we were at the top as to investigatin' and handlin' dangerous situations. Yet, when both Carl and I applied for the detective position, only Turpin was promoted.

It was clear between the lines race was the difference-maker thought Michael. It was obvious when the chief, Brady, in a morning briefing reminded us that Jacksonville was no Chicago. The city had a race problem. He emphasized there were more murders in one day in the South side there than the yearly total for Jacksonville.

So, what else is new? Michael asked himself. All my life it's the hand I was dealt. Either place your bet or spend your life fightin' the man for cheatin.'

Michael joined Turpin in the police car. "Just thinkin' about you sayin' you are up to meetin' the hippies for happy hour this evening. Why do you think this crowd will give us anything?" Turpin asked.

"Booze loosens tongues. We may get some shit thrown our way, but some may give us some leads as to a possible motive in this case."

"My first impression is that this had to be a psycho homicide. But nothin' comes together so far. It's a tough nut to crack," Turpin said.

"Ya'll all need a nutcracker. Lean harder and someone'll crack," Michael said.

"Maybe you're right," Turpin said. "Their hospital staff have shut down our investigation at every turn. The pissing war between the old and new staff so far stands out. It's a nasty battle over what works best with patients and who's in charge. To be honest, it bores the shit out of me as to what it's all about. But something tells me, somebody, somewhere, has a different take," Turpin said. "As for patients somehow being involved, who knows? In short, I can see several leads could emerge at the same time that require an extra investigator."

"Is this your way of askin' for help?"

"Yes. You were in on this case in the beginning, I'd appreciate another set of eyes."

"Okay, if I'm not your water boy," Michael said. "If ya'll want my help—Let's get started. I need to check what the prints and blood guys came up with. Mind if we return to the department to check that out?"

"Not at all. I need to clear up another matter when we get back."

****

"Hi Chief, I gotta ask you a favor."

"The answer is no," Chief Brady yelled. "At the moment, my focus is on how to manage another war protest. Protesters have threatened to shut down a politician's speech scheduled at MacMurray College for the weekend on Sunday." Brady added, "Alumni donors want to honor Senator Everett Dirksen. Dirksen had given one of his last speeches on the campus shortly before his death last year."

"Is this the old foghorn who argued for the war but raised hell about the civil rights of protesters?" Turpin asked.

"That's him. What stirred the hornet's nest was his silence after Kent State. After Dirksen's death, these MacMurray alumni asked Senator Ralph Smith—Dirksen's replacement to give a memorial speech. Given Smith's continued support of the war, protest leaders made it clear they would be there in numbers to shut down the outdoor event," Brady said.

"That's all interesting, but back to why I'm here—what are you saying 'no' to exactly?"

"You know damn well what I'm gettin' at," the police chief said.

"If it's about recruiting Michael Dyson for the Hepp case, you've got a great radar gun between your ears," Turpin said. "My gut tells me we've gotta speed up the Hepp case or it's gonna go cold and stay that way for some time. I need some grunt work—doing background checks on a list I've put together."

"First, you need to talk with the state Attorney General Phil Grant," Chief Brady said.

"So, he can lecture me about patient rights and privileged communications?"

"Get off your high horse," Brady said. "You're still

a cop and I ain't seen a law shingle hangin' in your office. You are gonna need all the help you can get. For openers, I got an anonymous tip from some guy with a muffled voice claiming he had reliable sources from Springfield. The source indicated the AG's office was gearing up for a war with any hospital attorney or Commie ACLU prick shielding witnesses from answering questions. You outta' at least hear him out."

"I'll see what they have in mind," Turpin said.

"The second thing as I see it and not to bust your chops—you could use some expert outside help—may be the Illinois State Police or big-time, J. Edgar Hoover," Brady said.

The detective persisted. "Let me make one more pitch." Turpin paused for a moment. "How about adding Michael Dyson to the investigation permanently with his own office?"

"I can't spare anyone right now—especially with the hippies threatening to shut down a speech by that new senator this weekend," Brady said. "I need Michael for crowd control."

"What's your real reason? Put the cards on the table. Why did you pass over Sergeant Dyson for a detective position when you gave us similar reviews in terms of our service record? You need to clear the air," Turpin said.

"Hell, you can't win that one," Brady said. "You were my pick then and you still are. As you know, Michael filed a grievance with the police union. He claimed he was overlooked because of the color of his skin. The union buried his complaint. I'm sure Sergeant Dyson still holds a grudge."

Brady turned his office chair and looked outside the

window folding his hands behind his neck. "It really pisses me off Michael will not let it go."

Turpin with emphasis on each word said, "I learned in combat all this shit about rank is just that–shit when your ass is on the line." Turpin continued, "You get to know under fire what's in a man's belly if you want to survive one more day. Michael is the kind of guy I can trust. He's the one cop that I know more than anyone else on the force to do the right thing when the chips are down."

"That's not the argument I'm makin'. It's who's is best qualified to be a detective?"

"Look chief, it's time to move on beyond your view. As to qualifications, you underestimate Michael's investigative talents. We work well together. I need to get movin' now, not dilly-dallying bringin' another cop up to speed."

"Okay, I'll give him two weeks for a trial period. Don't want Michael to get any ideas this is somehow permanent——you know like bein' promoted."

Chapter 6

*Tensions*
*Monday Happy Hour*

Michael met Turpin in front of the Tav. "Why the cowboy shirt?" Michael asked. "Looks like y'all want to come across as the gunfighter with the badge."

"Like the 'Lone Ranger?' "

"Y'all the man with the silver bullets?"

"Let's save the putdowns for another time. I'm forcing myself to go through with this based on your call. Let's get it over with."

Michael opened the tavern's heavy door that resembled a century-old barn door. The penetrating shrieks of laughter gave him pause. Maybe this was a bad move after all.

"Good to see you both made it. Join us and take a load off," Cody yelled.

"Okay. The first thing I need is a beer," Turpin said. "Can I get ya' something Michael?"

"Nah. Need a clear head."

The detective ordered a bottle of Pabst Blue Ribbon at the bar. Both ambled to a bench table crowded with celebrators. Cody slid over to make room for Michael and Turpin.

"So, everybody this, as you know, is Detective Turpin and his partner Sergeant Michael Dyson."

"The detective didn't want to join us, but his wife must have given him parole tonight. Did you get off for good behavior?" Cody asked.

"I'm on a short leash—It's two-beer night, period."

"Let me guess. You missed your AA meeting," Toby Cohen said while exposing a half-chipped tooth. His wide grin diminished as the detective's facial expression tightened.

"Look smartass, dealing with alcoholism is not a joke. Nor is drinking and driving. I've seen too much destruction on those fronts," Turpin said.

"No disagreement man, but there are better choices—alternatives that create a peaceful and inner focus." Cohen smiled. He brushed back his long blond curly hair and looked to his wife, René, as she nodded in approval.

"So, you do drugs. Personally, I don't give a shit if you get wasted as long as it's in the privacy of your own space. But when it leads to harm of innocents, that's where I draw a bright line in the sand. Just two years ago I investigated a wreck where totally wasted kids wiped out a family of five. They gathered at the top of a hill overlooking Highway 67 and dared each other that night to run a stop sign at the intersection to the highway going at least 80 miles per hour. It was their version of auto roulette." Turpin paused and took a big swig.

"As I see it, getting wasted doesn't explain stupidity, it's just one factor. I'm curious to know how they got to that deal at the top of the hill?" Cody asked.

"All we know is it started as a dare that was repeated on weekends. While the deal was a factor, it's hard to say what came first, the deal or getting wasted? Just like this homicide case. Was it due to a bad trip, somebody snapping over a deal gone afoul, or someone goin' off the rails? We don't know at this point," Turpin said.

Toby Cohen shouted over the din of the large crowd. "Look man, we don't need any lectures from you on violence. You oughta' focus on your kind who use tear gas and riot batons to beat up war protesters."

"Aren't you the cat guy?"

"Make that 'Thumper' guy. That's his name. The cat and I have a lot in common," Toby Cohen said.

Michael smiled, making eye contact. "Does that mean you join Thumper and do a nightly booty call on your own?"

"Only if he shares the litter box. Sometimes he—"

Cody interrupted, "Time out!" Cody yelled again, "Time out! Toby, *Toby*. Could you just cool your jets for a change and be more observant of those around you?"

"And what might that be Sigmund?"

"Do you ever shut up and ever listen to others or better yet, yourself? How did your folks or others in the Queens neighborhood put up with this shit?" Cody asked.

"Aw Dr. Cody, I really care about you, really, I do and everybody else in the universe," Toby said. "It's just schmucks that make life miserable."

"Enough sarcasm. Let's put the deal on the table. We've got a big problem however you look at it. We've got a bad-ass cancer that's gonna bring us down. It's in everybody's interest to identify the killer as I see it. We've got enough on our table with our reform efforts. Already news reporters are pounding the idea there is a 'psychopathic' killer responsible. By implication one of our residents is responsible. In the end, we all lose if this gets out of hand. This will result in more emphasis on security and less on treatment," Cody said.

"What's your point? Somehow you expect these pigs to look beyond any of our residents as prime suspects?" Cohen asked. "You can't trust the police to act fairly on anything. Look at what their goon squads have done to peace advocates." "Cohen turned to Michael.

"Hey Dyson. How can you remain on the force after what they have done to the Black Panthers? And what about your pals who busted heads at our peace rally a week ago at MacMurray College? And how 'bout the Chicago 7 who are fightin' for your rights?"

"I'm not ready to give up the struggle. If nobody other than the status quo enforce laws, there's zero chance to change anything."

Cody turned to others. "Let me sum it up. Here's the deal. Carl and Michael have run into a brick wall. Koeppen's the gatekeeper," Cody said. "And you know what that means."

"Let me guess, Zeke. You and these two want to open up the wards to question residents, right?" René Cohen paused for a moment and shifted her attention to Turpin. "I can see where this is going—a 'crazy' gets ultimately charged because you narrow your search to a single resident who would confess to anything you goons would beat out of them."

Charlie Fitzgerald, the research director who was seated next to his wife, Carla, spoke out. "René, why are you so quick to assume the worst stereotype? Give the detective and the sergeant a little space for God's sake to explain how they want to proceed."

"I agree with Charlie," Cody said. "We don't know where any of this is headed."

Carla Fitzgerald, a social worker responded, "Zeke is right. All of us know we still have the old guard that will jump at any opportunity to tighten security and blame the incident on reform efforts."

Turpin sighed. "All I've uncovered today so far is office politics. How do we get to the bottom line—getting staff to cooperate?"

"I may be the only one here to say this out loud, but it would not come as a surprise if a resident or residents know a lot about who may have beheaded Hepp," Cody said.

René Cohen said, "Man you're losin' it, Zeke. There's no way that would pass the smell test. We're going back to the 16th century when innocents were burned at a stake for bein' crazy or possessed because they made a priest horny."

"So, that's why all the firewood has been piled at Scott's superintendent's house." Cody paused for a few seconds. "It's to burn witches. You know—'patients' who cast a hex on others—more commonly known as 'hexopaths.'" Cody did his best to maintain a deadpan look.

Charlie Fitzgerald smiled and cleared his voice. "I'm not a fan of outsiders deciding what's best for patient rights absent a review process. Let's not forget why we are here. This is the first asylum to shift to a community treatment model based on President Kennedy's 1963 Community Mental Health Act. It seems overlooked in this debate—the whole idea was to empty asylums and free patients to make life choices on their own. In that context, it's naïve to dismiss patient views of this tragic event based on specious arguments most on the Cook Center are incompetent as determined by a judge relying on flawed or absent witness accounts."

Carla Fitzgerald added, "I don't always agree with Charlie but this time he's right. Patients this last week zeroed in on the incident and asked if they are safe? Our residents voted on a motion to have security accompany patients going off the ward, and it was approved."

Turpin asked, "Carla, would you be willing to see us tomorrow?"

"Sure. Let's set a time in the afternoon. Say around two?" Carla Fitzgerald asked.

"Look at what you are doing Carla!" René cried. "What a slippery slope to evil—and you of all people– It's always the same. Bit by bit, you are like the prez Johnson who upped the ante in Vietnam to prove he was strong on national defense drafting thousands for the slaughter. Isn't this the same—only this time the 'Boogey man' is a mythical crazy, one of our residents. You got it right Carla. Send in the pigs to slaughter people without rights."

Charlie Fitzgerald yelled, "Why do you insist on stereotyping police, René? Does this mean you are a terrorist because you have similar goals as the Weathermen? That you want to get us out of war? But what about the other baggage? That you advocate blowing up labs and if necessary, killing a police officer. Does the terrorist label fit you? And what about the police? If a few overreact to peaceful demonstrators, does that make them all fascist thugs?"

Not waiting for a reply, Cody could see the exchanges going south. "It's the detective's turn. Let's see how he sees it."

Turpin chugalugged a big gulp of his Pabst and stood up from the bench seat. He parted, saying, "Time I get home to the wife and kids."

"I agree with the detective. Need to kick back with my wife and get some fresh air," Michael said.

Chapter 7

*Expedited Autopsy*
*Tuesday Morning*

Michael had not touched his eggs or toast. His coffee grew cold.

"What's wrong, sweetie. You ain't yourself," Hope, his wife, said. "Got your head buried in that little notebook. Let us know you still alive."

"Can't figure this case. In one way it looks like a mob hit, and on the other hand, a psycho at the asylum including the staff coulda' tripped off on Halloween."

"Can't forget your dad, right?"

Michael turned his head toward the early morning light at the kitchen window erasing darkness. He cleared his voice and blinked a few times to fight off a tear.

"Tell me again what happened baby," Hope said.

"I was twelve years old at the time, 1952 to be exact. It was a dangerous job bein' a cop on the Southside of Chicago. He got a tip that one of the goons from mob boss Ted Rose's outfit was 'bout to do his protection money run at a bar. My dad was waitin' and caught the muscle takin' the money. He collared the piece of shit not seein' his cover. Six slugs were directed to his head. His ears were cut off and put in our mailbox. Nobody ever was arrested."

"Know it grinds on you. Are you wonderin' if y'all

followin' your dad's footsteps?"

"I don't know. But I ain't gonna give it up either. A brother takin' out another can't be excused because it's jest mob business. That's what cost my dad."

"Do this case look like a hit job?"

"I don't know. There are too many missin' pieces. This mornin' maybe we'll get some leads from the guy who did the autopsy. Gotta go. Need to be at the morgue by eight."

Michael stood up and gave his wife a soft kiss and hugged each of his daughters Kayla, age ten, and Jezebel, age eight.

Michael directed his 1963 Dodge Dart to a parking lot just as Turpin exited his car. Turpin had called Michael late after leaving the Tav and informed him that Monty Hampton, County Coroner, had negotiated with Cook County for an expedited autopsy and a preliminary report was available. One of the best forensic pathologists in the state, Dr. Terry Kipper, agreed to make a weekend trip to do his analysis and visit his brother in Jacksonville. He finished the autopsy late Monday and was anxious to report his results and return to Chicago and complete previously scheduled autopsies. Turpin reminded Michael that Monty Hampton had the final say as to whether a crime had been committed.

"Ain't that obvious?" Michael asked.

"I'm no lawyer, but this routine happened here when a pharmacist killed an armed druggie during a robbery," Turpin said. "In that case, Hampton ruled it was a legal homicide."

Michael and Turpin met Hampton and County Prosecutor Abe Goldberg at the morgue entrance.

Goldberg was key in getting the expedited autopsy. "Glad to see the three of you this chilly morning," Hampton said.

The foursome made their way through the hall of the morgue to the autopsy room where the pathologist was examining the remains.

"Dr. Kipper, this is Prosecutor Abe Goldberg and homicide investigators Detective Carl Turpin and Sergeant Michael Dyson," the coroner said.

After pleasantries were exchanged, Dr. Kipper continued his inspection of the victim's head turned on the right side. Michael wondered how the specialist was so caught up in his role that he manipulated the human head not unlike that of a butcher at a meat market.

"Where do we begin?" Goldberg asked.

"This is a challenging case given the missing torso of the body. But I was able to find possible leads," Dr. Kipper said.

"Your long curly hair and greying beard styled with mustache and goatee make me think you look of one of the three musketeers," Turpin said. "You don't use a sword in your line of work, do you?"

"I only use a sword if the corpse rises off the table."

"I swear you look just like Aramis—you know one of the three musketeers," Turpin said.

"If you got to know me—really know me, I'm not that much of a cut-up, especially if I were in a sword fight," the scruffily-dressed pathologist said. "That's why I stick with the dead." Turpin smiled and Hampton laughed in a high-pitched sound that bounced off the barren walls.

"Now, can I continue?" Dr. Kipper asked.

"Absolutely," Turpin answered.

"I examined the brain and the skull. There was evidence of a large head wound and hematoma on the right parietal lobe. A skull fracture matched the location of the brain trauma. I initially concluded the cause of death was likely a blow to the head by a heavy object," the pathologist said. "However, examination of the victim's neck raised questions—notably was death caused by the blow to his head or possibly strangulation?" Kipper asked. "I think at this point that's an open question without the remaining torso. If I were to make a guess, it was strangulation. Likely the decapitation occurred later but that is open to question. I will go over that in a moment."

"When can we get your report? Think this case requires a quick turn-around given the setting and ghoulish murder," Goldberg said.

"Have it ASAP, say two days," Kipper said.

"How did Hepp lose his head?" Michael asked.

"I gave this a lot of thought. If you examine microscopically the skin and tissue where the head was separated, I expected to find evidence of a cleaver-like ax or large knife leaving tissue tears along with clean sever marks from a sharp edge. On the surface of the victim's neck, I was baffled to find clear evidence that a surgical device such as a scalpel had been used. The skin and muscle had been separated such that the expected swelling of organs you would find with an ax or large knife forcefully decapitating the victim was absent. A few bits of bone were discovered in neck muscles that suggested some kind of saw was used to sever vertebrae," Kipper said.

"That would involve a bloody mess to pull this off as you described it, right?" Turpin asked.

"Of course."

"What drives me nuts is not finding any traces of blood in Hepp's office," Turpin said. "Even if Hepp was killed by a blow, how is it that his head is put in a fish tank without any traces?"

"That's your department to figure out," the pathologist said.

"So, in a nutshell, Hepp was whacked with a blunt object and was still showin' signs of life. The killer finished him off by stranglin' him and whackin' off his head, right?" Michael asked.

"That could have happened, though hard to prove. The region of the decapitation and the surgically removed head are not, in my opinion, consistent with the use of a knife or ax," the pathologist said. "If that proves to be the case, perhaps part of the motive for using an instrument such as a scalpel was to cover up ligature traces as to the cause of death."

"Did you find such marks?" the coroner asked.

"No. But that may explain the use of a scalpel was to remove any evidence of ligature traces."

Turpin rubbed his nose. "It is baffling that anyone would go to such an extreme. Is there any way to nail down the time of death?"

"Unfortunately, his blood samples were compromised by the water temperature in the fish tank and with no torso, there was no way to determine the onset of rigor mortis. Given it was not clear when the time of death occurred, I have concluded either the blow or asphyxiation could have caused death." The pathologist gathered his instruments. "This will all be in my report. If that's all you have for now as to cause of death, I've gotta head back for Chicago to make an afternoon appointment."

"Thanks, Doctor. We'll keep in touch," Goldberg said.

Goldberg, the coroner, Michael, and Turpin headed for the exit. "Appreciate your efforts Monty in getting this expedited autopsy."

Michael and Turpin met at the police station parking lot. "So where does this take us?" Michael asked.

"Let's revisit the aquarium. Think the fish guy and the campus cop…ah what's his name?"

"You mean the professor, Wentz, and Riley, the campus cop," Michael said.

"Yeah. They might give us some leads as to where the tank was obtained," Turpin said.

Michael agreed to meet Turpin at the police station to take a plain squad car with no obvious warning lights or insignia to the hospital. On the way to the aquarium, Turpin nodded to a motorcycle cop with a radar gun. Such courtesy was expected for speeding twenty over the limit. Turpin parked outside the featureless brick building housing the aquarium. To Michael, the building seemed out of place with other old brick and limestone structures still standing over decades.

Dr. Wentz and Chief Riley met them at the entry. "Do you still have keys to get in the building? We would like to get to the scene," Turpin said.

"Sure," Riley said.

They entered and scanned the tanks holding bright tropical fish along with an assortment of local species and a special jellyfish collection. Riley led them to the victim's office door. He searched for a master key and fumbled to get the key to work. Turpin pulled out a handkerchief and opened the door. He glared at the tank.

The bloody-red liquid brought back that queasy feeling. Dr. Wentz stood outside the office.

Turning to Wentz, "Do you have any records or memory of this particular tank's origin or use as a fish exhibit?"

"Yeah. This tank as well as other tanks was a gift from the university. Our university replaced all of our research tanks. As to this particular tank, it was an extra tank from our storage locker we have here," the professor said.

"Who has access to the storage area?"

"Only maintenance staff who inventoried them when first arriving."

"Could anyone else, say a volunteer, have access to any of the equipment?"

"Not really. Most are fish admirers or collectors who on occasion help with cleaning tanks and replacing supplies. I do have one of my graduate students, William Lazzo, who helps care for the aquatic animals here. He has a key since he sometimes needs a tank for captured species. His specialty research project deals with the study of the reproductive cycle of the Longnose Gar," Wentz said. "He's close to completing his Ph.D."

"Did your student ever have any contact with the victim, Fred Hepp?" Michael asked.

"Not that I'm aware of. Based on what I know, he rarely had interactions with any of the staff here at the hospital. He's very devoted to fish. He samples eggs from fish he's caught from the Illinois River. He is collecting such data for his doctoral thesis."

"Has anyone other than your volunteers shown high interest in the exhibits that led to patient or staff contact?" Turpin asked.

"After our spring opening, several hospital staff and local townspeople showed a lot of interest. Attendance fell somewhat when the superintendent announced more focus should shift to patient visits," Wentz offered.

"How many patient tours did you do?"

"Only four before the Cook County group."

"So, it's fair to say the number of patients who have toured the aquarium is limited. What would you guess, say 200 or less?" Turpin asked.

"I'd estimate fifty or so."

"Is the building and the storage room regularly locked?"

"Yes, except when William and I are either curating new arrivals or dealing with any problems with the health of the fish," Wentz said.

"Look, I've got to run. Lunch is reserved for my wife and daughter. What's the best time to schedule a follow-up if needed?" Wentz asked.

"I'd like a time when y'all and your student Lazzo are available," Michael said.

"Most any time you are free, I can set that up. Fridays are good."

"We'll be in touch."

Chapter 8

*Witness Protection*
*Tuesday Afternoon*

Michael and Turpin exited the aquarium and headed for the Cook County Center a couple of blocks away. Social Worker Carla Fitzgerald had previously conveyed a message the best time for an interview was during the lunch hour.

The large administrative building loomed to their right and a colorful forest of varietal trees to their left. "My dad knows a lot of secrets about that building," Turpin said.

"Sorry to hear."

"No, no, he was not looney. He was a Morgan County deputy sheriff for thirty-five years. He dropped off the insane there at the main entrance of that old building. A few had to be cuffed and forced to enter the locked wards."

"Maybe they put up a fight cause' they knew they'd never get out."

"Dad would have agreed, but he was simply doin' his job. If they resisted his job was to get them to the rubber room located near the nurse's station where staff took over."

Looking to his left, Michael spotted a bird that to him looked like Woody Woodpecker. The bright red crescent on its head flashed back and forth in a rhythmic fashion to enlarge a large hole in a dying tree. The loud knocks resonated among what he guessed were native oaks and maples amongst several trees he could not identify.

Carla Fitzgerald met them at the marbled entryway. "Did you have any trouble finding parking?"

"No. We decided to get a little fresh air and take a tour after visiting with Professor Wentz," Turpin said.

"Before we get started, have y'all ever seen a real Woody Woodpecker jest outside the center?" Michael asked. "I first heard this 'knock-knock-knocking' and looked up to see this bright redheaded bird peckin' on a dead tree."

"Can you point to the tree from the lobby window?" Fitzgerald asked.

"Sure. See that snag. About halfway up. I don't see him now."

"Not surprised," Fitzgerald said.

Michael turned to the sunshine highlighting her sparkling light-brown hair. She looked healthy in her bright maternity gown with a grey silk scarf.

"I'm no expert. Just an amateur birder—but I think you spotted a rare sight at least for me, a pileated woodpecker."

"I'll tell my kids tonight I saw the real Woody Woodpecker," Michael said. "I know my oldest daughter Kayla will get on my case. She'll likely rag me 'bout reading comic books rather than chasin' bad guys."

"Is this her way to get your attention?"

"Maybe, though she'd never admit it."

As the three made their way back to Fitzgerald's office, René Cohen signaled to Carla to step aside away from the officers. In a hushed voice, Cohen said, "Sorry I missed our previous Monday morning get-togethers. Can we make it up after you finish with the screws?"

"I'm booked solid today. Is there something, in brief, you want to discuss?" Fitzgerald asked.

"In a word, I'm all for resident democracy, but this Shannon Audrey you are counseling—the one who went directly to Hippo's office, she's poisonous. She has to be stopped," Cohen said. "She's accusing my husband, Toby, of hitting on Blaze Hepp and screwing her. She revealed this at the last patient government meeting. You know this will get out one way or another. We have to stop these lies."

Fitzgerald interrupted, 'Let's stop right there. There's way too much to sort out now. Let's try again to meet—say tomorrow at 8 a.m.?"

"I get it, Carla. You'll side with Shannon making some phony sick excuse, you know, 'mentally ill,' rather than be honest and see this for what it is. She's a bitch. Staff on the ward who want us facilitators canned are all too ready to believe this shit. Toby is in their crosshairs. It's all about our efforts to reform the wards," René said.

"Enough, enough! This is not the time or place to discuss this," Carla said in a firm but muted tone. The social worker turned away and stepped in the direction of the detective and Michael.

"Sorry about that. A misunderstanding."

"Couldn't help but notice there was a little heat," Turpin said.

"Nothing that can't be resolved. Would either of you like a cup of coffee?"

"Not this late," Turpin said.

"I would like a cup — make it black," Michael said.

Fitzgerald invited the pair into her office. The office was compact. Michael thought of the front room of his Mama's house in Chicago. The paintings of hummingbirds and winter scenes from the Northwest Cascades sprinkled here and there with a variety of colorful houseplants. Two sofas dating back to the forties faced each other and were nestled in the corner of her office.

"Take the load off—Have a seat," Fitzgerald offered. "Here's your coffee Sergeant Dyson." Both officers sat on the same sofa and Fitzgerald then seated herself across from them.

"Have sofas replaced the couch in your business also? Your boss—the superintendent—Scott—He has a similar layout in his office?" Turpin asked.

"Depends on who's office. For me, it's what works. Researchers have found clients are more relaxed and forthcoming with this arrangement rather than facing somebody behind a desk."

Michael grew impatient. "If you don't mind, no disrespect, but just bein' honest— shrink talk is jest that, talk. I'll admit I don't get it and maybe never will. But for now, there are bigger fish to fry—gettin' to witnesses who knew Fred Hepp and his history here. My gut tells me you know a lot about what may have happened on the wards but y'all are between a rock and a hard place, right?"

"If I say 'yes,' does that mean you will pull a good cop—bad cop routine on me?"

"Yes, I'll play the bad cop," Michael said with a smile. "Trouble is nobody wants to play da' 'good cop' role. They like to think they all Humphrey Bogart like in the movies."

Carla smiled. "So, I play the role of another dumb dame, right? Who is sweet-talked at first into believing it's safe to keep my mouth shut? Suddenly, the bad cop turns on me. If I fail to come clean, he slaps me around 'til I spill the beans?"

"You've got it." Turpin loosened his tie. "Of course, we're jokin' just to be clear. Most of these cop shows get it wrong. There's no seducing good-lookin' suspects or slapping them around in my playbook."

"You have to understand like your playbook, I have my own. I've got things I will not do. So, before we get too far into spilling the beans, there are simple constraints. I could not gain patient confidence to engage in treatment if I could not be trusted.to honor their most trusted secrets. You would demand the same protection if you were in their shoes. Think of all the private thoughts no one knows."

"If I knew something about who committed this murder, nothing would keep me quiet." Turpin rubbed his cheek. "You may have a point about confidentiality. But, if someone confesses to you that they murdered Hepp, how can you justify remaining silent? What about protecting the community? And what about the sicko who did it? If they belong in the looney bin, that's where they should be permanently locked up. Otherwise, most everyone would agree they need to sit on ol' sparky. Honestly, can you ever let a psychopathic killer out and assure the public they're no longer a danger?"

"I can tell from your reactions last night and now you have had your fill of our worries over patient rights and treatment philosophy," the social worker said. "But since you asked, key staff agree with the Superintendent's perspective that too many individuals are sent to a facility like this not because they are sick and hopelessly incompetent—but rather have for one reason or another failed to adapt to their environment due to undeveloped or under-utilized social strategies to take on life challenges. That's why some staff like me prefer the label 'resident' over 'patient.' It's a recognition that the medical model is a poor fit for far too many."

"Not sure I follow this squabble—but for now let's get to the main entrée on the menu. Straight up. Do you know of grudges, grievances, or beef either patients or staff may have had against Fred Hepp?" Turpin asked.

"I'm no detective. But what I know at this point is not much beyond what little gossip I hear. As to residents or 'patients' if you prefer, no comment," the social worker said.

"Let's get ta' the reason we are here," Michael said. "Who was out to even a score with Hepp?"

"None that I know as to the staff. I'm not in any of their loops."

"There's more than one loop?"

"I'd rather not go there. But it must be apparent from what you observed yesterday, there are strong—make those passionate views over hospital reform."

"Could some of these passions lead to murder?" Turpin asked.

"Not saying that," Fitzgerald said. "You need to go to other sources if you suspect as such."

"Where might that be?"

"If I were you, I'd start with the bottom and go to the top."

"How about some names?"

"At the ward level, Mahalia Ross is a ward coordinator and president of the Licensed Practical

Nurse union. Even though historically LPNs have been at the bottom of the pecking order here, the reality is they have more clout than anybody else where it counts. If you want a reading on a patient and their treatment, nothing gets past Mahalia Ross. And that goes for most ward staff. Mahalia has close ties with all the shift supervisors including Blaze Hepp," Fitzgerald said.

"Blaze Hepp's an important witness. Haven't been able to make contact yet. Outta' respect for her loss, thought it best to try again later," Turpin said.

"I can't speak for Blaze's grieving process, but let's put it this way. She's a good source to uncover ward incidents."

"It's a little odd she has not answered any of my phone calls," Turpin mused. "Let's switch gears. Toby Cohen seems to have heartburn with anyone in authority and that goes for his wife. Do they clash a lot with these nurses?"

"You have to put everything in perspective," Fitzgerald said. "The LPNs have been here much longer than most of us, some a decade or more on the wards. Flare-ups have occurred over the roles of these new recruits. To nurses, their job titles of the newbies as 'change agents' or 'actualizers' have created confusion and resentment. It implies that LPNs are the problem and not the solution. The LPNs worry their next in line to be phased out just like hydrotherapists."

"Is that a reality?" Michael asked.

"Not as I see it. But you have to see it from the LPN's point of view. They do not feel appreciated or even recognized. Observing these recruits labeled by multiple titles show up on the wards at odd times and minimizing contact with patients does not go unnoticed.

It's too bad because some are quite bright and often have insights that would improve resident care. Critics among staff see the recruits as slackers which in some cases is unfair. However, it is a fact that these new mental health workers draw a bigger paycheck with few if any patient responsibilities. I don't have to draw you a picture of why conflict erupts."

Michael thought of how this sounded all too familiar. Maybe someone with a first name of Mahalia, a possible sister, might cut through the bullshit. "Would y'all do me a favor and contact Mahalia Ross if she is on duty? I'd like to speak to her."

Carla Fitzgerald punched an auto-dial and made the request. "She's on the line—I'll step out."

"Hello, this is Sergeant Michael Dyson of the Jacksonville Police Department. Would y'all mind answering a few questions?"

"Sure."

"Could y'all tell me a little more about Fred Hepp's role at the center?"

"Fred Hepp was a hydrotherapist," Ross said.

"Yes, but according to his personnel file, his job was phased out. Didn't he somehow transfer to bein' a nurse of some kind?" Michael asked.

"Y'all got the record. Y'all tell me."

"Lists him as Licensed Practical Nurse. How did that happen?"

"After some trainin', he got his certification."

"You're head of the union, right? Seems like I read in the paper, that the union filed a lawsuit against the hospital over 'liminatin' hydrotherapists and Fred Hepp was the guy who filed the suit backed by your union, right?"

"I've said too much. You really caught me at a bad time. I need ta' git our meds ready. I have nothing more ta' say."

"I'd like to ask some follow-up questions. Do you have some time tomorrow after you have completed your shift?"

"That's not a good time. I need to be home for my grandkids. Their mom's away," Ross said.

"Look I won't take that much time. I can meet you during your break if that fits your schedule better."

"I want to level with ya', Sergeant. Much of our staff need this paycheck to make do with the bills. Me gettin' headlines in this case—trust me—is a ticket to the poorhouse for me and our rank and file. It's been bad enough to hear tell they aim to shut this place down. But with these kids on our wards floatin' around like they own the place tellin' us nurses big changes are around the corner, makes it clear why they're here. I'm fightin' to make sure we still have a job the next mornin' and every other mornin'. That means not givin' the big bosses another chance to chase us off. I know you gotta' do your job but I can't be pointin' fingers," Ross said.

"I respect what you're telling me, but we need staff to open up like Blaze Hepp. You know her, right?" Michael asked.

"I leave it to Blaze to speak her mind when she ready. Of course, we all upset what happen to Fred. Some are clamorin' that I should file a grievance to git more security on and off the wards 'til the killer is found, but that just puts us in the headlights," Ross said. "Gotta' run now."

"Before you hang up, is there a number where we can reach Blaze Hepp? Haven't been able to make contact."

"Best you reach her brother, Maxwell Covington. He lives in Pearl and I don't have his number. Bye."

Carla re-entered her office and announced, "Sorry to end our chat. I have a patient scheduled in five minutes."

"Thanks for your help," Turpin said. "We'll be back."

Chapter 9

*Threats*
*Late Afternoon Tuesday, November 3*

Shannon entered the bathroom stall and locked the door. In her journal she made the following entry:

*Scheduled a meeting with Carla Fitzgerald this afternoon, I want to trust her. But I need to be honest. The ward staff go out of their way to avoid me. It all started when I brought up in patient government that I had observed certain staff engaged in sex while on duty. Nurse Best said these were very serious charges and to be fair to all that staff members' names should not be sullied if there is no evidence to back up these charges. I made it clear I had observed one encounter and was made aware by other patients the pair had been seen hugging.*

*To be fair, some argued I needed to find a witness to back up my accusations or not bring it up. I told them what I saw and they could judge me however. Toby Cohen and Blaze Hepp were having sex in the utility room. I did not tell them why I was there. I was looking for a place to hide my journal.*

Someone entered the bathroom. Shannon put away her journal and rushed for the dormitory. The journal was placed under her mattress. Shannon awaited Art Tinsley, one of a handful of male LPNs hired at the Cook County

Center, to escort her to Carla Fitzgerald's office for a scheduled Tuesday afternoon appointment.

"Keep your hands off me, you pervert!" Shannon said. As they approached the social worker's office, the LPN knocked on the door keeping a firm grip on Audrey's arm.

Social worker Fitzgerald greeted the pair at the door. "Thank you, Mr. Tinsley."

Audrey interrupted, "Stop pawing me. I don't want anyone touching me."

"Thank you again, Mr. Tinsley. Shannon and I will take it from here," Fitzgerald said.

Shannon headed for a divan and cuddled in a fetal position. She cradled her head between her knees. "I'm ready to end it. There's no hope—the staff retaliation just gets worse. All this talk of giving patients a voice is bullshit. It's window dressing for those who control the wards." Tears flowed. The sobs grew louder. Fitzgerald offered tissues.

"I'm listening.—Let's start with what has made you so upset?" Fitzgerald asked.

Shannon looked up still crying. "All of this shit we've covered about the past has not affected anything…the abuse, the abusers,…the…the…reason I keep resisting… You…you…tell me who has the fairy dust to make any difference?"

"You need to know I take your complaints seriously. You are facing serious headwinds which are only getting worse the more you strike back."

"You're the only one I trust. But look at what's happened. Whoever I befriend becomes a target when I open up. And you may be next."

"For now, let's focus on you and your situation right

now. You can't survive if you give up your grit that you can move forward. You are not unique. Everybody has setbacks," Fitzgerald said. She paused a moment while Shannon blew her nose. "Give yourself credit for speaking out. As I see it, things have changed—hydrotherapy is gone, patients now can have a say on ward policy, and abusers are on notice."

"Okay, you tell me how any of this has given me an exit ticket out of here?"

Shannon again blew her nose. "And now I've got to convince everyone I had nothing to do with Fred Hepp's murder."

"An exit strategy is in the works. I have contacted your guardian and he has agreed to petition the court to have your rights restored. It's now up to the judge to put your case on the calendar. Yesterday, I was informed today your trial is scheduled in a little less than two months. Let's see—December 23rd."

"Believe me, that'll never happen. One way or another, someone will shut me up—most likely, Dr. Koeppen."

"Let's talk like friends. I want you to know I am convinced there is persistent pushback and possible retaliation for your complaints. And what is pushing staff to be so hostile is obvious to me—The reality is you are very bright. I don't need to spell out what that means. We've covered this before. You have admitted suffering from wide mood swings. If it's a bad emotional day for you, staff may find this to be a confirmation that you are the bad actor rather than them if you strike back verbally," Fitzgerald said.

"Some weeks are better than others—you know the mood swings," Audrey said. "But I'm not Jesus. I can't turn the other cheek every time. What I can do is keep my journal up to date. It's all there and nobody but you know it exists. It's well hidden but I fear not for long. Would you store it in your office?"

"Who would want to steal your journal?"

"Let's start with Dr. Koeppen and his loyalists. They would destroy it in a heartbeat to cover up what I have documented daily is happening on the wards," Audrey said. "And there's one more who would like to get their hands on my journal—my ex," Audrey said. "He wants to see me dead!"

"You realistically believe Daryl Audrey is a threat to kill you?"

"From the start, he has done everything possible to make me disappear. He had me committed to this hell-hole so he could take up with a secretary at the insurance agency where he worked."

"That was six years ago. I'm missing a piece. Do you think he's a threat to kill you? Explain."

"Just look at the past. He schemed with a doctor to have me committed for stuff he made up. It all started when I caught him cheating on me. And yes, when he came home late, I reacted. I threw a plate cutting his head, and pounded on his chest. He got really angry and beat the shit out of me, everywhere but my face. I managed to get free and locked myself in the bathroom. He called the police. Blood was flowing from a gash on his head when the cops arrived and they bought his story. They yelled at me to come out or they were coming in. I opened the door and told them Daryl had just beat me up, but they didn't believe me since he was careful not to mess up my face. He told them I was crazy and jealous—that I made it up—and, I was getting worse. Police and later his doctor agreed I was crazy and signed some commitment papers. After hearing Daryl's version, a judge agreed that I was dangerous and mentally ill. He ruled I was to be committed involuntarily to protect Daryl and the community," Shannon said.

"That's the past. How does your ex represent a threat now?"

"You figure it out. He works at an insurance agency. While he set up house with his secretary, they schemed to cash a half-million-dollar life policy on me to buy an upscale house in Chicago."

"So, tell me more."

"Vesta Diaz on our ward warned me about the life policy. Marie, her sister, worked at the same insurance office as my ex."

"Vesta Diaz is a good friend, right?"

"That's true. My best friend was permanently 'cured' with one swipe of a surgical icepick to her brain. Bingo! She no longer yells and screams about staff abuse. Now she babbles word salad. Her memory is shot. Before the surgery, she brought me up to date on my ex. Her sister had overheard my ex and the tramp making plans to buy an expensive property in Chicago suburbs—think it was Oakbrook," Shannon said.

"Help me out. If I understand, you are afraid your husband wants to cash the life policy on you to buy the expensive home?"

"That sums it up. I know even you might think I'm crazy, that I see enemies everywhere. But I know damn well what is happening. I trust Vesta. The one thing that stands out, my ex was quoted as saying he knew how they could acquire a half-million-dollar down payment," Shannon said.

"Let me play devil's advocate. How does your ex represent a threat as long as you are on a locked ward?"

"I can't tell you now. I'm still putting the facts together. I don't trust any ward staff at this point. Like when I raised hell last week in our sham government meeting over having to beg for sanitary napkins, Blaze Hepp spoke up and accused me of constantly stirring up trouble—that this was no place to bring up such an embarrassing topic. I told them it was no more embarrassing than to catch her fucking Toby Cohen. I spotted the pair when looking for the ward storage room to hide my journal. The door was slightly ajar and I heard moans and couldn't believe what I was seeing."

"Were there consequences for speaking out?"

"Not directly. René Cohen was really pissed, confronting me after our patient meeting. She said I wanted her husband fired for simply doing his job. I told her she ought to keep an eye on Toby–that Toby–that he had even been hitting on me whenever he found me by myself," Shannon said.

"Did Blaze react?"

"She did. It was the first time Blaze ever agreed with René on anything. Blaze lost it saying I was out of control and was harming innocent staff. Blaze made it clear René was right—If any of this left the ward there would be a serious look at my treatment plan," Shannon said. "It was clear that meant another lockup in seclusion."

Chapter 10

*Disclosure*
*Wednesday Morning*

Ty Crowley walked across the hall thinking events were unfolding as he anticipated. "Hi, Belinda. Is Sam in? I would like to brief him before the planning committee commences."

Crowley thought Belinda, Scott's secretary, could be an asset if there was a meltdown of the reform. After all, he had brokered the deal for Belinda Fast to be hired a year ago despite nine candidates were more qualified. All had more experience and administrative skills. The attractive young secretary had worked on the governor's campaign. In the tradition of patronage politics in Illinois. the governor's staff contacted Crowley. He recalled how the governor's representative agreed to a settlement where the hospital could add additional mental health positions if hospital administrators agreed to hire campaign supporters such as the young secretary.

"Sure. I'll check." Belinda Fast buzzed Scott. "Ty's here. Okay. He'd like to see you now."

As he entered the superintendent's office. Crowley felt buoyed. Scott was reacting just as he had imagined. His eyes were twitching and he was rotating his pencil. It was best to wait for a better moment to bring up the bad news. Scott remained detached. He continued to flip his number two pencil between his fingers like a miniature baton while reviewing a file. Crowley speculated he was looking at options to save the hospital.

Scott reached for his phone. "Get members on our Strategic Reform Planning Task Force together ASAP and remind them of our scheduled Thursday meeting at 10 a.m. Emphasize being there on time," Scott told his secretary.

"Sam, I think we got a maelstrom brewing in the Cook County Center. From my sources, tensions are building over this Hepp investigation. The old guard is hunkering down and threatening union action if the administration does not do more to ensure their safety. I don't have to remind you the whole reform movement comes out looking bad if we emphasize democratic reform on one hand and the other hand ignore organic input from the LPN union of what likely outsiders will see as legitimate concerns," Crowley said.

"So even you have succumbed to thinking we are in a silo," Scott said with a familiar wry smile and squint of his left eye. "Maybe I should reassign you to our old farm operation here on the campus. Based on your reasoning you would insist on keeping the silo full to feed livestock at all costs during a severe drought forcing the farm to go bankrupt."

"To use your metaphor," Crowley said, "the farm goes broke either with lack of feed-crops and/or…uh, uh…shutting down livestock production. The silo storage is a measure of where we stand, but hardly limits our options."

Crowley thought maybe he had gone too far as Scott's face brightened and his eyes widened.

"Goddammit! If you don't see the bigger picture,

how do we convince anybody else? Look. This grand experiment involves everyone, and I mean everyone connected to the metaphorical farm—the planting of feed crops, the cows, the farmer, the banker -anyone having skin in the game. We either collectively step up to this challenge and get all of the stakeholders involved or it will be curtains for us all," Scott said.

"You know where I stand on our paradigm shift plan. We knew going in there would be blowback." Crowley pushed back his horned-rimmed glasses.

"Save it for our planning meeting." Scott stood up from his desk and headed for the committee room.

Crowley felt confident as he followed Scott to the antiquated conference room with a large nineteenth-century oak table and chairs room. All the key players were here which was perfect Crowley thought. Dr. Gomez was the first to arrive followed by Keegan Murphy, Public Relations Director. Next, Dr. Walter Canfield, Chief Psychologist, Phil Carson, Human Resources Director, Gary Stanfield, Head of Social Work department, and Ed Zinke, Director of Systems Operations. Last to arrive were Charlie Fitzgerald, Research Director, Craig Sweeney, the Assistant Superintendent, and Mahalia Ross, president of the Licensed Practical Nurse Union.

Crowley debated whether he should set the right tone by opening remarks or wait? Keegan Murphy who had started as a standup comic and ultimately a local radio personality spoke before all were seated. "With all due respect Dr. Scott, if you are here to tell us heads will roll if we don't get more positive news out of this joint, you first outta' look at all the publicity already. Just think 'bout it, you only need one, count 'em, only one head to roll in a fish tank to get all the publicity we need."

Murphy's boisterous laugh exposed his gold caps and reddened face. He could be heard on the entire 4th floor. He reached into his right lapel and gathered a cigarette from his silver container and placed it in an ivory cigarette holder. He lit up. He opened his tan jacket and grabbed his flask. He opened it and took a big swig.

This was the price Scott paid to get a harness race track and remodeled barn for the horses located on the hospital campus Crowley thought. Murphy's norm-breaking routine was his shtick in the old days on a talk radio show to break the ice for laughs. His popularity grew and ultimately, he became a favorite with the harness racing crowd.

Scott broke the silence. "Murphy, your timing is way off. You're not Dean Martin or W.C. Fields, not even close. There's no humor in what's happened to Fred Hepp and how it has affected everyone. Now if we can ignore Murphy's sick joke, let's get down to why we are here."

Crowley told himself not to jump the gun and reveal his negative message too soon. First, Scott needs to drive home the hospital is on the brink.

"I've called this meeting to advise all of you we are at a point where we either get our positive message out there or negative news sprouting from the murder investigation will stick and take us down."

As Scott shuffled through his notes, Ty Crowley told himself now was the moment. "Sam, if I may provide a footnote. This looming threat can be framed in a social contract context. We need to negotiate with all stakeholders that we all have the same aim—to ensure everyone's safety. Tensions over resident rights have evolved because security concerns inexorably lead to oppression of their rights. Such erosion, in the long run, distorts the commonality between those labeled abnormal with those not so tagged. This battle has persisted going back to the inquisition where the extremely lopsided negotiating power of the establishment oppressed those labeled mad. Even in the modern era, the same challenge exists. Are we going to remain silent as once more civil rights of our residents are muted to calm the fears of an angry cabal of politicians and a myopic public? My answer is to beware of the pitfalls of either or. We cannot fall prey to Kantian categorical judgments. Instead, we should seek contracts that include both protection of civil rights and criminal justice—but with our finger on the scale to correct for vast differences in negotiating strength of each party at the table. This is the only way a fair agreement can be reached. We've already demonstrated how this approach has improved the lives of individuals mislabeled and robbed of their humanity here. Negotiating for the common good should remain our focus—good negotiating such as exemplified by the public's response to our seven-lively arts exhibits," Crowley said.

"Hold on to that thought Ty! Spell out how we 'negotiated for the 'common good' when residents were never at the table?" Fitzgerald challenged.

"Charlie, you need to get over 'concrete-itist' mindset—something we were taught to avoid in Psych 101. Patients have never had a seat. In a nutshell, we are about to change that. Our staff of change agents are serving as proxies for residents until they are capable of assuming such a role," Crowley said.

"Shut up—both of you," Scott yelled. "We're here

to deal with the actual cards on the table, not intellectual gotcha games. What's at stake in the direst terms is the survival of the Center of Human Actualization. The renaming of Jacksonville State Hospital was not a rebranding of the old—packaging a new label for a dying state hospital. Rather, it serves as a model to fit President Kennedy's dream—to transition from a human warehouse to a community-based comprehensive mental health center."

"I appreciate your call to get down to what faces us," Dr. Gomez said. "We cannot turn back a century of ward cultures overnight. New staff, in my opinion, are woefully naïve as to dealing with long-tenured ward personnel. And if I may be blunt, there is no evidence that such reforms attempted here lead to recovery. Where is the science?"

"Let me address your concerns Santiago," Crowley said. "Our treatment philosophy can be reduced to empirical and epistemological arguments. Clinical outcome studies on chronic populations have shown somatic therapies are ineffective and in too many cases harmful. The so-called science of psychiatry has failed due to the faulty premise of assuming the medical model will cure human problems of adaptation. This has led to regressive practices such as a lobotomy performed on JFK's sister Rosemary. The surgery reduced her mental capacity from a challenged adolescent to that of a two-year-old. Her speech was incoherent and she could not walk without aid. So, so, so, we are not vilifying science—only bad science."

Fitzgerald said, "Crowley, you are very talented at muddying the waters. Your criticisms are so hypocritical. Those you target are easy marks–

Specifically, the crude primate studies during the 1930s that served as a model for Freeman and Watts' psychosurgery techniques. These techniques were ultimately applied to Rosemary Kennedy because over the last four decades the public bought the notion some residents on chronic wards were deemed incurable. It was the 1948 Columbia-Greystone project that exposed both the degradation of post-surgical patient functioning and serious abuse of informed consent agreements. That said, where's the science to validate social reforms you promote to correct the treatment paradigms you rail against? How do your philosophical arguments for contract theory improve their lot?"

Fitzgerald continued. "To be clear, Crowley, you, like the past psychosurgeons, seem to have more interest in rhetorical justifications rather than empirical outcome studies."

"Enough of your vitriol, Fitzgerald," Scott interjected. "Research outcomes will not solve what ails us. We need to focus on an immediate concern. From a macro-view, research is irrelevant. We could be shut down in literally months if negative messaging over this tragic event at the aquarium gets out of hand. Sources close to our state legislator friends have told me they do not have the votes to extend our funding. Fiscally conservative legislators have silently lobbied to shut us down. Their primary argument centers around the lack of hospital security due to relaxed lockup policies."

Crowley thought it was working. This was the time for the coup de grace. "What at first blush looks like an enigma… Sam's…Sam's problem in 'actuality,' no pun intended, is a wonderful example of how social contract…"

Talking over Crowley, Mahalia Ross said, "Can I get a word in? *Can I get a word in*?"

"Lookin' around this table, any fool could see why this hospital's goin' to hell in a handbasket." Ross pulled the starched collar from her neck. "We do all the shit-details and who sits at this table? My, my, I need some new specs cuz all I see is white faces, *Wow*. And lordy, lordy, I must be the only woman who knows anything 'bout runnin' this place. How could that be? Maybe, just maybe, most of us women are wipin' butts or feedin' a poor soul who'll waste away if they don't eat. Or I know, be tryin' to stop someone from bashin' in their head on a wall. No, most of y'all don't know a thing about the business of carin'.""

After a pause, Dr. Gomez spoke up. "You are brave, Miss Ross, to say what many around this table know to be true. Caring for sick patients is a very demanding job. I witnessed this first hand at Boston General and here. We lean on the nursing staff to handle intractable psychotic episodes when all else fails."

"Nurse Ross, not to dispute anything you've said, but contrast the present with past administrations," Scott said. Not waiting for a reply, he brushed his balding head while blinking his eyes. "We have turned this place upside down—no more top-down organizational constraints minimizing your role and others delivering the goods. Currently, we are actively recruiting LPNs to serve in administrative roles. As you likely know, we recently appointed Pam Smith to the position of East Center director. Everybody here has the same mission— to decentralize administration of treatment and give frontline staff a voice in treatment strategies."

"Why ain't y'all offerin' us those type a' jobs at

Cook County?" Ross asked.

"We are in the process of finalizing administrative positions for your wards with Human Resources," Scott said. "The problem is Springfield."

"That's right. The Springfield bottleneck has prevented any placements for this position," Phil Carson, Human Resources Director, said. Crowley recalled how Carson was hired. He was another candidate from the patronage list hired after the governor's election. Carson, who formerly was a regional Ford dealer sales manager, was not selected based on his qualifications for the position. It wasn't his handsome looks or well-dressed appearance that impressed the governor's political team. It all came down to the fact he had delivered the key Peoria region in the governor's campaign.

"My sources tell me that the job title and job description for the Cook Center do not conform to other approved administrative positions," Carson explained. "Technically, Pam Smith was appointed as a hospital administrator charged with oversight of nonclinical functions. That's the hang-up on the Cook County Center administrator position."

Scott said, "That's on my plate. I'll have Craig Sweeney contact Springfield and get this settled. We'll lean on our friends to resolve this so an administrative position will be offered on Cook Center."

"I'd caution you Dr. Scott to keep an open mind as to who you approach," Sweeney said. "If we lobby for a new position to Chicago legislators sympathetic to mental health, this will only fuel intense blowback from those outside Cook County. They will push for even greater security if we don't act. The political rivalry between Cook County and the rest of the state has been at times so intense that there were serious discussions Cook County should secede from the state."

"I agree with Carson," Scott said. "Craig Sweeney's background with the legislature is solid. I trust he will avoid these political land mines. If he doesn't, he'll be back to sacking groceries as he did before he obtained his political science degree."

Scott looked briefly at his notes. "I think we laid out what we face. But we need to nail down immediately concrete plans to mitigate against the political storm ahead. I propose we do a media release on our newly constructed trotter's race track. It makes for a positive story as to how the old hospital barn was converted to horse stables for these horses and significantly how chronic psychiatric residents have bonded with the horses. Get horse owners to comment on how these residents have developed this special bond. These are special horses, requiring special treatment and hours of training. Emphasize how horse owners see this as a win-win. Their horses are well cared for and they have a first-class track just constructed on our campus to train and compete in harness racing. We need to emphasize how residents who rarely communicate with others have found ways to communicate with horses both on and off the track as they assist in their care."

"Hi Ho Secretariat, I'll get a press release to your desk ASAP before my flask needs a refill," Murphy said with his loud low baritone pitch. He added, "Look, for you who know little about trotting—It takes days, weeks to train a trotter to not break their stride. We have built this race track and provided stables for the horses with volunteers. Our patients have been key to reducing skittishness during their training sessions. We are scheduling our first race in three months. We expect over 500 harness-racing fans to show. Stands are almost completed and track groomed to standards of the racing commission."

"That's a start," Scott said. "My next priority is to emphasize our security efforts in response to this ongoing investigation. I realize this runs counter to our treatment priorities, but we have to look long-range at first weathering this pending storm before charting another course setting. As of today, residents will be escorted and monitored at all times off the ward. Locks will be changed and all ward keys turned in for exchange. Only ward staff and security will have new keys. Others entering the ward will use a buzzer and voice-com to enter."

Crowley exited the meeting feeling smug. This was exactly what he had planned.

Chapter 11

*Loyalty*
*Wednesday Afternoon*

Michael wondered why Blaze Hepp had not returned to work or left word with anyone after her husband had been slain?

Maybe Mahalia Ross would open up if he made one more try at her home.

Michael dialed her number listed in the phonebook.

Mahalia answered, "Hello. Who's this?"

"This is Sergeant Michael Dyson. "Y'all got a few minutes?"

"If ya' make it quick. This is my day off. My baby needs ta' be fed."

"Let's start with what is known about Fred Hepp's activities before the incident. Did he show up for his shift? If so, when?"

"Yes 'bout 3:30 and checked out after midnight."

"Did Fred Hepp have any ongoing beefs with staff members or patients?"

"Y'all need to check with my boss, Dr. Koeppen."

"Let me try it another way. This involves murder. I would guess this has hit home to many on the wards— 'specially those close to the victim like Blaze Hepp. Is everyone muzzled?"

"Don't put that on me. I keep my nose clean. Ya'

gotta' understand we all been 'round the block 'nough times to keep the chatter down. Leaks cost jobs."

"I get it. But muzzlin' staff ain't gonna help us figure out who's behind this murder."

"Don't tell me nothin' bout how folks get shut down. My mama and papa were forced off our lil' Mississippi sharecropper farm with a burnin' cross," Ross said.

"What you and your family went through, we'all gotta eliminate. But yieldin' to the man ain't gonna solve anything. The way I see it y'all maybe protectin' those who got some scratch in the game and makin' the bucks. I'm tryin' ta' do my job the right way. You must know a lot that could break this case open."

"No comment."

"I'd like to switch gears. Blaze Hepp's a union member and you must be aware that your LPN members discussed and agreed to file a brief supportin' Fred Hepp's suit against the administration. News reports indicated Hepp was suing the state claiming that he and other hydrotherapists were canned over a dispute about treatment."

Michael reached for a news clipping. "According to the suit, 'administrative claims of patient abuse were totally unfounded and had a chilling effect on his future professional career as well as other hydrotherapists. Damages for 1.6 million dollars were sought in addition to claims for pension and sick leave.'"

"That's union business. Like I jist' told ya'—finger pontin' never pays for those at the bottom."

"But still, why did the union stick its nose in the Hepp suit?"

"Y'all can read for yourself. Fred Hepp was an LPN

union member. That's all I gotta say. If you don't mind, gotta' go now. Some of us have a real job."

"I respect where y'all comin' from. But aren't ya' concerned 'bout Blaze Hepp's disappearance? That needs ta' be cleared up."

"She needs her privacy now."

"I'm cool with givin' her time to grieve, but we need to make sure she's safe."

"Okay. Know this is a mistake, but we'all in this together. Gotta have your word y'all protect your source."

"Ya' got a deal."

Michael jotted down the info and headed for Turpin's office. "I got a lead on where Blaze might be holed up."

"What's your source?"

"Can't say. Here's what you need. Blaze Hepp is with her brother Maxwell Covington. He lives in Pearl— a little town nearby located near the Illinois River. I want y'all to handle this contact. Here's the number."

After a couple of attempts, a gravelly-voiced male answered the phone. "This is Detective Carl Turpin. I'd like to talk with your sister, Blaze Hepp."

"She got away from Jacksonville to get time to grieve. She don't need any more upset," Covington said.

"I understand she needs some space, but I only have a couple of questions."

"Sis, it's some detective. He wants to talk to you."

"Okay."

Turpin introduced himself and pressed for a meeting. He offered, "We can drive to Pearl or we can meet here at a local diner. How about the Star Cafe, for coffee at least?" Blaze Hepp paused and asked Maxwell,

"What do you think?"

"It's up to you Sis."

"I guess it's okay. I was just leaving to return home. What time do you suggest?"

"How about three this afternoon?" Turpin asked.

"That'll work."

Michael and Turpin arrived at the 50s diner a few minutes before three. They took a seat at a corner booth. Turpin flipped the tunes on a nickelodeon in the center of the porcelain table. He searched for Johnny Cash's latest hits. While Turpin focused on the offerings, Michael caught a glimpse of a well-dressed woman in a red-chiffon outfit that clung to her body entering the diner.

With no hesitation, the lady approached their booth. "Are you Detective Turpin?"

"You must be Blaze Hepp. Have a seat. The coffee is barely drinkable here, but I see a new pot is brewing."

Turpin stood up and introduced Sergeant Michael Dyson. Michael nodded at Blaze. There was something out of whack about this picture thought Michael. What a fancy bag and matchin' shoes. Fred Hepp was at least fifteen years older, maybe more based on seeing his face at the autopsy. His facial features stood out despite the grisly scene—certainly no stud whitey like Paul Newman or even a Burl Ives. Michael wondered what this guy used for bait to land this beauty?

"I appreciate your efforts to find the monster who killed my husband. But I'm still in shock thinking about the horrible suffering Fred must have endured." Hepp reached for a tissue to wipe her eyes.

"I can appreciate your mourning and I understand how hard it must be to revisit the past," Turpin said.

"Right now, I would like your help. I realize you may not want to talk about the past, but it's vital to explore your husband's dealings with others. To your knowledge, do you know of anyone at the hospital who may have had a beef with Fred?"

"My husband took his job seriously. He made it clear when we first met, the job was off-limits. We didn't talk about the wards. We both agreed to leave our jobs there."

"Surely, you talked about his job transfer—from bein' a hydrotherapist to taking a job as a ward attendant?" Michael asked.

"We only discussed his disagreement with the administration to cut hydrotherapy. He was convinced the therapy was effective—even more effective than pills or talk therapy."

"That resulted in a lawsuit, right? Didn't you talk that over?" Michael asked.

"Not really beyond what was in the paper."

"Did he ever complain about a particular staff member or patient?"

"None that I remember."

Michael watched her eyes focused on Turpin. Not unusual for white women around black men. But damn, Turpin's deep look into her eyes—What was hookin' him? Was it the high cheekbones and small nose and curly hair cut short with a ducktail in the back? Maybe it was the whole picture including her perfectly rounded bright red lips?

Turpin paused and looked at his notepad.

Michael asked, "Isn't it true, y'all and your husband were assigned to the Cook County Center?"

"Yes, but we were assigned to different wards and

had different shifts."

"And you never checked out what was happenin' on the wards?"

"Not really. Fred made it clear when he got off his shift, that he wanted to be left alone to watch his favorite TV shows and knock down a few brews. We went our separate ways. I liked movies and romance novels," Hepp said.

"Did you go to movies alone or with friends?"

"Most of the time with girlfriends like back in high school."

"How about staff from the hospital?"

"Not really. We had enough of each other on the wards."

"What about Mahalia Ross?"

"Yes. We get along, but it's mostly professional."

"Does that include union activities?"

"Where is this going? I don't see how this has anything to do with the loss of my husband?"

"Nothin' in particular. Only didn't you talk about union business like grievances sometimes, right?" Michael asked.

"Stuff like that was rarely discussed."

Turpin declared, "You mean to tell me you never discussed the local news report that your husband represented by the union had filed a grievance against the administration?"

"I promised Mahalia Ross that I would not speak out about Fred's case. That involved hydrotherapists, not LPNs."

"Yes, but the LPN union had their attorney draft a brief in support of re-instating hydrotherapists. You're tellin' me you never had any discussions with Mahalia about this?" Turpin asked.

"As I said before, I stayed out of it."

"And, I suppose you did not discuss this with your husband."

"Not really. Fred only talked about the Cardinals baseball team and hunting. He kept me out of the loop about his job."

"When did you last see your husband?"

"Can you give me a moment?" Blaze Hepp reached for another tissue and carefully blotted her eyes. "It's so painful."

"I regret asking, but it's necessary to establish a timeline." Turpin said.

"Necessary for what? Look detective, Fred was a private person. He did not make it a practice of telling me when or where he was going. I heard the door slam around 3:30 in the afternoon, the night before that awful call from the hospital the next day. That's all I know," Hepp said.

"Your husband's shift ended at midnight, right? Y'all were not concerned that he had not returned at the usual time?" Michael asked.

"Is this your way of asking whether I give a damn about Fred?"

"Just establishin' what is known about your husband's whereabouts before and after the incident."

"To be clear, it is insulting to suggest I was not concerned. For the record, I took my sleeping pills that night and conked out from exhaustion. I did not realize he was missing until the call woke me that morning."

"Sorry if we offended you," Turpin said. "Maybe, we should end it here and try it when you feel you are ready to visit the past. Thanks for your help." Turpin grabbed his notepad and left a ten on the table. Michael and Turpin headed for the car.

Chapter 12

*Closure*
*Thursday Morning*

Santiago Gomez adjusted his tie and combed his hair straight back. On his way to the emergency plenary session Scott scheduled yesterday evening, he felt determined to not allow Crowley to dominate the meeting, once again.

Santiago was the first to arrive taking a seat at the head of the table. The remainder of the selected administrators came in shortly, one by one. That included Ty Crowley, Systems Analyst, Walter Canfield, Chief Psychologist, and Craig Sweeney, the assistant superintendent. Sam Scott took a seat across from Psychologist Canfield.

Craig Sweeney opened the meeting. "Can I say before we get started, that we all recognize Dr. Scott's progressive strides toward true reform despite the unexpected brush fires? We would not be sitting here if not for his leadership."

Santiago folded his hands and turned his head looking out the window unable to face Sweeney's obsequious smile.

Scott reacted, "Craig, it depends on how you frame it. If I left it to Crowley, he would wrap the current existential threats in a holiday box with a big bow and tell us in his effete way everything can be resolved with his enlightened negotiations using a social contract strategy. That's fine for academic types and recruits, but certainly not now. It's like arguing with your wife whether it's Karma or God's will of a pending tornado that is about to take your house as it closes within a few hundred feet. Similarly, we do not have the luxury of debating the causes of the threat. Our house will be taken out if we don't move hastily A) to clean up this investigation mess and B) to figure out a survival mode in the event the twister makes a direct hit," Scott said.

"Despite your snarky assessment which I do not take personally, I would argue this is precisely the right time to invoke contract theory." Crowley was cut off.

"Spare us your take. For God's sake, we have yet to identify the true believers dammit." Scott threw his pencil at his folders. The pencil rebounded to Walter Canfield who caught it in midair.

Canfield laughed. "Dr. Scott. You just projected a classic defense mechanism—reaction formation, but at the wrong target."

"Now Canfield that you enlightened us about the unconscious. Take good notes on my conscious thoughts as to your survival—you might find them useful."

Canfield reached for his pipe.

Crowley saw his chance to expose this nonbeliever. "As a licensed psychologist Dr. Canfield, would you not agree using antiquated measures such the Rorschach and paper-and-pencil tests like the Minnesota Multiphasic Personality Inventory (MMPI) to assess diagnosis and prognosis of residents is unprofessional and unethical given their poor reliability and validity?"

Crowley continued, "Most unsettling, you have held

fast to traditional therapies linked to the medical model and ignored recommendations of change agents assigned to wards."

"You conveniently overlook I am protected by civil service regulations," Canfield said. "My duties as defined by HR are well spelled out. Given my credentials, I am protected from your overreach as an administrator, Mr. Crowley. Firing me over my clinical preferences as a licensed clinician is hardly persuasive to any oversight agency."

"That means little if the legislature shuts us down," Scott said. He glanced at his notes and continued. "Here's what we face as I learned last night. The backlash is no longer a small brush fire. Plans are being drafted by legislators and the governor's staff to shut the hospital down within six months. I was told it is no longer if, but when," Scott said. "We also are scheduled for a special review by the Joint Commission on Accreditation of Hospitals (JCAH). Staff complaints of inadequate staffing and proper hospital security for 'dangerous' residents have reached Springfield. These shortcomings have 'forced JCAH,' in their words, to reconsider our accreditation."

"Let's not over-react," Santiago. cautioned "I learned a valuable lesson while in Colombia. The Columbian government over-reacted to revolutionary forces, FARC. The government crystalized the poor to oppose government efforts to irradicate the revolutionary forces. Many poor farmers ultimately joined FARC as their survival increasingly became dependent on the cocaine drug cartels. Over time, many were convinced the government was corrupt and the president and his cronies were lining their pockets. But the government survived by pulling back. Just as in this case, you have staff who have complained about ward conditions, arguably credible complaints in too many instances. And then on top of that, some staff have grown cynical to change—they've been down that road too many times. Even with our modest changes in treatment, a culture of distrust and lack of appreciation has grown. Put it all together and it will only get worse if we keep making the same arguments for reform."

"That seems to be an accurate reading Santiago," Scott said. "I agree we need to reverse course. We will make it clear that security is our exclusive priority and reform efforts on these wards have been curtailed for now. New staff will be placed on furlough. With salary savings, we will beef up both security and ward staff to cover every center 24-7. It's win-win if we pull this off. Chances for accreditation improve and at the same time attenuate all the noise from Springfield about hospital security."

"I hate to be the source of bad tidings over labels Dr. Scott, but my old friends in the legislature really can't get past your letterhead—'Center of Human Actualization,'" Sweeney said.

Scott chided, "Let's see now Craig—If I take Crowley's approach and look at this as an implicit negotiating tactic, we would go back to the former letterhead— 'Jacksonville State Hospital.' Magically, legislators and the public will see us as credible—that this is a safe and secure facility for our residents, right?"

"Not to be insolent, but why not?" Sweeney asked. "You can keep the framework of the reform in place while publicly reviving the old labels."

Crowley could no longer remain silent. "This does

not comport with our supporters' moral code—to put it in the vernacular—the 'smell test. Our major focus from the onset was and is to maximize individual negotiating skills in social contract deliberation involving both explicit and less familiar implicit codes of conduct. We are digressing like prison inmates from any moral codes of conduct to implicit codes that say everybody is on their own. Just as in prisons, this promotes distrust and paranoia and forms a breeding ground for bad actors."

"Can I get a word in before the rest of you?" Santiago asked. "Ty Crowley has an art for theoretical double-talk. His words work for academics, but have little to do with the lives of mentally-ill patients."

"Enough debate. Let's bring closure in a Gestalt fashion—seeking a whole solution rather than summing in a piece-meal fashion," Scott said. "Let me say from the onset, none of you mentioned the seminal event that got us in this mess—the murder investigation of Fred Hepp that has precipitated our challenges."

Scott turned a page of his typewritten notes. "Let's start with the legislature and governor's office. Sweeney, you've got two tasks. The first is to expedite the murder investigation. Use all of your chits to make sure the State AG assigned to the case is a 'law and order' guy who will insist the resident or residents police want to question be interrogated. And we need to get this to the right judge, one who has a history with such cases who is leaning toward protecting the community from the 'dangerously mentally ill' over their privacy rights. Secondly, get Murphy on a press release that hospital staff along with the administration that campus security is our priority—that we are fully committed to assisting law enforcement access to witnesses to solve this case."

Scott gathered his notes and stood. "Now before anyone here makes a grandstanding speech that you will resign in protest for ethical reasons. For the record, all such letters of resignation will be accepted."

Securing the Journal

At the same time administrators were meeting, Tinsley escorted Shannon back to the ward unconstrained. Carla was helpful but Shannon's focus drifted to Koeppen. There was no way to get around his insistence she still suffered from a mental illness, manic-depressive disorder. Behind all the jargon, Audrey sensed the psychiatrist was bent on preventing her from ever revealing anything connected to Hippo's murder or other instances of patient abuse and neglect. As to the murder, what could he be covering up?

Shannon headed for the bathroom to update her diary:

*Koeppen must realize I know about the sexual assaults. Before Vesta Diaz's psychosurgery, Vesta revealed how she had been sexually molested by Dr. Koeppen. During a visit to his office, he closed and locked his office door. Koeppen insisted she lay prone on his couch. He rubbed her inner thigh telling her this form of massage was an effective technique to help her relax and reveal her inner thoughts. He emphasized the root of her problems centered around her conflicts over sexual release. Vesta pushed his hand away when he penetrated her vagina with his finger. He moved his chair closer. He told her she should relax and free her body from conscious inhibition. Vesta recalled the doctor saying something to the effect if she relaxed and let her sexual response happen, this would make her hallucinations go away. As Vesta tried to lift herself from the couch. he pinned her shoulders back to a prone position. He positioned himself over her and unzipped his pants. Vesta was frightened and screamed. Koeppen retreated. She said he told her again to relax. She had to free herself of moral anxiety—that it was such a high level of anxiety that led to her psychosis—hearing voices condemn her to hell.*

*Vesta Diaz left the office upset, feeling guilty that she had somehow been responsible. She told me no one on the staff would ever believe her story, so she never complained. A week after the assault, Vesta disclosed to me how Hippo had isolated her in his hydrotherapy office and told her to cooperate just as she had with Dr. Koeppen or face the knotted wet towel. Vesta described the rape in detail. It was violent and disgusting.*

*Vesta's psychosurgery was scheduled three weeks after the rape. I tried to get more details after the surgery. I asked Vesta how did Hippo know Dr. Koeppen had sexually assaulted her? Vesta could not give a clear answer. She could only put a few words together that were slurred and unconnected.*

Shannon exited the bathroom and hid the journal under her mattress. She realized her journal carried risks if ever discovered by staff. It was clear. The journal needed to be left with someone she could trust. That was Carla Fitzgerald. Otherwise, she could end up like Vesta.

The next morning, Shannon stood in line for her meds. The line was quite small. She wondered why other patients had not been called. Blaze Hepp poured herself a cup of coffee at the counter behind the nurse's counter. Shannon took her meds with a cup of water.

"Mrs. Hepp, could I make an appointment with

Carla Fitzgerald today? I want to get an update on some questions I had about family visits," Shannon said.

"That can be arranged if you promise to be a good girl. No more name-calling and resistance to anyone who escorts you there, right?" Blaze asked.

"As long as they keep their hands off me, I'll be a good girl as you put it," Shannon said.

"I'll let you know if that's possible, okay?" Blaze asked.

Shannon left the station and returned to a large dormitory with beds lined in rows. She sat on her bed with her eyes fixed on the entry to the room. Waiting a few more moments seeing no one in the area, she lifted the mattress. The journal was missing.

Chapter 13

*Background*
*Thursday Afternoon*

Michael and Turpin went over their next steps. "The forensic report suggested someone with a surgical background was implicated in the murder," Michael said. "Maybe a careful background check of docs both on and outside the psych wards was in order—docs who did surgery for the hospital could provide background on staff who had trainin' to do the head removal."

"A place to start might be the hospital infirmary. Dr. Gomez indicated that's where patients are treated for physical ailments," Michael said.

Michael called the infirmary and talked to Dr. Omar Chaudhry, infirmary director. He agreed to meet them in his office after rounds in a half hour. The duo drove to an isolated grey infirmary building a few blocks from the wards. Michael and Turpin skipped up the stairway lined with shrubs and cultivated flower beds. While waiting for Dr. Chaudhry to return to his office, Michael picked up a pamphlet that gave a brief history of the infirmary and listing of staff.

"This is interestin'," Michael said. "I wondered why this buildin' was so far from the other buildings? Says it was built during the late teens and early twenties in response to the 1918 Spanish flu epidemic which took a heavy toll of deaths at the asylum."

Michael continued. "So, this is why it's so remote and never torn down. Other infections came along such as tuberculosis. It says medical services since the 1960s had been dedicated to hospital ER treatment and long-term convalescent care."

"Greetings. Let me guess. You are Sergeant Michael Dyson and you must be Detective Turpin. If it's those parking tickets, I'll write you a check for whatever the amount. My wife does not understand, or knowing her, ignores 'No Parking' signs when she's shopping," Dr. Chaudhry said.

"Not to worry. My wife has let the meter expire more than once while getting her hair done and the tickets pile up in the glove compartment. And guess what? There's a notice in the mail. And no. I don't get a 'Free Get Out of Jail' card," Turpin said.

Pulling a pen and his notepad from his lapel Turpin said, "I'd like to get background information as to who has surgical assignments in your hospital?"

"I do most surgical procedures. Our other two physicians treat other disorders other than minor cuts and bruises which nurses handle. Why do you ask?"

"Let's get to why we are here," Turpin said. "Did you or anyone on your staff have regular contacts with patients or staff on the Cook County unit?"

"Not really. We are isolated from other staff here. As for others on their unit, I had lunch maybe twice a month at the staff cafeteria with Dr. Koeppen and his head nurse, Linda Best."

"They lunched together often?"

"I can't say how often–only that they invited me to their table the few times I could get away. Regular lunch breaks are rare given our staff shortage," Chaudhry said.

"Do you know of any other doctors on your staff who had contacts with the victim Fred Hepp?" Turpin asked.

"Dr. Davis collaborated with him on his research project which focused on somatic therapies for geriatric patients."

"What does that mean? Were they investigating Hepp's specialty, hydrotherapy?" Turpin asked.

"Not as I understand the project. They looked at whether radical changes in body temperature combined with certain medications reduced psychotic episodes."

"Did this Dr. Davis have any specialized training in surgery?"

"I'd rather not speak to specialization. You need to check with the Illinois Medical Licensing Board of Physicians to get a complete answer," Chaudhry said. "But I can say our medical staff is competent to handle our mission here including ER duty."

"I'll look into the licensing," Michael said. "Off the top, has anyone else sought you out to discuss any aspects of surgery?"

"Only Dr. Gomez—but that was linked to accreditation standards."

"What did you discuss?"

"Dr. Gomez reviewed our medical records to see that we complied. He was looking for cases where I or the two other physicians here might be unqualified to perform certain procedures—an example would be hip replacements. Such specialized surgeries are referred to Jacksonville Hospital—now the Passavant Area Memorial Hospital," Chaudhry said. "I might add, they are far more equipped and staffed than we are, especially after their expansion in 1968 to a five-county regional health hospital."

"So, may I ask in terms I might understand. What are your surgical specializations?" Turpin asked.

"I did my residency in thoracic surgery at Sloan-Kettering for two years. That involved surgery to treat diseases involving defective organs in your chest such as your lungs."

"That sounds very specialized. Does this include neck surgery?"

"No. That is another specialty. Most of these surgeons deal with severe neck injuries of one kind or another," the surgeon said.

"So, excuse my ignorance, but your background seems out of place here. Why would you accept a position here when you could get on with larger outfits like Memorial?" Michael asked.

"I don't want to get into the politics of recruitment of physicians. I was so fortunate to get the very best training in the U.S. after obtaining my medical degree from India. I'm happy where I'm at," Chaudhry said.

"Do you have any more questions, Sergeant Dyson?" Turpin asked.

"No. That's it for now."

"Thank you for your time. Do you have any questions?" Turpin asked.

The middle-aged physician who had very dark skin and eyes with coal-black hair asked, "Why are you so curious about surgery? Do you believe whoever did it was a surgeon or had surgical skills?"

"Maybe, maybe not."

"So, am I a 'person of interest' as they say in this country?"

"No. As you can tell, I know squat about what docs like you do. I appreciate your cooperation, Doctor," Turpin said.

Chapter 14

*Audit*
*Friday Morning*

Charlie Fitzgerald agreed to meet at Superintendent Scott's home at nine o'clock. Fitzgerald wondered why did they not meet at the hospital? Scott's wife. Rani, met him at the door and invited him in. She excused herself and said Sam would be with him shortly.

The large parlor room was occupied a month earlier where key members of the hospital reform were invited to celebrate their success. Memories of a flying pig were hard to forget. Rani Scott had put together Indian dishes including a roasted piglet with an apple in its mouth placed on a silk rug. Virginia Gomez, Santiago's wife, attempting to sit on the floor to take a place at the feast fell backward with her leg kicking the piglet launching it into Scott's lap. Scott laughed. He asked, "Who said pigs can't fly? Was this the first solo landing Virginia?"

Fitzgerald scanned objects in the room. Folk art from Africa was affixed to one wall. A large sculpture of Buddha in the corner of the room was surrounded by furniture that appeared to be of Indian origin. He turned to a large painting on the wall. His eyes remained fixated on the erotic oil female nude portrait oblivious to the presence of anyone in the room.

"So, you like what you see. I do too, That's my

wife." Scott smiled. He led Fitzgerald to his study. "Just a minute before we get started. I have to get another folder."

While Scott left his study, Fitzgerald scanned books in his library. Most were commentaries on psychiatric reform. One stood out, "The Myth of Mental Illness," penned by a psychoanalyst, Thomas Szasz. Scott had often cited the author who characterized psychiatry as a "pseudo-medical enterprise." Fitzgerald recalled how Scott highlighted in seminars this was compelling evidence psychoanalysts were breaking ranks with medical school departments of psychiatry. At multiple conferences during the 60s, Scott had argued that the Freudian's stranglehold on academic training of psychiatric residents was even more damaging than traditionalists adhering to the oppressive medical model. Fitzgerald recalled Scott's main pitch in persuading Illinois politicos to hire him was to rid the Jacksonville asylum of years of oppressive abuse based on outdated paradigmatic approaches. A shift toward a new paradigm based on the primacy of social contracts and emphasis on social learning potentially could empty state hospitals.

Scott returned and shut the door to his spacious study. He headed for an Indian silk rug on an oak tongue-and-groove floor and seated himself on it, Yoga-style.

Fitzgerald picked a very large velour red pillow in front of Scott and awkwardly seated himself.

"I see your youth offers little advantage when flexing your ass." Scott smiled broadly with a twinkle in his squinted eyes. "On another note, Charlie, what's the status of that drug audit you initiated six months ago?"

"Stalled initially for lack of cooperation from the

pharmacist, Gary Smith," Fitzgerald said. "He insisted on the release of medical information forms for every patient audited. I could see no way to complete an internal audit in six months. We tried another strategy. After a lot of back and forth with nursing staff on the wards, I managed to get them to provide records of drugs dispensed on the wards based on confidential case numbers linked to residents. Everyone was on board except Cook County. Dr. Koeppen ordered a halt of the audit citing patient privacy was not sufficiently protected."

"So, despite all these shortcomings, what have you found?"

"Holes in drug accountability so far. Meds are not getting to patients," Fitzgerald said. "I alerted state auditors to our preliminary results. They agreed to do their audit of our drug pharmacy and ward records. Their audit has the weight of law given licensure requirements."

"Have you heard from state auditors?"

"In a nutshell, state auditors refused to disclose any general findings. But my source did say in passing they identified five patients who had been dead for two years but were still being dispensed their meds," Fitzgerald said.

"Dammit! Why not a heads-up on such info Charlie?"

"For one, I wanted to deliver their complete audit and our incomplete results to date. And two, I've been preoccupied with other research projects currently in progress." Fitzgerald tried to find a better position on the pillow.

"By now as you should realize unless you live in a

cave, we face an acute crisis here. Consider how these revelations look to outsiders—missing drugs, a barbaric murder, and ward staff who remain intent on wiping out our reform efforts with their bile. I don't have to spell out Springfield's reaction. Too many legislators see our wards as insecure and understaffed due to changes implemented by the current administration," Scott said.

"I get it. But, I'm not a politician or a PR guy. The job of directing research is my preoccupation."

"Charlie, there is no such world. Everything is political. How in the hell do you think we carved out your position here and support staff? What about the state stipend we obtained for you to complete your degree?" Scott challenged. "I want you to bury that state drug audit. You can dispute their findings based on your independent audit. Say that you found inaccuracies with the state's audit. You can argue most irregularities were due to clerical errors."

"Wow! Let's take a pause." Fitzgerald sensed this was more than a warning shot. He had to make a stand he thought. "I want to start with you, Sam. You've pulled off a reform effort here that for me is revolutionary. History will judge whether such reforms make a difference in treating behavioral disorders. You did it with effective messaging that the old hospital could be modernized and transitioned from serving as a human warehouse to a patient-first comprehensive...a...a community-based treatment program. I came on board thinking this could work if outcomes promoting the reform were based on principles of science rather than politics."

Fitzgerald sighed and inhaled deeply. "But you must see reform through a different lens. Bottom line—I'm not about to cook the numbers. If you are serious about skewing the numbers. That will ultimately bite you in the ass."

"What is it you don't see?" Scott asked. "Who is gonna listen to your sermons about accountability and science? You're simply parroting what you garnered from some tenured mossback who plagiarized his student's research thesis for advancement in the department. And it goes on and on. The serf becomes a prince who has his pick of the litter to carry out the same game - to build bloated vitae full of publications that mean nothing where a variable is tweaked using the same methodology over and over adding virtually no original knowledge," Scott said. He looked directly at Fitzgerald and said, "Hostile critics are growing. This is *realpolitik.* They could give a flying-fuck about science in this instance. The real game is to engage them on their turf now, not next week, next month, or whatever. We don't have decades."

Scott shifted his yoga position. "It's who is last standing that counts. Machiavelli was right. Consider the Medici family war with the Vatican in Rome. No one in that struggle could claim ownership of moral high ground to achieve power. When it's all said and done in our situation, voters don't give a shit about who played by the rules if in the end we humanely empty asylums and engage them in their life choices. If we play this smartly and maneuver our way out of this mess with the right rewards and punishment to the gatekeepers, we can survive so that ultimately you can then showcase outcome studies. That should work for even a skeptic like you Charlie."

"I'm skeptical for the right reasons," Fitzgerald said.

"How do we know whether your reform efforts have impacted patients? Without such evidence, who will consider such radical reform measures? So, let me point out the obvious. Research ain't easy. It's time-consuming to construct reliable and valid predictor and outcome measures that can be quantified in the first place. We've spent six months on that alone. Secondly, there are several potential confounding influences on patients' mental status that require statistical control. Despite those limitations, Cody and I think we are making progress. We're checking out structured interviews that show better reliability. Multivariate statistical methods have been identified that show promise toward modeling complex causal outcome such as ours. Bottom line, it all comes down to whether such a grand scale research effort will stand up to scientific scrutiny. As to your Machiavellian argument, I'll sum it up in eight words–I have faith in both science and humanity."

"Charlie, such ignorance!" Scott said. "Science cannot define faith. That's a dead-end, period."

"Of course, science is limited. There are many unanswered questions such as predicting the flight of a leaf from a tree to understanding the origins of life. As for our awareness of the unknowns, it ultimately comes down to that word you despise, 'faith,'—faith the scientific method continues to reduce mysteries of the unknown," Fitzgerald said.

"As I told administrative staff, you can get on board and engage in the fight or hand in your letter of resignation. Think it over Charlie. To paraphrase Machiavelli, 'Moral imperatives have no place in the political arena.' That includes faith arguments for damn sure. I'll give you two days. If no response, I will terminate you and your staff effective immediately."

"So, meeting here was all about a loyalty oath?"

"Everybody who has signed on to reform in one way or another is gonna have skin in the game when it gets hot. There's no question some bastards on board with our mission will turn critical on their way out the door. If they are true believers, they will play by the same rules as our critics do now or get the hell out."

"Count me out. I'll have a letter for you as soon as I get back to the office. There is another alternative going forward, but I doubt you want to hear it. Better that I spend that time shutting down current projects." Fitzgerald lunged forward off the large pillow and bolted out of the house.

Chapter 15

*Credentials*
*Late Friday Morning*

It was Michael's day off. The phone rang. "Need to ask a favor," Turpin said. "Meet me at Memorial Hospital at ASAP. Come as you are. Forget the uniform."

"Is this an emergency?"

"Not really. We need to check out a tip I got."

Michael met Turpin at the hospital entrance parking lot, "What's up?" Michael asked.

"I just got a tip from the state AG office that drugs dispensed at the state hospital are not making their way to patients. We need to run down drug OD cases here at Memorial for the last year and locate those where the docs ran into problems over identifying the drug or drugs abused to see if the missing drugs are getting to users in the area," Turpin said. "This will involve working with our drug unit for leads."

"You know damn well hospital staff will not give out those names," Michael said.

"No. So, we do our own investigation. Investigating local drug traffic means shedding your police uniform permanently for this case Detective Dyson."

"I ain't a detective and I'm not interested in a token promotion if this is what you or the chief has brewed up.

I earned my stripes. So, let's keep it that way, okay?"

"We've traveled a lotta' miles. Just consider we pulled off calls at dangerous scenes with nobody killed or maimed. That's remarkable. Let's face it, there were many times you had a target on your back as a black officer," Turpin said. "I know where you've been in this department and what you're up against. You put your name in for the detective position believing you would make a damn good one. Now prove it."

"It ain't gonna happen. Even if it did, you know damn well this crew would see it as window dressin'. I can just hear their reaction like, 'How y'all doin' Detective 'Token?'"

"There's no reason not to call 'em out on that. I got your back if that shit spreads. We go at 'em one at a time," Turpin said.

"Save this for later," Michael said. "I repeat, I don't want favors. If you are askin' as a friend for some help on this case, then let's get it on."

Turpin nodded. The pair headed to the surgery wing of the hospital where Dr. Timothy Blake, chair of surgery, had been scheduled for an appointment.

Turpin and Michael were ushered to a Spartan-furnished office with anatomical displays of internal organs. Blake headed for his desk and leaned back in his chair. "I'm Dr. Blake. Can I help you?"

"Good to meet you, Dr. Blake. I'm Detective Turpin. This is my partner, Detective Michael Dyson. We're here to ask a few questions. We want to know what surgeons at your hospital or elsewhere have had training in one form or another to perform neck surgeries?"

"Off the bat, none as specialists. Depending on the

diagnosis, most in ER could handle trauma cases involving the neck," Blake said.

"Have you collaborated with medical staff at Jackson State Hospital on surgical procedures," Turpin asked?"

"None to my knowledge," Dr. Blake said. "We treat referrals from JSH on occasion… Wait a minute…there was one physician from their infirmary who requested access to our medical library. I don't recall his name. I remember he also asked if I might answer a few questions as a follow-up."

"I have a list of physicians on this pamphlet practicing at the JSH infirmary. Would you scan the list and see if any jog your memory?" Michael asked.

"Yeah. That's the one, Dr. William Davis. He never contacted me."

"Did he visit the hospital library?" Michael asked.

"He never checked in with me. You'll have to ask our part-time librarian," Blake said.

"Could I ask a dumb question? Do docs get basic training like medics in the army on basic surgery techniques?" Michael asked.

"For the most part, yes."

"But ain't it true, some have the book understandin' but short on puttin' it to use," Michael said.

"No question."

"If I get this right, this Dr. Davis would've checked in with his boss first, if he visited here?" Michael asked.

"There's no way to know that from where I sit. You'll have to ask Dr. Chaudry."

"Thanks for carving out time for our investigation. We may call on you again," Turpin said.

"Before you leave. Just curious. Why the queries

about surgical training?" Blake asked.

Turpin stood. "As you may have figured out at this point, we are investigating the Hepp murder-decapitation case. We're wondering if someone with surgical skills was involved? The forensic pathologist concluded there was evidence of surgical techniques used in the homicide."

"I'd like to see the report."

"It's best to keep this confidential until we get some solid leads. However, your review would be very helpful," Turpin said.

Walking out the glass-door entrance, Turpin commented to Michael, "You know where this going. Curious what this Dr. Davis is up to?"

"You don't listen very well. Drop the *detective* bullshit, or count me outta' this investigation," Michael said.

"I get it." Turpin turned and walked toward his rig.

Michael thought I can't let this go down. He stepped hurriedly toward Turpin and stepped in front of him. "Now let's get back to why we're here. I'm gonna jist' be a cop—not a token detective. To be clear that starts doin' police work. I will be checkin' all JSH docs on their trainin' and those sheepskins on their walls."

"Now we're talkin'," Turpin said.

****

Michael arrived at the station before Turpin. Without greeting anyone, he scanned the offices to locate a private phone. Every phone was used or near someone except Turpin's phone.

He noticed Turpin coming toward his office but halfway stopped and seemed headed for Chief Brady's office. I wonder what Carl's up to? I will get plenty pissed if he's makin' a play for me.

A few minutes later Turpin approached his office door. "You don't fool around Michael. I'm guessing you're already on those docs," Turpin said.

"Ya' got it." Now was the time to clear the air he thought. "So. What did you hit the chief up for—a new badge for me?" Michael asked.

"No. He did not have any available. But he did have a temporary office you can use for the investigation."

"God dammit! What don't y'all git?"

"There's no point in you not having some privacy in your calls. Ya' know damn well this office has all kinds of leaks—leaks we don't need for a lotta' reasons."

"So, y'all think there's no way in hell I could make it happen one way or another?"

"Of course, you can, Michael. But this department ain't gonna cut ya' any slack."

"And y'all think you are the equalizer? Let's get one thing straight Carl. I'll fight my own battles. I'm the dawg they wanna' be hauled to the pound. Just back off. It's on me to man up."

"Okay, okay. Just for the record, you have an office. You can take Shirley Quin's office. She's on furlough to have her baby. Betty Stern's taken her job as a meter-maid. She doesn't need an office."

"Is this a makeup call for not being promoted to a detective?"

"Look Michael. I'm not lookin' for a fight but that's where it's goin'. I'll admit you were screwed. But don't take it out on me. You know Brady and like it or not he's still the chief."

"I'll deal with Brady. Just stay out of it."

"I'm guilty. Just figured the case is getting colder.

Losing patience with all the delay."

"Just let it happen," Michael said. "You ain't gonna change centuries of racism in a day."

"Okay. Now, can we get to the investigation? For starters, we need ta' get access to that drug audit my anonymous source revealed. And, we need an update from the guys we've got on drug enforcement. They might turn up an angle," Turpin said.

"Yes sir master. First, I gotta' return to my cabin."

"Not funny. Let's get to work."

Michael ignored the stares when entering the assigned office. His first call proved productive. The state department of licensure agreed to provide credentials of physicians practicing in the Jacksonville area. Michael took notes concentrating on those with an M.D. employed by the hospital. Most at JSH got their medical training outside the U.S. One exception stood out—a new hire at the infirmary. Dr. William Davis had a degree from the University of North Carolina. He was last employed at Dorothea Dix Hospital in Raleigh North Carolina. He had served as a psychiatrist at the facility for thirteen years.

Michael thought it odd that an experienced psychiatrist would take a position at an infirmary treating primarily physical health issues from what little he knew. His specialty was psychiatry. Why did this doc not do his thing on one of the wards? Maybe, it was best to run all this by Turpin, On the other hand, he knew Turpin would not wait for approval from anybody.

"Hello. This is Michael Dyson from the Jacksonville Illinois Police Department. Is this Kyle Carrie, Human Resources for Dorothea Dix Hospital?"

"Yes, how can I help you?"

"A Dr. William Davis who is currently employed at Jacksonville State Hospital has listed your hospital as his last employment. What years did he serve as a psychiatrist at your hospital?" Michael asked.

"You sure you have the name right—a Dr. William Davis?" Carrie asked.

"Yes, I'll double-check—a Dr. William Frank Davis who lists his last employment as a psychiatrist at Dorothea State Hospital in Raleigh North Carolina," Michael said.

Unless there's some error in spelling the name, something's amiss. Let me check with our recent history and see if there may have been a visiting psychiatrist or faculty from other institutions with that name," Carrie said. This will take a few minutes. Can I put you on hold?" Six minutes later, Carrie called back. "Hello, I've got information. Before giving you details, would you mind if I did a security check? If you give me your badge number, full name, and rank, I'll call your department and see if you are who you say you are."

"Fine with me. Tell 'em it's regarding the Hepp case. I'd like ta' hear what you found out ASAP if that works for y'all?"

Carrie agreed. Michael offered his badge number, his rank, and phone number.

Michael dropped the receiver on the cradle wondering if his accent brought on the security check. What did she mean when saying "something was amiss?" While waiting Michael scanned the hospital list one more time. Dietrich Koeppen's training stood out. He reread his resume. Koeppen completed his medical degree at Munich School of Medicine in 1948. A three-year residency was completed 1950-1953 at Wesson

Maternity Hospital in Springfield Massachusetts. Dual residencies were listed in obstetric surgery and pathology during this period from 1953 to 1955. Another two-year residency was completed 1957 at Oklahoma Medical School. Koeppen earned certification in psychoanalysis from the American Psychoanalytic Association.

Impressive credentials from what little he knew about training docs. Questions jumped out. He recalled his dad was assigned occupation duty in Munich at the end of WW II the year Koeppen completed his medical degree. Something didn't jive. His dad had said little about the war when he got back other than tellin' him 'bout the bombed-out city, Munich. Michael recalled his dad described it as a scene from hell. After the war ended in 1945, troops were ordered to hunt down Nazis. Michael recalled his dad gave it a fancy name, "the denazification initiative." He told him stories of Germans begging for food and shelter. Little was left standing—no water you could drink. He went on to say it was like huntin' starvin' ducks on a dried-up pond. It was not hard to root 'em out. Most surrendered all skin and bones. Few knew little or no English. Most Americans did not believe them when they said "No Nazi." He remembered his dad sayin' most were shipped by truck by the hundreds to the West and imprisoned in POW camps.

His dad emphasized since Munich was the breedin' ground for Hitler's movement, most soldiers showed little mercy. Over the months, allies encountered less and less resistance. Their orders changed in January 1946. Denazification was suspended. After that, he was given a discharge and returned stateside.

That's what did not add up. How did Koeppen get his medical degree in such a short time? Assuming somehow a medical school opened in 1946, how did he get a medical degree in only two years? And, what about his varied specializations in obstetric surgery and pathology? What skills did that involve?

Michael collected his notes. The phone rang. "Hello. Is this Sergeant Michael Dyson?"

"Ya' got it right."

"This is Kyle Carrie, Human Resources at DDSH. Just talked with your Chief Brady. He told me you were investigating a homicide case."

"Yeah. I'm checking on the backgrounds of the staff here at Jacksonville State Hospital. Did y'all come up with any info on a Dr. William F. Davis?" Michael asked.

"I looked back in our files going back two decades," Carrie said. "I checked to see if one of our staff with the same last name but a different first name may have served here and moved on to your facility. I checked with our visiting specialists and teaching faculty and came up short. The bottom line, there is no mistake in the record. Dr. William F. Davis. served with distinction here for thirteen years in a clinical capacity as a respected psychiatrist. Sadly, William Frank Davis passed away July 16, 1968."

"That's interesting, to say the least. Is there another Dorothea Dix Hospital branch in your state?" Michael asked.

"None."

"I'll double-check with HR and state records. Maybe there is a mix-up somewhere in the records. Thanks for your help." Michael clicked his pen several times as he wondered what was the right move. "Hello, Carl. Need to update you. Turns out I've found two docs that raise questions. Let's start with the shrink who works at the infirmary, a Dr. William Davis. Turns out he's dead. He met his maker in July 1968. We got an imposter seems to me. Our next move is above my rank."

"Goddamn, what a bomb! You sure you got it right, right?" Turpin asked.

"Yeah. Double-checked the name and there's no question. He died at the age of 45 of heart failure," Michael said. "So, Detective, what's next?"

"Enough already. Drop that shit," Turpin said.

"You the man dammit. This looks like one for the feds and you gotta' make the call if that's where we take this," Michael said.

"You know how I feel about contacting the FBI."

"Right," Michael answered. "So, we make like the Lone Ranger or punt. It's clear at my paygrade makin' any call without goin' through the ranks would land my ass out on the street."

"Here's the deal. I need your help. Not all this shit about rank. I value your take on where we go next. We can't screw this up," Turpin said.

"I suggest we sit on this 'til we figure out who else may be of interest," Michael said.

"Now, who else is on your list?" Turpin asked.

"As to the other doc, I got a lotta questions about this Dr. Koeppen," Michael said. "As best I can determine, somehow, he got a medical degree in two years in Munich right after the war. That don't seem possible. And while here in the States, he got some trainin' in surgery."

"Now on Koeppen we need to map out the goods on

him before we do a follow-up," Turpin said. "He's a smart dude evading direct answers. What about checkin' out his record on the QT with Dr. Gomez? He comes across as a straight arrow?"

"Again, you the man, Detective Turpin," Michael said.

"What the hell? Are we back to 'step 'n fetch it?'" Turpin asked.

"I ain't askin' for anything other than tellin' it like it is," Michael said.

"It's time ta' soldier up," Turpin said. "We're still a team. If I'm full of shit, don't hide it. Use your instincts, hunches, whatever, and go for it. Now let me lay another egg. I just found out from the guy in charge of the state drug audit most of the phony scripts were on the Cook County unit. So, give me your take—where next?"

"If it were me, I'd track down the drug connection for starters," Michael said.

"We think alike. Could be a major supply link right here in sleepy historic Jacksonville, Illinois," Turpin said.

"Maybe. Still don't see how docs fit in?" Michael asked.

"I have a feelin' you'll figure that one out."

Chapter 16

*Freddy*

Charlie Fitzgerald thought of how he would miss the gang and the research projects started. He looked at his notes on pilot research studies thinking how he had totally misjudged Scott. As he packed the files, one stood out labeled "Freddy."

Charlie recalled his encounter with Freddy one month before the dustup with Scott over the drug audit.

The goal was to identify and treat a regressive resident who exhibited acute mutism. Cook County Center was selected for the study. Staffing charts were avoided to make sure selection was based strictly on behavioral observation, not clinical impressions from others.

The purpose of the pilot study was to demonstrate the validity of emerging behavior modification techniques residents considered hopelessly "psychotic." One resident seemed to fit such criteria. He was sitting in the corner of the dayroom rocking back and forth making facial grimaces. These repetitive behaviors were timed over a five-minute period.

Unknown at the time, the "psychotic" patient named Freddy Brown had been an entertainer during the '50s, 'Steppin' Freddy,' as he billed himself then. He survived earning less than fifty dollars a week with tips when tap-dancing at Chicago bars catering to blacks. Early after his admission to the state hospital, he claimed he had opened for blues legends such as Little Walter, Muddy Waters, and Howlin' Wolf. But the gigs dried up as television viewing kept more and more home. He took to the streets and while very drunk one night he told staff he was jailed.

At Freddy's arraignment, his admission papers cited the judge's conclusion that Freddy was incoherent. The judge asked the defendant what he did for a living? He smiled and said, "I do the beat with my feet." He was asked what that meant? Freddy said, "It's from my head," The judge at that point said he had heard enough. He ruled the defendant was mentally ill and legally incompetent to be tried for the charge of vagrancy. The judge signed involuntarily papers that the defendant was to be committed to the Jacksonville State Hospital for time indefinite until his competency was restored. That took place on June 6, 1958.

On the ward, I grabbed a chair and placed it in front of the resident (aka Freddy). He continued to lunge forward with his mouth closed, as his grin grew larger.

I questioned the resident as to the place he resided, the current year and month, and his name. No verbal responses were offered. Only the repetitive stereotypy of lunging back and forth.

The plan was to employ behavior modification techniques to reverse the apparent mutism by shaping his verbal sounds one word at a time. The first target word was "Hello." I divided the word into five syllables.

With exaggerated facial expressions, I introduced the word "hello" one syllable at a time. The first target was "Heh." I positioned myself to make eye contact with the resident. Orally and visually, I exaggerated the sound and movement of my lips. He continued the same repetitive back and forth motions with his eyes partially closed. I gathered a handful of M and Ms from a package in my pocket and held them in one hand while repeating "Heh. Heh." He continued rocking. After the fourth repetition, the resident said in a low-volume audible voice, "Heh." He grabbed the candy from my hand. In a single motion, he threw the sweets in his mouth. Using his gums, he chewed the candy when thrusting forward. His closed-mouth smile widened.

Next, the "EL" sound of hello was modeled. The syllable was exaggerated by splitting the "eh" sound from the "L" sound. After rocking three times, Freddy made the "EL" sound, and grabbed the candy immediately. His cheeks ballooned as he chewed the candy rocking back and forth.

The last syllable, the "O" sound was offered. He rocked back and forth multiple times not uttering a sound. Next, the whole word, "Hello," was modeled. This was to aid him respond to the entire sequence rather than depending entirely on what behaviorists termed "chained S-R sequencing."

Emphasis was placed on each syllable, "Heh el O." He did not respond. He continued rocking back and forth with his familiar grimace. The procedure was repeated a dozen times and still no response. A large handful of M and Ms was offered as a reward.

As resident lurched forward for the eighteenth time, he stopped and made eye contact. "When in the hell are you gonna give me the rest of da' candy?"

\*\*\*\*

*Friday Afternoon, November 6th*

Cody headed for the male ward to sample first-hand what residents were up to. "Steppin' Freddy" yelled, "You got more of dem sweets?"

"Freddy. No, I don't have candy—but how 'bout a cigarette?" Cody asked.

"Nah Man. I ain't got no teeth," Steppin' Freddy cackled. "But I still gotta' a sweet tooth."

"Havin' no teeth don't prove a damn thing. I'll check with the candy guy to see if I can get you some," Cody said.

"That fool gotta' big supply."

"Yep, Freddy. You played him for all he had."

Freddy started rocking to and fro as before.

"I promise Freddy. I'll try ta' talk the candy man into bringin' you a couple a bags," Cody said.

Freddy stopped and said, "What's ya'all's gig? Ain't, I suppose ta' fetch da ball if I's to get da' treat?"

"No fetch the ball. But somehow, I think you know a lot about this joint. For starters, what da' ya' know about Hippo?"

"I ain't got no nothin' 'bout 'forcers."

"Do you mean 'enforcers?'"

Freddy started rocking again. "What would it take to explain what you mean?" Cody asked. Freddy remained silent exhibiting a broad smile with each forward lurch. Cody pulled out a pack of Camels and offered one. Freddy halted and took one. He returned to the rocking motion with the cigarette dangling in the center of his mouth. Cody offered him a light. Freddy inhaled deep into his lungs. He continued rocking. Each drag on the cigarette produced head movements that seemed inspired by a silent beat to a melody from the past. At least that's the way it seemed to Cody.

Freddy lunged forward, took an extended drag, and swung his elbow sideways hitting Cody in the ribs. He exhaled with streams of smoke out of his nostrils and mouth. He turned to Cody with an exaggerated smile. He pulled the cigarette from his lips, turned his head up toward the ceiling, and opened his mouth wide. He placed the half-smoked butt on his tongue, closed his mouth, and swallowed it with even a wider smile. Smoke drifted from his nostrils.

"You got my attention, Freddy. Now, can I get yours?" Cody asked.

Freddy's wide grin turned to a deep laugh. "Sure. Still gots a sweet tooth butta' ya' got no candy."

"How 'bout something on Hippo?"

"Why don't ya' ask his lady?" Freddy asked.

"You mean Blaze Hepp?"

"She gotta' a lotta my pills."

"You mean the pills at the nursing station? You don't get your regular meds?" Cody asked.

"I need my pills. Trade 'em fa' Baby Ruths."

"When's the last time you got your meds?"

"Don't mess with outfits. Sure as hell miss those Ruths." Freddy resumed his rocking motion turning his head toward the black and white TV placed at the upper corner of the dayroom. He concentrated on the rotating weather dials on the screen ignoring Cody's further questions about who else did not get their pills or who traded them for candy bars.

"So long, Freddy. We'll talk later and I'll get ya' some candy," Cody said.

On the way out of the ward, Cody chatted with those like Freddy. They said little, but nonverbally seemed to connect. Some responded with a few words. Others voiced repeated expressions—sometimes a flurry of word salad. Cody reached for his keys to unlock the ward door. He considered options of returning to the nursing station to check out how meds were dispensed or calling Turpin.

Either choice had a downside. Considering Fitzgerald's take on the drug audits showing scripts were not getting to the residents, snooping for the current ward drug protocol could tip off those involved. Notifying Turpin potentially could harm Freddy and compromise his privacy rights.

"Hello, Detective Turpin. This is Zeke Cody the moon guy."

"What's up?"

"I have some info that could be useful in the Hepp case. Before we get to that, is this line private?"

"Let me switch to a buddy's office phone," Turpin said. He made his way to an empty office and closed the door. "Okay, what ya got."

"I think you're the kinda guy who would honor this as an anonymous tip, okay."

"At this point, the answer is 'yes.'"

"Just say from sources, I have learned there's some kinda' monkey-business with prescribed drugs not being dispensed to residents. One name mentioned was Blaze Hepp," Cody said.

"Can you give me a source for a follow-up?"

"That would get us both in trouble. But there's no reason you can't get access to a state drug audit. Should give you some idea of who's skimming the drugs," Cody said.

"I don't quite see the connection—the deal with psycho drugs? If I recall right, you said at least with one of them…I don't remember the name…could kill a horse," Turpin said.

"One angle you might consider is their value on the street. They could be substitutes. At least that was reported in the drug scene at the Haight Ashbury's free clinic in San Francisco. Docs there were having trouble identifying drugs leading to overdose because substitutes were used. To max profits, dealers cut popular drugs like amphetamines or heroin with substitutes such as high levels of caffeine and psychiatric meds," Cody said.

"I'll check that out. Got anymore leads?"

"There might be a connection to outfits, but needs to be confirmed. For any future contacts, we need to set this up differently. Phone calls or bars are too risky. Any suggestions?" Cody asked.

"How 'bout a ride in the country with my Volvo 1800 sports car?"

"That could work. We could trade rides. Like to show you my 1967 Mazda rotary sports ride. Gotta' go," Cody said.

Chapter 17

*Deal*
*Friday, Late Afternoon*

Fitzgerald continued clearing his office. Cody had to be notified. He dialed his number. "I've got some bad news. I just delivered my letter of resignation to Scott."

"Whoa. Let's slow down. Say we talk this over after work."

Zeke Cody found his way to a corner booth of the Andrew Jackson pub. Regulars were scattered at the bar and tables. Most of the jukebox selections were psychedelic and folk-rock. Cody was energized by Grace Slick's haunting voice. The music overpowered laughter and high-volume conversations.

Cody pondered over what led Charlie to such a drastic move? They had been close friends and colleagues for nearly a decade. Maybe it was domestic.

Charlie Fitzgerald spotted Zeke and rushed to the booth. "Thanks, Zeke, for showing up on short notice."

"So, what's up?"

"I resigned. Think we've gotta' tie up some loose ends over what's going on," Fitzgerald said. A young waiter asked, "Can I get you anything?" "Sure, a quick draft—make it a Bud. I promised my wife to get home early."

"You're shittin' me, right?" Cody asked.

"No. It's the real deal. The letter is on Scott's desk. It came down to cooking data or resign."

"You, you, musta' misread him. You know he can't always be taken too literally. He likes to argue the opposite point of view to check out where you really stand on what's a big deal to him."

"I know. But in this case, this was no high school debate. I refused to go over the line. His ultimatum was unambiguous. Either I was all in or clear out," Fitzgerald said.

"Slow down Charlie. Let's sort out what the hell is going on. The vibes at our human warehouse are quite negative now. I can see it everywhere. It would be naïve to think when you try to slow down an entrenched agenda baked in over decades, you're not gonna get serious pushback. Scott's gotta' pull out all his weapons to survive. Otherwise, it's get outta' Dodge for most of us, the sooner the better."

"Walk it back Zeke. How far would you go to 'win' the struggle? Who are the actual enemies? Early on we did not ask those questions because we stepped back and bought the argument. We had a plan—a plan for changing stakeholders towards recognizing social intervention at this point is superior. Scott has now changed the plan in the short-term for minimal gain as I see it," Charlie said.

The attractive waitress with hair reaching her waist placed the cold brew in front of Fitzgerald. "Just in time. Thanks." The mug was nearly emptied with one swallow. "You see this at ground level Zeke. What's got everybody so stirred up?" Fitzgerald asked.

"Everybody at one level or other senses there's a wacko somewhere in their midst. Yet on top of that, there's a staff backlash building against the kids we hired," Cody said.

"And there's one more negative vibe Zeke. Gomez informed me Scott is planning to reverse our reforms and cut the new mental health workers and lock down the wards to quiet his critics. If that's true, how come you are not in the loop to review these reversals?" Fitzgerald asked.

"It's simple. Scott sees this as window dressing to turn down the heat while maintaining the status quo. I don't need a playbook to figure it out."

"Zeke, you know we've been through a lot. Remember the early days when we got our first job at a Kansas State Hospital in the middle of nowhere? They branded us as the young Turks because we were such a pain in the ass to the 'real' docs. Back then, Scott was our iconoclastic leader. He was so smooth at manipulating M.D.s into taking his schemes for reform and getting them to claim them as their own," Fitzgerald said.

"That's the man and look, Charlie. Who has changed? I mean Scott is being Scott now because when you get right down to it, Scott's still engaged in the same battle. It's the same play with different actors," Cody said.

"He's changed Zeke. He was different then. His debates were not with politicians, rather with like-minded academics and administrators. Back then, he was recognized as a growing leader of his brand of reform, social contract theory. That led to heavyweights like David Premack and O.H. Mowrer somehow finding their way across the Kansas plains to visit our small hospital and offer seminars on human learning applied to patients in state hospitals. Those were heady days when Scott recognized gaming medical staff meant little absent true reform—acquiring legitimacy in the academic world. He was a true believer back then in the purest sense and he's lost that now. It's all about staying on top whatever it takes," Fitzgerald said.

"The reforms that led us here are still in play," Cody said. "I get it. Again, what else matters Charlie? If he goes down in flames, it's over. When it's over, it's over,"

"So, what's your point?"

Cody swirled his beer. His smile disappeared. "That drug audit you're doing we both know is flawed. There's no way to verify the reliability of sources reporting data where you have no direct access." He sipped the foam from his beer. "You know damn well in this case you're fucked. And another thing. Koeppen and the human subjects review committee that he chairs have shut down any drug audits of residents citing privacy arguments. My point is scientific legitimacy goes beyond whether you play by the rules. Being credible comes down to winning negotiations with gatekeepers who could care less about our mission or science."

"Yah, I know. And this is where Scott and I are at loggerheads. Cheaters may win in the short run, but long term they get ensnared in their lies. It's the supporters who break rank that are the most dangerous. Scott knows this but his priorities have been tainted. As I see it, he's being driven by his primitive brain—you know the reptilian centers that dictate survival over intellectual strategies," Fitzgerald said.

"Whoa! So, he's growing a long tail and his skin is turning rough and he changes color depending on how best to eat you before being eaten. Sounds like a killer to me. Better get Dyson and Turpin on this," Cody said with a wide grin.

"Touché. But the confluence of events has exposed his darker side," Fitzgerald said.

"What's happened to you Charlie? You sound like Inspector Clouseau, the pink panther guy. What did you do over at Scott's place? Get caught leering at the large nude painting of his wife?" Cody asked. "And there it was, I'll bet. You spotted a book in his library on the history of decapitation next to a copy of "The Prince."

"Clever. But let's get real. Scott made it clear. Get on board or get the hell out." Fitzgerald finished his beer. "Simple request Zeke. I'd like you to consider writing me a letter of recommendation."

"You gotta do what you gotta' do even before knowin' how this airplane lands."

"This airplane's got no landing gears and the pilot's power drunk," Fitzgerald said.

"Let's get to what caused the change of direction Scott is taking," Cody said. "It's being harassed about phony issues of security. Stringin' out the murder investigation over weeks will only increase the volume to emphasize security over treatment," Cody said. Musing for a moment, "So what's needed is for Turpin and Dyson to get more info. That starts with the wards. Just sayin' if a lead suddenly emerges, this could take the spotlight off the security argument."

"You could be right. To me there's one source that stands out. It's Koeppen. Yet, where's Scott headed on that front? He's opted to shield this guy. What gives?"

"Let's make a deal. If you agree to cool your jets for a week, I'll check out what's behind backing Koeppen. I'm not gonna give you any sources. But you know I don't bullshit on my end of any deal," Cody said.

"I trust you—but my letter is on Scott's desk. It's outta' my hands."

"I'll fix that too. Just stick around. Take your time packing."

Chapter 18

*Blaze*
*Saturday Morning*

Turpin called Michael to meet him for early coffee at the office to review the status of the case. Michael agonized 'bout givin' up another day off. "I know we need to speed up the investigation, but unless y'all got somethin' new to bring to the table I'd rather visit my family in Chicago."

"Got a potential break in the Hepp case."

"Okay, I'm good for an hour. But then off to Chicago."

"Thanks for comin' in on your day off. We ain't got time to let up. The clock is tickin'," Turpin said.

"I'm with ya' on that. I think it's best, for now, I stay focused on the drug angle. Plan to visit my brother in our old neighborhood on Chicago South Side," Michael said. "Want ta' check out the neighborhood."

"Think you're right. Drugs may have played a role in the murder. I've scheduled a get-together with my source. Something about drugs stolen off the wards— Blaze Hepp could be involved. I think she's a major link to crackin' this case."

"Hope yawl's investigatin' skills with her are better than your golf game," Michael said. "Remember never up never in."

"Get the hell outta here!"

Michael liked going back and forth as it was before Turpin's promotion. He wondered if maybe he was right? Turpin was a prime target to be manipulated by what he had observed in the café. That could be a disaster if anything got out of hand.

****

While Michael retreated to his makeshift office to make a call. Turpin shut his office door and dialed a number written on a napkin.

"Hello. Is this Dr. Cody or is it the Joker? This is Detective Turpin. Do you have a couple of minutes?"

"You, you must have the wrong number. I don't know either one of them."

"How 'bout 'Zeke?"

"Ya' got it, Batman. What's up in Gotham City?" Cody asked.

"Why don't I swing by with my Volvo and take you for a spin?"

"That could work. How 'bout the city library in a half-hour, okay?" Cody asked.

"See ya' there."

"Roger. Will you be the guy with the bat cape and your bat library card? I hear you never leave the cave without it," Cody said.

Turpin chuckled and said, "See ya' shortly."

Turpin entered the library. "There you are," Turpin said. Cody was thumbing through a car magazine.

"This ain't gonna work if you brought your bat mobile. Think it's a little obvious, don't you?" Cody asked.

"So is my Volvo. But we can take some backroads,"

Turpin said.

"Yep. I need to get back to some stuff in an hour."

Turpin and Cody headed for the shiny red Sportster. Turpin unlike Cody had to duck his head to get in the car. Turpin started the engine and eased out of the parking lot. He found a country road and pushed the RPMs with each gear. He spotted an opening and pulled off a road near a gravel pit.

"Thanks for goin' to this much trouble," Turpin said.

"For what?"

"Need a favor. How well do you know Blaze Hepp?" Turpin asked.

"Not that much. She's a shift supervisor and the rest you know."

"What about her background, say past work, friends, how she met her husband, what connections she has with other staff of the ward?" Turpin asked.

"Why the focus on Blaze?"

I'm not sure, to be honest. It's the way she comes across like she's been around the block a couple of times," Turpin said.

"Whoa. Sounds like she's the Cat Woman."

"Not likely. She didn't exactly expose her claws when we met for coffee," Turpin said. "She was just the opposite—a little too familiar. But that could be on me. To get back on track, do you know her friends or who she hangs out with or former employers—stuff like that."

"Blaze is the best source of course, I'm guessin' you've already tried that and came up empty," Cody said. "Other than Mahalia Ross, none off the top of my head."

"Did Blaze ever socialize with the gang at the Tav?"

"She was not a regular likely because she was tight with the union and Mahalia. But about a month ago I do recall she showed up which was weird. She brought a friend. Her friend was about her age. Remember Blaze said they had met in Chicago. Trying to come up with her name…something to do with a coin…a nickel…a penny… Penny something. I remember. Penny McQueen. Said they use to work together," Cody said.

"Did you catch whether she's a local or not?"

"Not a local, only that they laughed about how life had changed. Something about not having to depend on tip money anymore."

"I'll see if I can track her friend down. One more favor. How much do you know about this Dr. Koeppen's medical training?"

"He's a piece of work when it comes to gettin' any background on him other than he's from Munich. He brags about his correspondence with Erik Erikson. He's a famous psychoanalyst who made quite a reputation in his study of child development. If you're around Herr Doctor very long, all he talks about is his status. He's a member of an elite outfit, The American Psychoanalytic Society," Cody said.

"I don't know shit about the shrink training," Turpin said. "But let's switch from his knowledge of the mind to his medical training on the medical side. Have you ever gotten him to loosen up and talk about how he landed here at Jacksonville and why?"

"Could I get one thing straight? I don't like snitches," Cody said. "But I see this situation you're facing in a different light. There's a lot of secrets in this joint. Some need to see the light. I too wonder as you do. Why did Koeppen pick JSH? You have to wonder with his psychoanalytic training, why is he practicing in a state hospital in the Midwest when he could be making big bucks in New York, D.C., or L.A."

"As for him loosenin' up, at least around me, never. We keep it professional. We don't step on each other's turf. I send in my psych evals on residents that he likely never reads."

"What about his love life?"

"I know nothin' other than he is not married that I know of," Cody said. "Santiago Gomez might be a source. Doubt if you'll get much outta' Linda Best."

"That's all for now," Turpin said. "I will keep the lid on as to sourcing what you've told me. Just want to inform you with one exception, Michael Dyson. I'd like to run this by him?"

"The info. Not the source."

"You got it," Cody said.

"One more thing. Again, you must honor our confidentiality agreement. Keep this buried. If drugs were involved somehow in the murder, who knows where this might go," Turpin said.

Turpin returned Cody to the library. Back at the police station, he headed for the phone and asked the operator for a Jacksonville phone number. The operator said that there was no local listing for a Penny McQueen. He next asked to search the Springfield area. The operator after a short delay reported there was a Penny McQueen on Spruce Street. "Try that number."

Turpin dialed the number. The phone rang several times. He hung up. Maybe she was at work or away from the phone. He dialed the number again thinking maybe he'd get lucky. After ringing several times, Turpin was about to hang up when a woman with a mid-ranged voice answered, "Hello."

"Is this Penny McQueen?"

"Yes. Who's calling?"

"First, I want to make sure I have the right party. Are you acquainted with Blaze Hepp?" Turpin asked.

"Yes, why do you ask?"

"I'd like to ask you a few questions regarding a murder investigation. I'm Detective Turpin from the Jacksonville Police Department."

"Why ask me? Blaze can tell ya' all you need to know," McQueen said.

"Blaze is still in mourning. It would be helpful if you could fill in a few details about Fred Hepp—questions that Blaze found too painful to recount when we met," Turpin said.

"I read about it in the paper. That's all I know."

"You knew Fred Hepp, right?"

"Sure. But, not well."

"Any background on the victim would be helpful. How 'bout getting together in Springfield, say tomorrow afternoon?"

"Look detective I've gotta run. I'm late for work."

McQueen hung up without notice. Turpin turned to his watch. He concentrated on the hour movement. A quick trip to Springfield seemed right he thought. The Springfield Police had more resources to look into McQueen's background.

A call was made to their detective division. "Bob Lee on the phone. How can I help you?"

"Need your help on a background check for a Penny McQueen. It's regarding the Hepp case. I'd like to make a quick trip to your outfit today if possible and see what we can dig up," Turpin said.

"Fine. See you when you get here."

"Hi. I'm Detective Turpin from Jacksonville. A Detective Bob Lee, Is he in?"

"Yes. He's waiting for you," the desk officer said.

"You made a quick trip. Step back this way," Lee said.

Turpin found a chair and pulled out his notepad. "Thanks for taking my request on short notice. Something tells me this potential witness will disappear if I don't make contact today. Know nothing about her other than she's a friend, or acquaintance at least, of Blaze Hepp, wife of the deceased," Turpin said.

"Here's the skinny on this Penny McQueen," Lee said. "She's a hairstylist at the Capital Salon in the legislative district. She's single. Her age is 27 and add a hundred and you have her weight. Here's her driver's license record. Yu can get the rest—her address and eye color and so on. I checked on a hairdresser who knew her and agreed to answer a few questions. She's been at the Salon for two years. Before that she told this source she was a barmaid at 'Via Veneto' in the Chicago North Park area. This joint during the 1930s was a mob hangout. Politicians made their way there to drink, gamble, and seek out ladies of the night. Drug trafficking in heroin came later during the '50s. It was an open market with few arrests."

"Thanks for all the effort. This is a big help. Owe you a drink or two," Turpin said.

"Glad to be of help. Anything else?" Lee asked.

"Come to think of it—one more background check. Fred Hepp the victim listed Springfield as his address before taking a job as a hydrotherapist. Anything on

Hepp's background here would be appreciated," Turpin said.

"Sure."

"Gotta' get to the salon before closing," Turpin said.

Turpin scanned his road atlas and located the Capital Salon. He drove by the salon to check out the business. Sign on the door invited both women and men for hair-styling appointments. He surmised the business could be thriving given the longer hairstyles and the politicos needing to make an impression.

He parked a half-block away, dropped dimes in the meter, and headed for the salon. He approached the receptionist. "I'd like a haircut from Penny McQueen. Heard she gives a great cut."

"Let's see her schedule. Looks like you lucked out. She can take you next—about fifteen minutes," the receptionist said.

"Which chair is she at?"

"Number three, the middle one."

Turpin took a chair and scanned a magazine assortment. None that appealed. He picked one at random. Pretending to read the magazine, he watched McQueen style the hair of a well-dressed male who could have been an elected official or a bureaucrat. Turpin found it hard to ignore how the stylist went to lengths to please him. His hair was cut such that it fell in place when blown dry—yet long enough to cover the upper part of his ears. The hair at the nape of his neck was trimmed to accentuate his natural curls. The stylist loosened the cover around his neck. She stroked his shoulders and massaged his scalp. Her customer closed his eyes and took in the sensuous touches near his ears and scalp. A blow dryer was directed to his neck and shoulders. After rubbing his scalp and neck with a fragrant cologne, the stylist removed the chair cover. He remained closed-eyed. As the chair was lowered, Turpin could see that he was touching her thigh with the back of his hand. She remained in place momentarily as he moved his hand back and forth. The stylist moved back to shake the cover. He stood and reached for his wallet. A couple of bills were paid. He whispered in her ear. She smiled.

"Whoever is next, I'm ready," Penny McQueen, the stylist, said.

Turpin seated himself in the chair. "Just a trim off the top and a military taper in the back."

"When did you get your last haircut? Looks like it wasn't that long ago," McQueen said.

"Like it trimmed often. Never know when it pays off such as being around the ladies," Turpin said.

"Can't imagine you having problems in that department," McQueen said.

"I'm guessing you don't have any problems either," Turpin said.

"I couldn't help but notice you look my way as you read that magazine."

"Guilty. Kept thinkin' I've seen you somewhere before like some watering hole."

"You're not a regular here, right?" McQueen asked. She circled his neck with a disposable neck cover as she prepared to fasten the chair cover.

"No, just passin' through. Have you ever lived elsewhere, like Chicago?" Turpin asked.

"Maybe, maybe not."

"I have done my share of bar-hoppin' in the windy city. My favorite bar was in the North Park area…the Via

Veneto. Good lookin' women like to hang out there," Turpin said.

"Did you go there to drink or get laid?"

"Both, now that I think of it. That's where you look familiar. I gotta ask. By chance did you ever hang out or work there?" Turpin asked.

"I got to know when first hangin' out there if someone gets too nosey to shut my mouth and leave."

"No need to pry. Just noticed the way you handled your last customer. To be honest, that's when I made the connection."

"You sound like somebody from vice."

"No. I'll level with you though. I'm Detective Turpin from Jacksonville Police Department."

"Your voice did sound familiar. If it's about Blaze, forget it. She's been through enough hell," McQueen said.

"What do you mean by hell? Does it have anything to do with her past such as the Via Veneto?"

"We've been through a lot—a lot that'll get us killed if our tongues wag," McQueen said.

"Is that why you left Chicago? Someone forced you out of town?"

"Your time's up. My next customer is waiting."

"If Blaze is in the same boat, I need to know that. That's particularly true if her husband was somehow connected to the business out of the Via Veneto," Turpin said.

"Are you finished?" McQueen asked. Her body stiffened.

"Just one more thing. Was Fred Hepp abusive?"

"That's for Blaze to answer."

"Here's a tip for your trouble."

Turpin quickly exited and headed west for Jacksonville. It was clear. Blaze's connections to the Via Veneto needed to be checked out.

Chapter 19

*Saturday Afternoon*

Michael found a parking spot half-block from the family home located in South Chicago. The two-story home had a porch filled with several flower pots prepared for spring planting. Nothin' had changed.

"There's my baby. "Ain't you a sight for sore eyes," Matilda Dyson said.

"Happy I made it. I needa' hug, Mama," Michael said.

"If youse lookin' for David he ain't here."

"Is he on the streets?"

"Nothing's changed. All he wants is cash. It all goes to da' dealer. I tell 'em if he want a bed and sumpin' to eat, he knows his bed's still empty upstairs. But I ain't spendin' my hard earnt money on all that crap goin' into his veins."

"I need ta' connect with 'em again. Like ta' see if he'll listen to his little brother and get himself cleaned up," Michael said.

"He showed up yesterday tellin' me he was hungry and needed money to buy some grub. I told 'em y'all be comin', but he paid no mind," Mama said. "Wait a minute. Did ya' hear that that knock? It musta' got through to him after y'all comin' round."

At the front door, David Dyson stood with a soiled

blanket over his shoulder and a shirt and pants stained by whatever surface grim had been beneath him. He was sockless with holes on the top of each sneaker.

"Michael's here, David. Come in and sit down a spell with your brother. Y'all got a lot to catch up on," Mama said.

"I ain't here for no sermon—just some bread to get me somethin' to eat."

"It's been too long brother. Won't ya' stay a while and catch up on what's happen'?" Michael asked.

"Not if that means hearin' you jive 'bout your clean life and sellin' out to da' poo-lice."

"Can we just be bros again? Y'all always be my kick-ass big bro."

"Don't bro' me. You sold out and let Mama rot."

"Let's go back on a little history. Mama never let us down even when Dad was taken out by soldiers. She didn't complain. She got herself a job at the laundry and earned enough to buy it and put a little money in the bank. She bought this nice house and has a nest egg to live on. She was demandin' but fair to us brother."

"Come clean. Whadda' ya' after? To show Mama who turned out to be a piece of shit compared to y'all— A black-turned-whitey man in blue?"

"I got nothin' to be ashamed of. Looked up to Dad as a cop. Just like Mama, I've worked my way up whitey's ladder. I ain't gonna argue Michael. We make choices. Sometimes like with Dad a choice where ya' can't see what's out there. Maybe that's happened to you also. But if you're still in the game, at some point ya' gotta have a little respect for yourself and fight your way outta' this. I know as a kid there was nothin' you couldn't kick ass. I want that brother back."

"I'm cool with the way I am. Don't need any scorecard."

"You may not wanna hear this but you're gettin' your ass kicked by the shit. It was the mob outfit that spread this poison that's killin' you—heroin on the Southside."

"Where did ya' hear that? At some poo-lice convention? Some mick told ya' everything 'bout the hood, right? Let me bring ya'll up to date. It's black brothers that control skag all up 'n down the line. Black gangsters have wiped out the wops. Ya'll don't know shit 'bout the business."

"Right on, brother. But answer me this, was the purity of skag better or worse when black brothers took over?"

"Users 'ODed' from whitey's skag."

"So, the skag sold by the mob was cut with some kinda' shit, right?" asked Michael.

"For the most part, yes. But now, it depends on the mule and pusher. It gets 'round the hood, like minutes, if the shit has been cut. The soldiers track it down and take out any outlaws on their turf," David said.

"So, the mob still controls some areas?"

"Not for long. Sam Battaglia has a price on his head. He's whitey's pimp sellin' the shit. Why all these questions? Are ya' gonna bust your brother's balls?"

"Why can't we just be family and get along?" Mama asked.

"Amen, Mama," Michael said. "Here's the deal, David. Y'all want cash for your stash. Here's three hundred. I'm leavin' it ta' you David to make the next call. If we still family y'all do the right thing by kickin' ass or fold like a candy-ass. You can shoot it all up and forget family or get a pair of balls and clean yourself up. Whatever. Let's not split with last-minute words we'll regret. I'll not bring it up again. Let's go away still bros."

David turned away and started for the door.

"Not even a hug big brother?" Michael asked.

David halted. "You trashed me in front of Mama. Flashin' those bills makes you a big dawg, ain't that right?"

"Ya' got it all wrong. It's just a small way to say I still look up ta' ya' that you're still the baddest dawg. Forget the money. Just show yourself you're still my kick-ass bro. You can beat this on your own."

"Still know I can whip your ass. I ain't makin' any promises but we still family," David said. He extended his arms. Mama extended her arms and joined her sons. Mama teared up and looked up. She cried, "Glory, glory, the Lord do work in mysterious ways."

David turned and left the house without looking back. Michael tried to hide his tears. He pulled Mama's hand and put the cash in her palm. "You'll know best what to do with it."

Michael headed back to Jacksonville Sunday morning after breakfast and sayin' goodbyes to Mama. Michael mulled over what David had revealed. It was clear those hooked on heroin were very sensitive to purity. Battles for turfs were still in play between the old guard, the outfit guys, and black gangsters. Anyone cuttin' the drug absent approval from drug lords was at risk to be taken out. If this outfit dude, Sam Battaglia, was losin' money, could Fred Hepp and Blaze be targeted for gettin' too greedy by selling the cut drugs to the wrong users Michael wondered?

Battaglia may have seen the pair as bad for business.

Michael reasoned the pair likely had help to move the psycho-substitutes. Somehow, insiders were involved. That meant patients' prescribed drugs were intercepted regularly throughout the hospital. Likely, a few patients, if any, would complain about their missing medications. Michael thought if true, docs would be informed. What if docs knew about the stolen drugs and were involved in a coverup?

Chapter 20

*Credentials*
*Monday Morning, November 9*

Michael was jotting a few notes in his temporary office when he heard Turpin knock on his door. Turpin had a couple of cups of coffee.

"Here's a wake-up. We got a lot to talk about," Turpin said.

"Right on. Did you score with the lady?"

"All business, and just to clear the air, I'm just fine with home-cookin' and my wife," Turpin said.

"We cool on that for now. Been thinkin' about where we at now. Still some dead ends," Michael said.

"I did come up with a couple of leads," Turpin said, . "Blaze and Fred Hepp may have a business connection with Chicago mob bosses. Blaze's friend, a Penny McQueen who I tracked down in Springfield, hung out a Chicago bar, the Via Veneto. Blaze frequented the same bar. Doubt two attractive young women were there to sell Tupperware."

"So why da' ya' think Fred or Blaze is tied into the business?" Michael asked.

"Strictly a hunch. When I asked McQueen if Fred Hepp was involved with the business, she tightened up unlike how she came on so strong with her previous customer," Turpin said.

"Never doubted your radar gun for the ladies."

"You taught me all I know," Turpin said. "Did you get anything out of narcotics about a possible hospital link?"

"Nothin' directly," Michael said. "But got a better idea from our drug unit of a pipeline that runs from Chicago to East St. Louis to KC. Drop-offs out of Springfield make their way to Jacksonville dealers, mostly heroin and cocaine."

"What's the Chicago operation all about?"

"From what I could find out, mob bosses' frown on drug dealing but some in the outfit are not listenin'. A black gang, the Gangster Disciples, have forced the white outfit outta' dealin' on Chicago's south and west side," Michael said. "Turf wars over territory along the pipeline have heated up with assassinations. That's because it's a cash machine. Supply chain that runs from Mexico to Chicago is major distribution center east and west."

"Here's a possibility. Suppose Fred Hepp somehow was involved with the drug trafficking in Chicago and he got mixed up in this turf war. What da' you think?" Turpin asked.

"Sam Battaglia could be the boss pushin' drugs on the South Side. If Hepp was tied in with him, Hepp coulda' been targeted for cuttin' 'hard candy.' It's a business decision. Hepp got too greedy leading to reduced profits for the bosses."

"If Hepp is linked to Chicago, we gotta get some hard evidence. To me, that means we go after Blaze. And this fake doc Davis could be into this operation handin' out bogus prescriptions and maybe more. By the way, did you see your family?"

"Great ta' see Mama, Everything's cool. Let's change the conversation," Michael said. "Let me get this right. You're thinkin' the supply for the psych meds coulda' been funneled to made-guys like Battaglia?"

"That's the thinkin'. What say you?"

"The missin' piece is nailin' the mob connection," Michael said. "Let me put out a possibility. How 'bout income taxes? There's this tax agent, a Bob Fuesel if I got the name right, who might have the answers. He gave a talk on Chicago mob bosses last year. He worked undercover to infiltrate bosses operatin' on Rush Street and beyond. This dude could tell ya' more in five minutes than you'd ever learn in a year hangin' out at the Via Veneto."

"I forgot all about this guy. He sure had guts," Turpin said.

"Whatever, I do remember him sayin' he put 'em out of business because they were profiting from watered-down booze at their joints which amounted to tax evasion according to the feds."

"This sounds like a pattern that could apply to this case."

"It's like a tax in the drug business I learnt. You get paid by weight. Those who supply the pipeline gets ta' collect the extra profit if drugs are laced," Michael said. "That profit is hidden. If the tax guys get their tentacles into unreported income from soldiers, heads could roll."

"Sounds like a lead to me," Turpin said.

"Need ta' contact this Bob Fuesel," Michael said. "We also might get a lead from the Illinois State Police who investigate interstate narcotics. Here's a plan. Y'all call Fuesel and I'll get ahold of state police."

Turpin headed for his office phone. After a few

dead-end calls, he located Bob Fuesel's office. After answering questions about his credentials, he was put through to the agent.

"Hello, Special Agent Fuesel. I'm Detective Carl Turpin of the Jacksonville Police department. I'm investigating a local homicide that maybe you could be of assistance with. We have reason to believe a couple could've been involved in the drug supply chain out of Chicago. The husband was brutally murdered. His wife appears to have been a regular hangout at the Via Veneto. Does this pattern sound familiar?"

"Could be."

"We have a possible lead that the outfit is operating out of Via Veneto. Sam Battaglia may be the kingpin of a pipeline operating between Chicago and Mexico."

"That's a possibility," Fuesel said. "Let me give you a little background. The organized crime bosses are not on the same page about the drug business. Some have splintered off from the old businesses of the lottery or numbers racket, prostitution, and backroom gambling to the more profitable drug trafficking. We've gone undercover and infiltrated their joints getting some of them to talk. This has led to arrests of lower-ranked guys in the drug business. We have confiscated their big money that props up the peddlers. Such busts have led to reprisal killings of suspected snitches. So far with our witness protection plan, we have not lost any informants."

"We have sketchy evidence Blaze Hepp, wife of the victim, frequented the Via Veneto in the early 60s," Turpin said. "She allegedly befriended another lady who frequented the same bar who may have had mob connections. And there's indirect evidence Blaze Hepp has been raiding a hospital pharmacy for psychiatric meds here at Jacksonville State Hospital. It's just a hunch, but maybe she's supplying these meds to those packaging drugs to cut heroin dosage and maximize profits—just like mob bosses did when watering down booze."

"I can't talk about that. Just put it this way. The big bosses, guys like Sam Battaglia, second in command to Tony Accardo who arguably runs the Chicago mob— they both like steady flows of cash without any hiccups. That means keeping out of the news. Cutting drugs with prescription meds risks exposure in all kinds of ways as I see it. With all those profits, it's quite possible soldiers like your suspects could have let their greed get out of hand and that could be deadly," Fuesel said.

"Did the so-called Chicago outfit do drug business at the Via Veneto?"

"Entirely possible," Fuesel said. "We got to know most of them directly by simply visiting bars like the Via Veneto undercover. They were quite open in their joints about their business except for Accardo. Like the old days of Capone, they would sit where they could get a view of the front and back entrances. It was like telling the world they were not intimidated by anyone—friend or foe."

"Is there any way through your contacts you could find out if a Penny McQueen or a Blaze Hepp were connected to the Via Veneto?" Turpin asked.

"I won't promise you anything, but maybe our sources will cooperate. I gotta' another call. So, if that's it I'll let you know. Spell out the names and other identifiers to my secretary. Good day."

Michael ruminated over the holes in the Hepps' drug

conspiracy angle that required more proof. He recalled in a talk on drug investigations that the Illinois State Police had made big profile busts in their war on drugs. He located a possible resource, Terry Kelly, who had been quite involved in Chicago investigations. Michael called the number listed. After wading through a maze of underlings, he reached Kelly. From the onset, Kelly expressed little interest in the Hepp case. Instead, he dwelled on his record of drug busts and how traffickers were on the run.

To Michael, Terry Kelly was yet another law-and-order guy who was not colorblind. He emphasized to Michael the role of blacks behind a series of deadly fights over Southside territory going back to the 40s. It started with a black mob boss Ted Roe who terrorized blacks with extortion and bribery. Most of his income came from an illegal lottery. During the early 50s, the outfit led by Sam Giancana sought to control the Southside lottery business. His henchmen tried to kidnap Roe. Roe shot the kidnapper, Fat Lenny Caifano, a made guy. Roe was tried for murder. After beating the case, Roe was tracked down by the outfit and murdered in retaliation.

Kelly said, "Sam Giancana took over. The outfit brought down murder rates on the Southside. Side." He went on to describe how black-on-black wars between the Blackstones and Gangster Disciples erupted in the 60s. Anarchy reigned with escalating gang wars resulting in spikes in murder cases. He added, "They ultimately took over the drug business, but crime and violence did not go down unlike the Teddy Roe days when Giancana took control."

Michael thanked Kelly and hung up. The call

distressed him. It was the black-on-black violence Kelly emphasized while minimizing the number of hits by white mob bosses. He wondered if brother David knew this history? Whatever. He had to protect David.

Michael clicked his ballpoint up and down nervously worried that David could be targeted as a snitch if word got back, he made recent contact with his cop-brother.

Turpin sauntered back to Michael's office to give him an update. Turpin detailed his debriefing of the call to Fuesel. While Fuesel did not confirm the Hepps' link to any outfits, Fuesel agreed to check with his sources about any connections of Blaze Hepp and Penny McQueen to crime bosses.

Michael reviewed his call to State Police Investigator Kelly. "It was frustratin' that the major source of drug control was bein' fought out by black-on-black territorial wars indifferent to whitey's role." Michael sighed, "Cuttin' drugs for either the outfit or black gangs affected sales and invited consequences for those in the supply chain."

"So, where do we go from here?" Turpin asked.

"We gonna lose whatever leverage we got on the docs if we don't move before they disappear or lawyer up. Somehow, they're involved in this drug connection and maybe the murder," Michael said. "If it were me, I'd be all over this fake doc Davis and furthermore look into what Koeppen may be hiding that also could have somethin' to do with the Hepps."

"What's this 'If it were me' bullshit?"

"Y'all ain't never gonna get it. You open doors I can't pry open with a crowbar. Do you think the clinical director would set up a meetin' with the staff as he did for you?" Michael asked.

"Why don't we find out? Give him a call right now and let's clear up who this fake doctor is."

Michael called.

"This is Sergeant Dyson. My partner Detective Turpin and I would like to clear up questions about your staff. You are in the best position to fill in some missing pieces we found when doing background checks."

"How about in a half-hour?"

"That's a deal. Thanks, Dr. Gomez. See ya'll shortly."

Michael and Turpin arrived at the clinical director's office and were ushered directly into his office. Gomez offered them a seat and closed his office door.

Michael began. "Let's start with one of your docs listed on your staff, a new hire at the infirmary, a Dr. William Davis. Based on records from HR, he obtained a medical degree from the University of North Carolina and was employed at Dorothea Dix Hospital in Raleigh North Carolina for thirteen years. He listed his specialty as a psychiatrist at the facility. Is any of this in error as far as you know?"

"Not that stands out," Gomez said. "Dr. Davis came highly recommended. He did ask for a special assignment to the infirmary. He said he wanted to study somatic treatments for geriatric and mental illness disorders."

"So, there's nothin' unusual about a highly recommended psychiatrist workin' full-time in the infirmary? If I understand what type of patients are treated there, it's mostly old physically sick folks who ain't playin' with a full deck?" Michael asked.

"As to your first question, not in this instance,"

Gomez said. "We agreed this would be a temporary placement until Dr. Davis had completed his study on geriatric patients."

"So that means he had some kinda' research project involvin' sick ol' folks," Michael said. "Now just one more question. Did y'all get a chance to follow up with those who recommended him?"

"Not directly," Gomez said. "There was no need to. I knew three of his colleagues who each had an outstanding resume."

"That's interestin'. It turns out when I called HR back in Raleigh to confirm he was employed at the Dorothea State Hospital, a Dr. William F. Davis had been on their staff all right for thirteen years. But I was told he passed away on July 18, 1968," Michael said. "So, do you have any idea who is this doc on your infirmary ward?"

"You must be mistaken. Have you checked fingerprints or photos?" Gomez asked.

"Not yet. That would involve the feds. Before goin' there, Detective Turpin and I wanted to get your take. We'd like to know just how's he doin'? You know, have there been any complaints 'bout his performance as a doc?"

"His staff report he is responsive and effective with infirmary patients. Like any good physician, he consults with colleagues when there is a question of diagnosis. Bottom line, he has met our expectations given his limited exposure to treating geriatric diseases and ailments," Gomez said.

"How is it someone could pose as Dr. Davis and not be exposed given licensure requirements?" Turpin asked.

"No way that comes to mind. Our medical training is thoroughly vetted by the State Medical Board and the board exam requires two pieces of ID and a photo," Dr. Gomez said.

"Supposin' this 'Dr. Davis' did a fake set of papers and this medical board looked at his resume and made the same conclusion you did—that his trainin' and references were all they needed to give him a license to practice in the state?" Michael asked.

"Perhaps," Gomez said. "But those degrees and completions of residencies are very hard to fake with special seals, paper, and all the right signatures."

"But you don't have photos of those pieces of paper, right?" Michael asked.

"No, but that is a licensure issue as I see it. They review your transcript's endorsements very closely," Gomez said.

"Let's shift to Dr. Koeppen," Michael said. "I know squat about what it takes to be a doc. Is it possible to get a medical degree in two years?"

"In special cases like Dr. Koeppen, the answer is yes. He had completed most of his medical training during the war. He did the equivalent of three years at Munich Medical School early in the war from 1941 to 1945. He told me he took advantage of pre-med training in Munich with Hitler's effort to have a reservoir of replacement doctors for the offensive."

"Was he in combat or did have duty behind the lines with special assignments?" Michael asked.

"With casualties mounting two years into the war, he along with all able-bodied males were drafted into the infantry to join the German offensive through Ukraine and Hungary to the Soviet border. He survived many battles only to be nearly killed by a bullet or piece of shrapnel penetrating his neck. Dietrich showed me the scar on his neck."

"I still don't see how he got his medical trainin' in the middle of a war?" Michael asked.

"He was fortunate in 1942 he somehow found his way back to Munich to recover from his wound. While recuperating he was given a furlough and continued his medical studies. He rejoined his fraternity and enjoyed his former life of sailing, drinking, and entertaining the ladies as he put it. However, war reversals during 1943 on the front forced veterans such as him to reenlist. He was assigned to a medical company treating the wounded in an improvised hospital located near Budapest. Due to combat losses of medical staff, Dietrich acquired specialized surgical skills including amputation and treating head traumas."

"So, just curious. How does Dr. Koeppen finish his doc's degree in Munich?" Michael asked. "The city had been leveled with little undamaged after the war ended according to my dad. U.S. troops occupied Munich and most of 'em who fought for Hitler. Nazis were rounded up and trucked to POW camps. How did he avoid arrest and at the same time go to medical school—at least in 1946?"

"All I know is what he described after the war ended," Gomez said. "Dietrich was devastated by the destruction of Munich. Most of all he was scared and very bitter over his brother's capture and forced starvation and ultimate death at a POW camp, located at 'bad something'. I remember, it was Bad, Bad…Kreuznach. He told me close to a million German prisoners of war died in U.S. and French camps during the end of the war."

"Again, Whada' 'bout his return to med school?" Michael asked.

"He revealed to me he hid in forests outside of Munich until he was able to make contact with his father and mother who had relocated on their farm outside of Munich, near Eichenau as I recall," Gomez said. "As to the University of Munich opening, he told me that occurred in Fall of 1946. Upon contact with his old professors, given his war experience with medicine and his previous studies, he told me he passed his final exam in Fall 1948 specializing in pathology. Dr. Koeppen proudly told me he graduated with Magna Cum Laude distinction."

"So, is it right that Dr. Koeppen has had a lotta' surgical experience and training?" Michael asked. "And yet he winds up in mental health?"

"That's true. The wartime memories did not go away. For this reason, he returned to further study in psychoanalysis to get to the bottom of what made him so miserable."

"Thank you for giving us backgrounds on the staff here," Turpin said. "I know you have a busy schedule. Just one request. Would appreciate your confidentiality as to the status of Dr. Davis to be fair to him if it's a case of mistaken identity. Or if it turns out he's a fake, don't want him to disappear before questioning him."

"Yes, but I want this cleared up quickly," Dr. Gomez said. "We cannot tolerate such obvious malpractice if Dr. Davis is a fake."

Gomez squared the pad on his desk. "Just curious. Why are both of you so focused on Dr. Koeppen? I have a great deal of respect for his medical knowledge and service to the hospital."

"To be honest, we simply wanted to know how he obtained his credentials and medical specializations," Turpin said.

"I agree," Michael said. "We need ta' mosey out of here. I've got some phone calls comin' in. Thanks for y'all's help."

Back at the police station, Turpin followed Michael to his make-shift office. "We gotta' make a move on Davis now," Michael said. "He's bound to be on guard for any leaks about his past. That's especially true if he's been recruited for the pipeline."

"Hate to bring the FBI into this before we finish our investigation," Turpin said.

"We ain't got no choice if ya' look at the federal angle like drug pipelines across state borders and maybe even his fraudulent practice of medicine involving two states. At some point, we gotta' bring in the feds," Michael said. "However, I agree. Let's make the first play on Davis. We need to make a surprise visit at the infirmary."

"Ya' know, you sound more and more like a detective," Turpin said.

Michael shot back, "Stick it where da' sun don't shine. It's still *Sergeant* Dyson, okay?"

Chapter 21

*The Past*
*Monday Afternoon*

After the police left, Santiago Gomez reviewed files of the two questioned doctors. Dietrich's resume was beyond reproach. He thought about the many implications of recruiting an imposter doctor for the hospital. Maybe it was an error in the spelling of his name, but that made no sense. He recalled that a couple of classmates during his residency vouched for Dr. Davis's knowledge in psychiatry when applying for residencies at Dorothea Dix Hospital. This was no time to wait for events to unfold.

"Hello, Dr. Scott. This is Dr. Gomez. Detective Turpin and his partner, Sergeant Dyson, dropped by to give me an update. Based on their investigation, we have some staffing issues. I cannot give details but just want to give you a heads up. We face a potential scandal that will dwarf our other problems such as security."

"So, how can we react if you cannot reveal what we face?"

"Just let me caution you that we need to alert Phil Carson and his staff at HR to vet all new hires going back to 1968," Gomez said.

"For what? Being on the blacklist for screenwriters?"

"Of course not. This is no joke. It's much more serious. Just do as I suggest to validate our screening of applicants," Gomez said.

"Again, screen for what, venereal disease?" Scott asked. "At some point, you have to give me some idea, like staff screwing each other?"

"There are rumors on that front—of affairs to be accurate. That could surface as a scandal but that is the least of our worries," Gomez said.

"So, how many questions do I have left?" Scott asked. "Did this staff member get their degree from a course offered on a match-cover?"

"You never know. Hold on I've got an emergency call from Cook County Center. I'll get back to you later," Gomez said.

Gomez hung up and looked at the blinking call button. How convenient to get a call at that moment cutting off the superintendent thought Santiago. Knowing Scott, he would not let it go. One way or another he would unravel the nature of the scandal. If I read Scott correctly pondered Gomez, he was already on the phone with HR instructing them to review all new hires since 1968.

Gomez pressed the blinking call button. "Hello, Dr. Cody. What's up?" Gomez asked.

"I recently got some info about Dr. Koeppen that I think you should handle," Cody said. "It's a long story. Can we meet after work somewhere—say the Jackson pub?"

"I'd rather we meet at the Holiday Inn bar—more privacy and less noise," Gomez offered.

"If our conversation is confidential, that could work," Cody said.

"No problem. How about 5:30?"

"See you then."

After hanging up, Cody headed for the women's ward.

****

Shannon was pacing the hall wringing her hands. Shannon spotted the psychologist Cody heading for the dining area. This was no time to have an exchange with the psychologist. Shannon focused on finding her journal.

Maybe, someone spotted her hiding the journal, but who? She rubbed her forehead thinking she needed to replay events. Who may have been in the vicinity? She recalled passing by Maggie Nilsson seated at a table all alone in the hallway. Maggie's menacing leer at me was hard to ignore.

Maybe Maggie had suspected she like others were out to steal her thoughts. Maggie believed certain individuals on the ward were spying on her thinking about who should inherit her large stately home overlooking two sections of prime farmland. Maggie had whispered once to Shannon in a calm voice she had planned to will the estate to her eldest daughter, Wilma, rather than her son, Liam. She said Liam insisted that this was only right that he was the heir given the custom over generations back to their Nordic ancestors. As spelled out in her husband's will, the male son was made the heir. Maggie told Shannon Liam was determined to keep her locked up until she passed on. She told anyone who would listen that people were stealing her thoughts and passing them on to Liam to prevent her from ever returning home and making a legal claim to the property.

Shannon wondered. Did Maggie stalk her thinking

she had stolen her thoughts while in the dining hall? Maybe Maggie spotted her hiding the journal and suspected her thoughts had been recorded. Shannon realized she had little time to check this out. Any staff reading her journal would funnel it to Nurse Best who would pass it on to Dr. Koeppen. That would seal any chance of ever being discharged. There was a slim chance Maggie had taken the journal and hidden it under her own mattress waiting for an opportune time to peruse the pages searching for references to her stolen thoughts.

Shannon could see most staff were in the nursing station preoccupied with ongoing conversations. In the dining hall, Maggie was staring at Beverly who was yelling something about those around her to confess and repent their sins. LPN aide, Carol Taylor, yelled, "Quiet down Beverly." Nurses turned their attention to Beverly waiting for her to stop the yelling. At the right moment, Shannon quietly walked past the station and entered the bed dorm.

Shannon recognized Maggie's quilt on her bed. She opened the drawers to the small dresser nearby. A well-worn Bible was amidst her undergarments and gown. A marker was placed in the book of Matthew 5:5. The verse, "Blessed are the meek, for they shall inherit the earth," was highlighted with a yellow marker.

She looked toward the entrance. There were no sounds of steps in the hallway. Shannon lifted the mattress. There it was. Shannon shed a tear. This was no time to celebrate. This time, the journal had to be placed in a secure area. She exited the dorm.

From behind, a male voice called out, "Wait for me, Shannon. I'd like to ask you some questions about the ward," Zeke Cody said. "We are doing a research project."

Shannon cut Cody off. "I'm not able to answer any questions right now—maybe later."

"That's cool by me. You look a little uptight," Cody said. "Is it anything that we might fix?"

"No, no. I just need some time to myself."

"Not to pry, but is that a collection of your writings?" Cody asked.

"You might say so but they're not for publication."

"So, this is something personal?"

"I'd rather not say."

"Okay. But if there's something you want to chat about, I'm a good listener."

"How can I trust you?"

"Depending on what you mean, it all comes down to you. You have to make that call."

"I see you talking with patients often. I would guess they have told you things that they have observed on the ward or elsewhere, right?"

"Perhaps. I don't get into that aspect–you know askin' residents if they have had run-ins with staff or residents. I feel that's up to each of you to make the call as to who you confide in and go from there."

"To be honest, I don't know who to trust. It's best I keep silent."

"About what?"

"About the frightful scene of a head in a tank. If I talk about this, whatever I say, it will be used against me—that somehow, I was implicated."

"I dig where you're coming from. Maybe, this is something that you need to run by a lawyer if you're concerned about what you should disclose."

"Even if I wanted to open up, I can't. I am

incompetent according to the court. So, that means I am unable to comprehend or understand legal stuff including reporting what I witnessed. The only solution is to have my competency restored by a judge. And that will never happen as long as Dr. Koeppen insists I remain incompetent. In his eyes, he has concluded I have poor insight as to what brings on my mood swings and outbursts."

"Maybe, maybe not. There's a way to get a win-win. Just so I have this right you believe the court will not restore your rights because Dr. Koeppen will not sign off on your petition to have your day in court.?"

"That's it in a nutshell."

"And, somehow you feel anything you say about Fred Hepp will implicate you—maybe being charged with some kinda' crime, right?"

"It's what I know about patient abuse over the years. It's clear the staff have me pegged as a risk for assault or suicide as an excuse to put me in seclusion or worse for what I know. Look, I've said too much already. I just want out. I have problems but none that can't be managed."

"So, I think there's a way for you to get outta' here and at the same time expose the staff you see as being abusive or whatever. Come to my office, and I'll assess your status for the court. After we finish the evaluation, I will submit a psychological report to the judge. That way, the judge will have an alternative assessment to Dr. Koeppen's. As to identifying staff who have mistreated residents, I need names, incidents, and dates. And this is very important. You need to trust that I will convey this to investigators as an anonymous tip. I will never reveal the source," Cody said.

"How can I be sure?"

"Just know I'm stickin' my neck out to pull this off. If it ever came to light that I had used confidential information from a resident to finger staff, trust me, I'll be hittin' the bricks lookin' for another job," Cody said. "So, in a way, I'm in the same boat. I have ta' trust you to not reveal our discussion to anyone if you agree to be assessed. That way you can make your case in court and expose the bad apples on your ward."

"Are you including the Hepps as bad apples?"

"That's your call. Look, it's obvious you have been through a lot of stress over this incident. The way ta' move forward is to get at the truth in the final analysis. That is not happenin'. Your knowledge might help get to who did this horrific act. Just so you know, Dr. Koeppen refuses to allow detectives to interview you."

"I've only confided in one staff member about what is happening on the ward. I trust Carla Fitzgerald. In fact, I was headed for her office. All of the stuff about the staff is here." Shannon raised the journal and pointed at it. "I can't take the chance that the journal will be stolen. I have to find a secure place."

"Would you be willing to tell authorities what you know?"

"I don't know. You seem trustworthy. I do want to clear my name and find the killer. It's been tense on the ward. Patients are acting out more. I don't want this to get out of hand."

Shannon looked at her journal and gathered her thoughts. "To be clear, Fred Hepp was a monster. I could see how my descriptions of things that happened could give police the idea that I wanted revenge on Hippo. I hated him, but I'm no killer."

"We are on the same page. You are right. It has been hell for you and other residents. I have to be frank. We need to move this investigation forward sooner than later for a lotta' reasons."

"I have identified victims like myself who have endured sexual abuse and cruelty. How do you protect our identities?"

"I cannot make that promise. But if this information gives leads to identifying suspects, authorities will likely intervene on your behalf."

"I'll agree if protection from staff retaliation is a reality and not an empty promise."

"I'm confident you and others will be protected if the prosecutor can put together a way for you to testify in a deposition that protects your rights and safekeeping."

"Where do I begin?"

"You need to seek advisement from an attorney representing your interests as to how to go forward. That has to be initiated by your guardian ad litem."

"This apparently has been setup by Carla Fitzgerald."

"So, the first task is to take care of this competency issue. Can we go forward with an assessment?"

"I may be fooling myself, but I know I am competent, period. Any legitimate test will prove I'm right."

"That's a deal. We can schedule your assessment tomorrow."

****

*Monday Evening*

Santiago found a corner booth. The bar had few patrons. He ordered a very dry Martini. What had Cody unraveled? The juniper-vermouth taste of the drink brought on a welcome distraction from thoughts of the imposter physician under his watch. What else would Cody reveal?

Cody spotted Dr. Gomez and headed for the corner. He ordered a bottle of Pabst Blue Ribbon beer.

"Glad, glad ya' took the time to see me," Cody said. "Think ya' ought ta' be brought up to date. As ya' know, we need to put out some brush fires that are getting out of control. I just got word of one that you have ta' handle. It involves Dr. Koeppen."

"If it's about his relationship with his nurse, Linda Best. I heard a complaint from staff and I have settled the matter. They're two adults. As long as their alleged affair does not interfere with their professional performance, I see no reason to get involved," Gomez said.

"I'm cool with that. Have any patient complaints about staff abuse on Cook Center been referred to you?"

"None that have come to my attention."

"What about Dr. Koeppen's past? Is he possibly hiding something about his war record?" Cody asked.

"I see nothing along those lines. Dr. Koeppen has never hidden his involvement in the war," Gomez said. "He was apparently part of an elite group of students destined for medical degrees who were exempt from the draft. His studies ended in 1941 when his draft deferment was ended and assigned to a mountain division to support advancing troops on the eastern front. He and his buddies were deployed to Bad Reichenhall as I recall."

"Could this have served as a cover to stage their real mission?" Cody asked.

"And I gather you are suggesting this mountain division had some hidden assignment such as mass killings," Gomez said.

"I, I don't know. What little I know is there were special death squads sent to captured territories on the eastern fronts. Such squads organized and directed the mass killings of Jews, Bolsheviks, and gypsies."

"Let's be clear. There seems to be no evidence Dietrich was involved in the actual killings."

"Right. But, was he directing local partisans to shoot wave after wave of victims? Former partisans have identified Nazis directing these exterminations. If he had any role in directing these mass murders, this could explain why he did three residencies here in this country."

"This is shocking. Knowing Dietrich as I do. He may be autocratic, but he does not fit the profile of a criminal—a mass or even a serial killer," Gomez said. "I see him in a much different light. One time after a few drinks at his spacious apartment, he grew nostalgic and told me of the wonder and beauty of growing up in Munich. He studied hard at his gymnasium to earn entry into the university. Dietrich boasted he enjoyed drinking and sailing with a fraternity of like-minded students more than the politics. He said he was a nationalist. At the time of the invasion of Poland, he believed Poland was attacking Germany which he admitted was propaganda as the war came to an end. However, he felt for much of the war it was his duty to defend the homeland."

"Look, I'm not here to be the judge and jury over his patriotism—only to see if Dr. Koeppen has been entirely forthcoming about his past. Going from one specialization to another in medicine raises questions to me as to whether he's tryin' to get ahead of the disclosure of his war record of one kind or another? Or, has he taken up psychiatry to cure his long-term stress issues resulting from orchestrating large-scale exterminations?"

"You can speculate any of that could be true. Yet without witnesses, who's to say what war crimes were committed? The bigger question is what is the hospital's response to any of this if true?"

"It's your call as I see it. It's the clinical director who oversees questions of clinical judgment. I consider he needs to have the chance to tell his side, I know this, this, is out of bounds but I think we outta' contact the FBI and let them do their spooky routine. And, I think we keep this quiet and cooperate with investigators going forward."

"You have omitted to inform the Superintendent."

"You got it. If true, he can claim he never heard a thing 'bout it until reported by the news media."

"I'll agree to cooperate with investigators, but I will not prejudge Dietrich based on his military service or shifts in specializations."

Chapter 22

*Making the Connections*
*Tuesday Morning*

"We, we gotta' quit meeting this way. Did you see the stares we got in the library parking lot?" Cody asked.

"No and who gives a shit? We don't have that much in common," Turpin said.

Cody started the car and suddenly erupted with a burst from the parking lot. He raced through the gears of his 1967 Mazda rotary sports car to the same spot the duo had met before—a carveout in a cornfield for farm implements and a gravel pit.

"You have to realize there are big-time consequences if it gets out who you have been seeing and they find I've ratted them out," Cody said. "Maybe you see me as a prime suspect and you are using these contacts as a ruse to get me to slip and reveal info that only the killer could have known."

"No need to worry. That's for the screenwriters," Turpin said. "If you are involved in any way—just a fair warning. Don't expect a break. So, just sayin' know ahead of time I'll go where the evidence takes me."

"I had you pegged right. A no-nonsense-bring-in-the-bad-guys-cop who happens to have a sense of humor." Cody thought he had to be very cautious about how much he would reveal to Turpin. "So, so, what info

I have likely could put innocent people at risk in a lotta' ways beyond whatever suspect or suspects you indict. And to be clear, I'm referring to my sources. Their identity has to be protected. As for me, if you got the goods—bring it on."

"I'm not the hidebound cop who would sell out a key witness to break a lead in a case. But you are right in one respect. I'm damned determined to close this case. Everyone needs protection by gettin' this sicko or thug off the streets. So, whaddya' got?" Turpin asked.

"Let's start with 'Hippo' as residents have tagged him."

"Who in the hell is that?"

"He's the victim, Fred Hepp. For the record, Hepp was not a boy scout. My source indicated he often abused residents. That included rape and attempted rape." Cody looked at the cornfield and turned back to Turpin. "Just readin' between the lines of my source, Koeppen has stopped any complaints against Hippo from being leaked." Cody added, "I think Hippo coulda' made a deal with Koeppen."

"My source gave me a detailed account of his wartime record. Bottom line, Koeppen got his degree legitimately and developed surgical skills during the war treating head wounds."

"Who else may have known of this?"

"I don't know. But it's clear staff who were tight with Koeppen kept their mouths shut."

"Hepp raped at least one patient?" Turpin asked.

"That has to be confirmed. What is evident, Hepp was the enforcer on the wards. Residents understood if they refused to cooperate with staff or made complaints about staff abuse, they faced hell. For some that meant seclusion. Hippo was a powerful man who could do a lotta' damage without consequence. Bottomline, I think he controlled Koeppen. "

"I gotta' ask is your source, Shannon Audrey?"

"You know damn well I will never answer that question. And don't take my none-answer as proof of anything," Cody said.

"It seems on the surface Shannon Audrey could tell us a lot about Hepp and why she headed for Hepp's office when first visiting the aquarium."

"Maybe, maybe not. That's what whoever did this wants you to think. A crazy patient somehow pulled off a vendetta killing,"

"What did Hepp have on Koeppen?"

"I have no idea other than somehow Hepp may have had evidence that Koeppen was involved in some kind of war crimes."

"If you're shielding Shannon Audrey, that could be a mistake."

"Don't push it with Audrey if you want any more outta' me," Cody said.

"Okay, I get it. Do you have anything else?"

"If you're still putting the pieces together, one of our young mental health workers told me of rumors on the wards that Koeppen was involved with both Blaze Hepp and Linda Best. I'm tellin' you this to suggest infidelity can be a powerful motive as much as being crazy to take out Hepp."

"If I got this right, Fred and Blaze somehow made their way to the top of the food chain on the wards. None of this could have happened without making sure staff, 'see no evil, hear no evil.' Is that in the ballpark?"

"That's at least right in part. You left out 'speak no

evil.' And that's what has me most concerned. You gotta' make sure no one knows where you got these tips—not to just cover my ass but my sources. It's risky they will be exposed and could be in grave danger."

"You've got my word I will protect sources. But again, to make it clear. I will take this case wherever it leads us. Stay in touch. Right now, I need to get back to the station and start putting some pieces together," Turpin said.

**** 

"Glad you decided ta' come ta' work today," Michael said. "We need to go over some updates."

"Before we get started, you may need a caffeine jolt, okay?" Turpin asked.

"Not this late. Besides that's my job to fetch the coffee."

"What's it gonna take to have you knock off that bullshit?"

"That'll happen when whitey treats me like one of 'em. When I can go out ta' eat and not get those stares from the daddy of the family thinkin' I'm a threat to stalk and rob them or their greatest fear—rape their daughter."

"I get it. I can't change how people react to race other than calling it out when I see it. Can we get back to the case? I just uncovered some info that was right in front of us if we had only gone to the post office."

"What did we miss?"

"Before I got here, my wife this morning had asked me to pick up some stamps," Turpin said. "On the way, I stopped at the post office. Out of curiosity while waiting for a clerk, I went through the FBI's ten most wanted and there was one that stood out. A bearded male, named Gary Teagarden, was pictured along with a bio that he had ties to organized crime in New Jersey. He was wanted for murder and solicitation. The interesting part is that the FBI claimed he may be assuming another identity as a mental health worker such as a psychiatric aide. That was his line of work in New Jersey. He was listed as armed and dangerous. The picture suggested he was middle-aged and of average build."

"That's a big deal. Could this be 'Doc Davis?' If so, we gotta' haul ass. He's not gonna wait for some dick to figure out who he is." Michael clicked his pen. "So, I'm thinkin' first I need to make a follow-up call to Dorothea Dix Hospital to see if the name 'Teagarden' was ever on their payroll," Michael said. "I'll take that java after all."

Michael put in a call to Kyle Carrie, HR Director. "This is Sergeant Michael Dyson from Jacksonville Illinois. We just found out a suspect by the name of Gary Teagarden could be posing as a Dr. Davis at Jacksonville State Hospital. If this is the same individual the FBI posted as the ten most wanted felons, this Teagarden may have taken another assumed name at Dorothea posing as a mental health worker, maybe a psychiatric aide. Wonder if y'all could review new hires going back three years and look for anyone who fits this description?"

"So, you don't know whether he took a fake name while here? Somehow, seeing the poster would help us identify Dr. Davis's imposter?" Carrie asked.

"That would be askin' too much. How 'bout checkin' hires that were assigned to wards under Dr. Davis? Check with staff 'bout any ward personnel who had frequent contacts with Dr. Davis or who may have gained access to his office. Most important, check out any staff who resigned or disappeared after the death of

Dr. Davis. This felon is from New Jersey according to the poster."

"That's a tall order, but I'll get right on it. The identity of this imposter will likely lead to a lot of dead ends. The best chances to isolate the fake is to start at the ward level. Ward staff usually have a feel for the competent from the incompetent on their wards," Carrie said.

"Here's your coffee. Any luck?" Turpin asked.

"Good cooperation from the Dix hospital. Wouldn't be surprised to hear back today who this asshole is."

"Any more on this Dr. Koeppen yet?" Turpin asked.

"Not yet. I'm still checkin' out library books on death squads."

"There's a lot we need to find out from the doctor—his relationship to Fred Hepp and his wife Blaze Hepp," Turpin said.

"So, you think Koeppen had been played with blackmail threats if he ever disclosed any abusive incidents on the ward to authorities?" Michael asked.

"I doubt it. He's too smart to ever jeopardize his reputation that way. No, I think the Hepps had something on the doctor. His past is a good starting point. Maybe they somehow figured out he was a suspected war criminal. And there's the possibility Fred Hepp did the mob thing to protect his drug source from the hospital. He demanded Koeppen's silence about the drug thefts to avoid a hitman," Turpin said.

"I'm guessin' Blaze was in on whatever Fred Hepp had on Koeppen," Michael said.

"You could be wrong 'bout Blaze. You know, she affects people in different ways, right?" Turpin asked.

Michael thought this was Turpin's way of admitttn' that Blaze had gotten to him after their first interview. "How 'bout this? Maybe this Hippo dude treated her like Koeppen. She had no choice but to go along with drug dealin'. And maybe, just maybe, Hippo discovered his wife was cheatin' on him. Koeppen got wind of this and took out Hippo before he had a chance ta' whack the doctor," Michael offered.

"That's a possibility. Or, Fred Hepp was taken out by a hitman."

"I still think Koeppen's war record needs more investigation," Michael said.

"Am I missin' something?" Turpin asked. "Engaged in combat and doing the medic work does not mean he was involved with mass exterminations."

"Yeah, I don't have the goods yet. But I've got a couple of ideas—like he needs to be asked one-on-one about his surgical skills involving head wounds and what would be required to decapitate someone. But first things first, Boss. We gotta' make a move with the FBI or this fake doc's gonna vanish," Michael said.

"Whadda ya' recommend *Detective Michael Ray Dyson*? That I tell the feds we gotta' a 'ten-most-wanted' suspect who posed as a shrink and coulda' been involved with the death squads based on his service in the German army?"

"I do believe you pissed. If it's all on me that's cool as long as I don't make that call. You da' man," Michael said.

"I've got zero tolerance for any more of this bullshit. Michael. Just come clean. If you can't get over seein' me as another whitey—you know—Taggin' me as '*the Man,*' we ain't ever gonna' break this one open."

"I ain't an equal. It's that simple. But I'm still a cop just like my ol' man. He was a good cop. I woulda' turned out on the other side if he hadn't been for him. He was my hero, my idol. I dreamt of being a cop just like him," Michael said.

Michael turned his head upward peering at the pulsating fluorescent light trying to clear his unsteady voice and fight off a tear. "I was twelve years old at the time, 1952 to be exact. He got a tip that one of the goons from mob boss Ted Rose's outfit was 'bout to do his protection money run at a bar. My dad was waitin' and caught the muscle takin' the money. He collared the piece of shit not seein' his cover. Six slugs to his head. His ears were cut off and put in our mailbox. Nobody ever was arrested."

"I'm sorry to hear you went through this, Michael."

"Not to suggest this case is like what happened to dad except for one aspect.—This kinda' violence is the worst kind—where the killer or killers terrorize bystanders and silence any potential rats."

"Ta' me, I think it's a deflection. Whoever did it had figured a decapitated head in a fish tank at an asylum would point to a crazy," Turpin said. "Still haven't heard from the prosecutor about a possible meeting with Shannon Audrey. She could have a lot to disclose."

Chapter 23

*Cleaning House*
*Later, Tuesday Morning*

"Thanks, Dr. Gomez for takin' time for us," Turpin said. "We've got some updates. Sergeant Dyson has identified who we believe to be the imposter. Sergeant Davis will give you the details."

"Yes, I checked with HR back at Dorothea Dix Hospital who could've pulled off a fake identity," Michael said. "Through a process of elimination, they came up with a suspect who is posin' as this Doc Davis. His real name is Gary Teagarden who had ties to organized crime in New Jersey. As the feds moved in on him in New Jersey, Teagarden took on another alias as a 'Henry Kline' and posed as a psychiatric aide at Dorothea Dix for six years. It's a long story, but to get to the gist of it—Teagarden broke into Dr. Davis's office after his death and photocopied his degrees and resume. He found a good forger and made an application to Jacksonville State Hospital. The rest is history."

"You said he was or is a felon?"

"Yes. Teagarden was involved in sex and drug trafficking," Michael said. "He's wanted for the murder of a prostitute in New York City he believed was holdin' out on him. He fled to North Carolina and took the hospital job as a cover. When the real Dr. Davis died, he recognized his chance to once again to change his identity."

"I'm shocked to think he was treating patients in the infirmary with acute illnesses."

"Thank God he's identified," Turpin said. "This Teagarden is considered armed and dangerous according to his description on FBI's ten most wanted list. Did this alias Dr. Davis have any dealings with Fred Hepp that you are aware of?"

"None that come to mind. This Doctor Davis emphasized he was exploring the links between physical illnesses and psychiatric disorders. He made a special request to take an assignment at the infirmity to study such connections. He agreed to transfer to one of our centers after completing the study." Gomez paused and looked out the window. "Wait a minute, he did mention in passing he wanted to check out how body temperature is related to psychotic episodes. Something about he planned to review ward charts on patients treated with hydrotherapy," Gomez said.

"Did he mention Fred Hepp?" Turpin asked.

"No. But I got the impression he intended to review archived hydrotherapy files for specific patients and review their incident reports," Gomez said. "Hard to imagine he did not involve Fred Hepp for retrieving such records."

"Best this not get out before we take him in," Turpin said. "We want to get as much info as we can to see if he had anything to do with Hepp's murder. Two other questions—Whoever decapitated the victim appeared to have surgical skills. This brings me to ask you if you are aware of this fake Dr. Davis ever made any request for surgical training while here at the hospital?"

"Not that I recall."

"Are you aware he requested use of the medical library at Memorial hospital? According to the head of surgery there, he had requested to review some type of surgical procedure in their medical library," Turpin said.

"Oh, oh, yes. I recall this Dr. Davis complained that our medical library is quite limited," Gomez said. "But he never mentioned Memorial hospital."

"Did Dr. Koeppen ever mention having dealt with head wound cases during the close of the war?" Turpin asked.

"I do not find it unusual if he served in that role given his medical background then I fail to see how this relates to anything. It does not square with his character to commit such a barbaric act as I see it," Gomez said.

"We're not jumping to any conclusions at this point. It's a process of elimination. Let's go to Dr. Koeppen's relationships with staff. Are you aware of his intimate contacts with staff under his supervision?" Turpin asked.

"I think that goes beyond anything I want to discuss."

"I'm only askin' to see if his affairs were discovered and threats made?"

"No comment."

"Thank you, Dr. Gomez, for your time. I think that's it for now. We appreciate your cooperation," Turpin said.

\*\*\*\*

*Witness Protection*

Turpin and Michael discussed their next moves on the way back to the station. "Gotta' think others are tied in with this fake doc," Turpin said.

"Ta' get my two-bits in, I think we do not wait any

longer. It's time to make a move on Teagarden."

"We're on the same page. Agreed. We need to see how he found his way to JSH and his connections to Hepp. The prosecutor got an expedited bench warrant for his arrest. Let's pick up the warrant and make a visit to the infirmary."

"Hi-Oh Silver," Michael sang.

\*\*\*\*

Dr. Chaudhry returned from his rounds and greeted Turpin and Michael in his office. "Good afternoon. What's up?"

"Could we shut the door?" Turpin asked.

"Sure."

"For openers, how would you evaluate the performance of one of your docs, a Dr. Davis, over the last few months?" Turpin asked.

"I have received no complaints. He has consulted me occasionally on what diagnosis I would recommend for patients he is treating. I am flattered given his background that he would defer to me for consultation," Chaudhry said.

"What do you know about his background?" Turpin asked.

"To put it into perspective, I wish I had as much knowledge about psychiatry as he does. His training and experience are exceptional. Given his research interest in this population, I find it quite understandable he would seek out consultation," Chaudhry said.

"Would you mind asking him to come to your office? And please do not reveal who is in your office, okay?" Turpin asked.

"Is he a suspect in your investigation?"

"Right now, a person of interest, fair enough?"

Chaudhry made a call to the geriatric ward and requested Dr. Davis. "Hello. This is Davis. What's up Omar?" Davis asked.

"Could you drop by my office. I'd like to review a couple of your cases," Chaudhry said.

"Be there shortly."

Davis knocked on Chaudhry's door. Chaudhry opened the door and announced, "I'd like to introduce you to Detective Turpin and his partner, Sergeant Dyson."

Davis calmly looked at the pair. "Is this about going to the medical library at Memorial?"

"Tell us. Why before we've even met you, you bring up a library visit? Help us out. Why do you think we're here—to collect a fine for an overdue book?" Turpin asked.

"No. Just guessing it has something to do with the Hepp murder," Davis said.

"Explain why you think a library visit would be involved in the investigation?"

"Heard from other docs over lunch investigators were interested in a suspect with surgical skills. And I've been reviewing surgical procedures used here in the infirmary."

"Did you know Fred Hepp?"

"Let me get this straight. You call me in here because I did library research on surgical removal of a gall bladder? What do we have, the keystone cops? You somehow have concluded gall bladder surgery has something to do with decapitation? And as to your question of Fred Hepp, never knew this guy. Is this the one who lost his head?" Davis laughed at his joke.

"Tell me. Is this the kinda' joke a doc with your

credentials in the shrink business would see as funny?" Turpin asked.

"You mean shrinks as you put it don't have a sense of humor?"

"I'd wager a bet the real Dr. William Davis woulda' never told that joke."

Davis with no obvious change in facial expression turned and ran for the door. Michael bolted through the hallway in pursuit. Turpin was close behind. Davis headed for his car in the parking lot. Michael, a former safety for his undefeated high school football team, sprinted to close the gap with Davis. Michael launched toward his waist and made a tackle. Davis crashed to the asphalt. The two wrestled as Davis tried to get his hand free. Davis with a swift elbow to Michael's head freed his hand. He reached inside his white medical jacket and pulled out a .38 revolver.

As he maneuvered the weapon toward Michael's head, Turpin dove in the direction of the gun and slammed Davis's arm to the ground. The weapon flew from his hand. In short order, Turpin and Michael wrestled Davis to his belly and cuffed him.

Davis was spirited over to Turpin's police car, where Michael held him tight against the back door. Davis was searched for weapons. None were found. His wallet was removed.

"I know my rights. Wait 'til my attorney hears I've been arrested for going to a medical library."

"I have an arrest warrant for Gary Teagarden, alias Dr. William F. Davis, on charges of fraudulent credentials and forgery. "You have the right to remain silent," Turpin said. He continued reading his Miranda rights. As Turpin finished, Davis yelled, "Ya' have no proof I'm not William Davis. Look at my driver's license."

"How 'bout another alias—Henry Kline?" Michael asked "Ever heard of him?"

"I ain't got nothin' to say."

"Did I pick up a little New York accent Teagarden?" Michael asked.

"How woulda' boy like you know anything about accents?"

"Get in the car asshole," Turpin said. The backdoor was opened and Teagarden was forced to the back seat. Back at the station, Teagarden was booked and fingerprinted. Turpin and Michael directed him to an interrogation room. His cuffs were removed. A barren table with chairs and bright lights were features of the room. The door to the room was embedded with a small window reinforced by wire mesh.

"I need to make a phone call. That's my right," Teagarden demanded.

"You can make that call after you tell us how you made your way to the hospital impersonating a doctor," Turpin said. "Let's start with your real name. We know you were connected in Brooklyn with a sex and drug trade. Somethin' happened. How 'bout this version? You pissed off a crime boss and you did a disappearin' act. You switched identity and took a job outta' the city down south as a psychiatric aide—Do I have that right?" Turpin asked.

"Stick it up your ass, cowboy."

"Try this on for size. Somebody from your former life would very much like to know where you ended up. If this goes as other high-profile cases, your arrest will be leaked to the press makin' headlines. Who will protect you in that case?" Turpin asked.

"Who fuckin' cares what comes out. My lawyer will have me out in no time. Your charges will never hold up."

"You're goin' nowhere. The feds will see to that. Your problem is survivin' in lockup. Your old crime boss likely has a lotta' connections in federal prisons."

"I'll take my chances in court."

"I'd say y'all makin' a stupid bet to beat this rap. It's an open and shut case down to the forged credentials and writin' scripts for patients here," Michael said. "And, there are federal charges on top of that. Let's cut the bullshit. You were up to your ass in the Mexico-Chicago drug pipeline with the Hepps. Did Fred Hepp turn on y'all when he found out you were assigned to take him out."

"Keep yappin'. Tell me, boy. How *y'all* gonna respond to police brutality charges?"

"The facts are simple. Y'all's ass is grass if you wind up in any prison."

"Take that big dick of yours and cram it down your throat."

"If I were you, I'd be thinkin' 'bout my own nightrider bein' whacked. Blaze Hepp's got you in a corner. If she goes to victim protection, there goes Teagarden just like blowin' out a candle. She knows the whole network—the theft of drugs here and cuttin' stimulants and the blow."

"Never heard of the Hepps."

"Explain the big dawgs here sayin' you made special contacts with Fred Hepp to review his files on hydrotherapy—the water torture act?"

"I've said enough. Get me to a phone."

"Here's the deal. We think your survival is nil when the shit hits the fan," Turpin said. "You can opt to have this heard in court or cooperate right now. The wolves from all directions are comin' at you—the feds, Blaze, and your old Brooklyn connections. Oh, and maybe the Chicago outfit for botchin' the hit on Fred Hepp."

"You ain't got shit for evidence."

"There's little time left. Feds will be here to pick you up after we're finished. If you cooperate now, there's a chance we can argue you need to be considered for witness protection before being sent to a federal lockup. Think it over."

"Protection from what?"

"Make no mistake, you didn't leave Brooklyn and change your identity to please your crime boss. There's a score to be settled at some point," Turpin said. "And, Fred Hepp had friends as I'm sure you know, who were not happy with skimming profits. If you had nothin' to do with his murder, tell us what you know about Blaze. What was her role in the drug pipeline, and what did she have on this Dr. Koeppen?"

"Told you, I don't know Blaze Hepp."

"You're lyin'. I think Fred Hepp and y'all knew the drug business inside out before comin' to Jacksonville. The remaining question is whether Blaze was forced into the setup or she was the one who ran the show?" Michael asked.

"Why don't you go back to your kin? You know bein' a jungle bunny and fuckin' horny apes."

"Look you piece of shit. I've run outta' patience," Turpin said. Turpin grabbed Teagarden by the throat and slammed him against the wall. Michael pounced on Turpin's back and with all his strength attempted to pull

Turpin's hands away. Teagarden's face turned bright red. He gasped for air. Helpless, he struggled with no relief from Turpin's powerful grasp around his throat.

Michael yelled, "Back off God damnit, back off. How many times do I have ta' tell ya' I'll fight my own battles." With a knee to Turpin's back and a strong grasp of Turpin's forearms, Michael with a last surge of energy forced Turpin to release his grasp.

Teagarden gasped for air. Blood to his brain returned. "You just gave me a ticket outta' jail you fuckin' hick cop."

"Shut the fuck up," Michael yelled. "You must be confused. I didn't see anything. Did you, Detective Turpin?"

"No."

"This is jist' the beginning. Let's see how long you survive if I let my dawg off his leash? And it won't be where there are any eyes. Jist' doin' our duty. Arrestin' a fleein' felon."

"Fuck you."

"If that's the way y'all want it. Stand up to be cuffed. We takin' you to the crime scene—the Illinois River where you dumped Hepp's remains," Michael said.

"I demand my right to an attorney."

"You can make that call after we get back from the river—if you survive," Turpin said.

"You'll never get me outta' this building without one of your hick buddies seein' I'm bein' kidnapped."

There's a fire escape with no one between us and the squad car," Michael said. "Now, put your hands behind your back peacefully or maybe we hicks need to show ya' there are penalties for bein' so disrespectful." Teagarden lunged for the door. Michael tackled him, forced him to the floor, and cuffed him. He pulled up on his arms. Teagarden screamed. Turpin grabbed him by the scruff of his neck and pulled the weaker Teagarden to his feet.

"We're ready to ride, Dr. Davis." Turpin grabbed Teagarden by the cuffs and forced him to the door.

"Wait, wait. Maybe we should talk this over."

"Talk fast. After all those insults, you gotta' believe we have ta' hear the whole story or we are goin' down to the river not to pray but to offer the snappin' turtles something to feast on," Turpin said.

"Okay, okay. Let's start with Blaze."

Chapter 24

*Praying Mantis?*

"We gotta move fast on Blaze or you can bet she will disappear on some island with plenty of cash," Turpin said.

Michael sat on the passenger side of the squad car while Betty Stern, the meter maid, sat in the back. Turpin stepped on the gas as he made his way to East State Street just off the square. In front of Blaze's house, a U-Haul was parked in the street with workers loading the truck.

"Did we strike out?" Michael asked.

"Let's check it out," Turpin said.

A young, hefty twenty-something-year-old was struggling with an antique wing chair as he approached the ramp of the truck. "Is Blaze Hepp around?" Turpin asked.

"Think she went after somethin'. Maybe the bank to pay us," the worker said.

"When do you expect her back?" Turpin asked.

"Next half-hour or so. She promised to pay us when finished. We are almost done," the worker said.

"Thanks," Turpin said. Turpin and Michael returned to the car. "Think we best not attract any 'ttention," Michael said. "We can tour the neighborhood and count the number of black folks livin' on this end of town."

"You could drive in almost any direction and not

212

find any black folks other than the few who work at the hospital or are enrolled at MacMurray College," Turpin said.

Michael recalled a local history buff at a private museum had given a talk on the origins of Jacksonville. The stately two-story homes dating back to the 19th century built on State Street were indicators of a prosperous era when Jacksonville thrived as an agricultural and cultural center after the civil war. The city competed with Springfield economically and politically.

Driving east on State Street, Turpin commented, "If I get enough scratch someday, I'm gonna buy one of these attractively restored homes."

Michael seethed at the prospect of ever being a part of the neighborhood. This had always been the ol' south white neighborhood and not bound to change. A better spot was near Lake Jacksonville he reasoned where there were isolated cabins and homes. Seemed an ideal location for both his wife, Hope, and him upon retirement. There he thought he could catch all the bluegill and crappie anytime he put his line in the lake and not think about belongin'.

Turpin circled a block and headed west on State Street. He parked a half-block away from the truck. A Nova Chevrolet was parked in the driveway near the U-Haul.

On the small front yard, Blaze Hepp Turpin and Michael approached Blaze as she counted out cash payments to the lead worker. Betty Stern, dressed in her police uniform, remained in the car.

"Good afternoon, Blaze. Looks like you might be leaving. Are you moving permanently from

Jacksonville?" Turpin asked.

"I've got nothin' to say to either one of you. Now excuse me while I check out the house to see if something may have been left behind."

"Let's go inside. We need to clear up a few details," Turpin said.

"There's nothing to clear up. Now, leave or I will file a complaint. This is pure harassment. You would think a victim's wife would be given time to grieve without being tied into your wild speculations about my dead husband."

"Let's get to the bottom line, Mrs. Hepp. Y'all is in a swamp with alligators bitin' at your ass everywhere. A so-called Dr. Davis jist' ratted you out. He's pegged you as headin' up a major drug-trafficking operation," Michael said.

"What in the hell? Who is this Dr. Davis?"

"Let's cut the bullshit. You, Fred, and this Dr. Davis whose real name is Gary Teagarden are suppliers for a drug pipeline between Chicago and Mexico. Y'all shaved too much profit by cuttin' the drugs with the psych meds. We have reason to believe your drug bosses may have taken out your husband over lost revenue."

"I have no reason to listen to any more crap."

"Think y'all better hear the rest of this story. Your buddy Teagarden made the case y'all masterminded the hit job on your husband," Michael said.

Blaze turned and walked toward her car. Turpin stepped in front of her. "Let's do this without a scene in this nice neighborhood." Turpin grasped her arm and led her to the detective's car. Blaze did not resist. Betty Stern got out of the car. "Put your hands on the roof of the car," Turpin said. Stern did a body search for weapons and none were evident. Turpin cuffed Blaze while Michael read her rights.

"You are arrested for illegal narcotic sales and a suspect for the murder of Fred Hepp," Michael said.

Back at the station, Turpin booked and fingerprinted Hepp. She was directed to the interrogation room.

"Have a seat Blaze," Turpin said. Michael took a seat at the table in front of her. Turpin stood oblique to the side of the table.

Michael began the interrogation. "Let's start with what y'all face Blaze. Teagarden has made it clear y'all were behind the drug thefts from the hospital and distributin' blow cut with psycho meds. Your pipeline included the Chicago area, most of Peoria, Springfield, and East St. Louis," Michael said.

"Let me call my attorney."

"You ain't heard the whole story, Teagarden told us how you blackmailed your boss, Dr. Koeppen. Seems like Koeppen couldn't keep his hands off ya'. Your husband suggested you invite Koeppen to your house where he crawled into the attic and waited with his camera. Teagarden told us there was a small opening near a light fixture in your bedroom. Your husband got a great view of you two gettin' it on. He took some photos. Later, he talked you into other orgies with the doc. Your husband got off on the photos and live-action."

"I don't see how any of these sex fantasies this Dr. Davis or Tea…something…may have any connection to me or Dr. Koeppen?"

"The rest is easy. You had the photos. You spotted this tattoo under his left armpit. You asked him durin' a drunken romp what was that all about. At some point, he told y'all it was a blood type required in case of bein' wounded during the war. You pumped him 'bout whether he had been involved in killin' Jews? You told Fred and Teagarden he finally admitted bein' forced to give orders but never performed any executions."

Michael flipped a page in his notebook. "The three of ya' decided to make a move on Koeppen. You laid it out to him. To save his reputation, it was simple. You needed regular protection money for the photos and keepin' quiet 'bout his war record. And most important to you, keepin' the missin' drugs under wrap."

"You don't have any evidence for these wild shots in the dark. I repeat. I don't know this guy, whoever he is."

"We ain't to the part where y'all set up your husband for a hit. Accordin' to Teagarden, this 'guy' you don't know was recruited from the East coast. At the time, y'all didn't know he was on board to take over the business. Teagarden said you got word from Chicago from an old contact, 'Sal,' otherwise known as 'Salvatore the Cupcake,' your former pimp. He told you that the outfit had targeted you and your husband for a hit. Profits were down. Users were goin' elsewhere to get purer dope," Michael said. "Black Gangsters were controllin' most of the Southside because they had the best skag."

"Is that all?" Blaze laughed.

Turpin intervened, "You can laugh at the case we have 'gainst you. But Teagarden has made it pretty airtight what happened next. You convinced Sal you had no choice but to go along with cuttin' the drugs. Fred had been brutal and greedy. You gave Sal dates and contacts as to where Fred would be at the hospital in exchange for protection. Whoever was hired was told to leave a message for anyone skimmin' profits. Their days were numbered."

"Again, this is some guy I don't know makin' up stuff to beat a rap."

"A murder rap is at stake, Blaze. If you gave the outfit times and location of your husband corresponding to when and where he was murdered. You can be charged with conspiracy to commit murder. Prosecutors will show little mercy for such a barbaric act," Turpin said.

"Okay, okay. There's little to be gained with any more lies," Blaze said. Blaze put her head on the table and rubbed her face.

"What lies?"

"You have no idea what I've been through." Blaze wiped her tears. "I did not plot a murder. That's what you've got wrong. I realized at some point the whole operation was bound to crash. Fred pushed it over the edge. I warned him Chicago wanted new blood to handle the drug business. He didn't listen."

"How does that square with you setting him up for an execution," Turpin asked.

"I told Sal he should meet with Fred to settle the matter."

"So, your version is you knew your husband had set a date with Sal to settle their beefs. But you never knew the time or place. Is that right?"

"I never wanted any part of the drug business, but I had no choice. It was always his way after we met— make that when I was sold to Fred," Blaze said. She reached for a tissue and wiped more tears. "The price was cheap. I was so close to death with all the pills, booze, and air fresheners I inhaled. I looked like shit. I couldn't make enough to pay rent or even 'nough to feed the cat." Blaze reared her head and looked up at Turpin with intense eye contact. A single tear left a trail of mascara. In a slow, somber voice with a slight rattle, she uttered, "Fred saved my life but at a great cost. He controlled me just like Sal. This time it was much more brutal. He knew I'd jump every time he said jump to avoid the beatings. He also was my source for the good stuff."

"Blaze, you need to give us somethin' to go on if what you're sayin' is true. Did you ever call the police or go to ER when assaulted?" Turpin asked.

"No—and face another brutal beating?"

"Yet, you went along with this extortion of Dr. Koeppen?" Turpin asked.

"Fred schemed the whole deal. He wanted control of the doctor and the union."

"Looks like Koeppen did protect you and Fred as to any reports of drug theft. What about the union?" Turpin asked.

"It's a long story. But in a nutshell, Fred convinced ward workers they would all be terminated like him if they didn't support their union and put all their weight behind Dr. Koeppen. Complaints about anything happening on the ward were to be forwarded to the union steward. That was Fred. That's where any talk of patient abuse or worse ended, period. Everybody realized from the way he handled patients that he would break a few bones if anyone broke rank."

Michael cleared his throat. "Jist' wonderin' how would Fred react to what y'all said? Suppose he might say you were no victim—that you were the brains behind the drug business—that it was your idea to skim the meds for patients and increase profits by cuttin' the dope so it would go further."

"You think the Chicago mob would turn over such an operation to a wasted whore?"

"Isn't it a fact y'all stayed in contact with Sal and Sal warned you bosses were unhappy with the Jacksonville operation? Y'all fingered Fred. That he was greedy and outta' control. It was easy to set up your husband jist' like y'all tryin' to do with us now," Michael said.

"So, I'm the female praying mantis. I lure them with sex and bite the head off of every male who tries to fuck me?"

"Fred might agree," Michael said.

"Going back to growin' up in Chicago, Fred was like all the men in my life. They were locked into one thing, gettin' their rocks off. Whether it was my dad or after runnin' away—the miserable scum who rented my body to abuse it in every imaginable way," Blaze said. She turned her head toward the table. "Yeah, lookin' back on everything biting their heads off woulda' been too kind."

"And that applies to your husband?" Michael asked.

"Thoughts yes. Actions no. You did not get on the wrong side of Fred. Everybody understood that," Blaze said. "Ask Ty Crowley."

"Who's that?"

"Zeke Cody's administrative connection."

Chapter 25

*Key Witness*

Turpin intervened. "I'm not sayin' you are a saint, Blaze, but if we are to believe you, a lotta' what's happened to you was outta' your control."

"I have been swimming in a cesspool. I want to live and love again like on a riverbank with my brother and talk about those early years when Dad took us fishin'. You discover there's another life."

"Ya' know there's a way out. Witness protection could be in the cards for nailing those who built the cesspool."

"It's a big risk. I want to stay in touch with my brother."

With no words exchanged for almost a minute, Turpin could not resist Blaze's penetrating tearful eyes. Breaking the silence, Turpin said, "Trust me. I can make it happen."

"I need a break."

"That's fine. We can get back together whenever you've made your call," Turpin said.

Michael nodded in approval. The interrogation ended.

Turpin escorted Blaze back to a holding cell. Upon seeing Turpin return to his office, Michael headed for Turpin's office. "So, y'all bought her side, right?"

Michael asked.

"Blaze declined to make a phone call. Looks like we've got no choice. Take care of her 'til we figure out who iced her husband," Turpin said.

"Her eyes for y'all seems to be workin'."

"Ya' got it all wrong. It's clear beyond the tears she's marked however you judge her scheming. Without her cooperation at this point, we ain't got shit."

"Why did she take so much time gettin' outta' Dodge if the heat was on? Still think her eyes put blinders on ya'."

"You got balls to say that. Eye candy's one thing, takin' action another."

"And Blaze said somethin' similar. She may 've wanted to take out Fred, but action was out of the question. You believe her? She's softened you, and not your Johnson?"

The phone rang. "Hello. This is Detective Turpin."

"This is County Prosecutor Abe Goldberg. We struck a deal with the hospital and the State's AG office. They agreed to an interview with Shannon Audrey. There will be constraints disallowing one-on-one questioning with the witness. We can ask written questions read by a neutral party to her. Her guardian ad litem and an attorney will be present to advise her legally and intervene if questions provoke an emergent event compromising her testimony."

"What in the hell is an 'emergent event?'" Turpin asked.

"Skipping all the lingo, it's someone going around the bend. The meeting is scheduled for this coming Friday. I'd appreciate it if you and Sergeant Dyson could have written questions at my office by Wednesday. I will organize them along with my own. The interview will be at my office scheduled for 10 a.m. There will be no cross-examination or queries from anyone. The only person allowed to ask the questions is Psychiatric Social Worker Sarah Welker from Springfield," Goldberg said.

"This is not in any way ideal. We very much depend on follow-up questions to break open which could be vital info," Turpin said.

"I realize full well from my end we will have our hands tied behind our back," Goldberg said. "But this is the best we could do. And just between you and me, this testimony may not stand up in court. Let's make the best of it and see what is revealed."

"We sure as hell have a lot of questions based on new leads. One more thing. Don't be surprised if the FBI makes a move shortly on this case," Turpin said.

"Keep me posted. Gotta' run now. Good day," Goldberg said.

"Good news Michael. Shannon Audrey will be available for an interview. But we are limited to written questions. Not ideal. I'd like to get to a lot of areas, especially why she headed for Hepp's old office. What was she lookin' for?"

"Yes, and what else did she see on the ward? If Blaze is right, there was plenty buried that could expose others that may have had reason to take Hepp out."

"I'm curious. Who is on your list?" Turpin asked.

"I got my suspicions that the administration was in on some of the dirt but let it slide waitin' for the right moment to clean house. We need to follow up on this Ty Crowley Blaze fingered, whoever the hell he is. It's possible the pissin' war with the old guard may have gotten out of hand," Michael said. "Someone coulda' set up a contract killin' and made it look like a mob hit job."

"Based on what we know, no one has been identified as having a drug connection or motive to kill Hepp unlike Teagarden or Blaze," Turpin said.

**** 

*Friday Morning*

"Hello. This is Sergeant Dyson. I really appreciate all you did to make it possible to interview Shannon Audrey. I can't get in 'ta details, but I fear Shannon faces risks if she does not testify. Little can be done to protect any witness if potential threats are not exposed."

"I'm on the same page Sergeant Dyson," Carla Fitzgerald said. "At Shannon's request, I agreed to be present at all phases of the interview."

"That's good to hear. There's much we need to clarify about what's happenin' on the ward. Better cut it off now. See ya' shortly."

A local attorney Theodore Pauling who specialized in civil rights cases and Max Sheldon from Chicago, Audrey's guardian ad litem, along with Carla Fitzgerald agreed to meet Friday morning one-half hour before start of the deposition. Pauling outlined the procedure to be used. He stressed Shannon would not be subjected to the usual cross-examination of a witness. Her testimony would be terminated if her defense team found her to be adversely affected by any further examination.

Prosecutor Goldberg welcomed the witness, Shannon Audrey, and Social Worker Sarah Welker along with Pauling, Sheldon, and Fitzgerald. Goldberg directed them to a spare office with a large picture window. A mike placed in the middle of a folding table had been arranged for the interview. Speakers were placed outside the room for observers. Shannon was asked to sit near the window such that her profile view could be exposed without having to face observers.

After everyone inside and outside the office were seated, the interview commenced. "Thank you, Mr. Sheldon and you Shannon Audrey for agreeing to the interview," Welker said. Welker next read into the record the date, time, and individuals present. Welker outlined the procedure to be followed. Shannon then was read the oath as a witness "to tell the truth so help you, God." Shannon said, "I will." And with the oath affirmed, Welker started with written questions concerning her relationship with the victim. Shannon disclosed details regarding Fred Hepp's brutal hydrotherapy treatment of patients including her run-in with Hepp when refusing to enter the tubs. Shannon described how he used a knotted-wet towel to force patients to enter the tubs. Her persistent resistance led to solitary confinement. When freed, Shannon described her attempted suicide using a broken bottle to cut her wrists.

"My suffering pales in comparison to my good friend, Vesta Diaz," Shannon said. She explained how she came to know Vesta Diaz, their close ties, and Diaz's account of being raped by Fred Hepp. "It was brutal and sick," Shannon said. "Complaints to Nurse Best of Fred Hepp's sexual assault of Vesta Diaz went nowhere. A couple of months later Vesta Diaz was subjected to psychosurgery which left her quite impaired. Most upsetting to me was what happened before Vesta was raped," Shannon said. "Dr. Koeppen sexually molested Vesta and then told her this would lead to her recovery. It's clear Hippo…Fred Hepp…was somehow informed this had happened and I believe encouraged him to take liberties with Vesta."

"What was your relationship with Blaze Hepp?" the social worker asked.

Shannon related how it was poor particularly after speaking out in patient government she had observed Toby Cohen having sex with Blaze Hepp in a storage room. "After I had revealed this, both Blaze and René Cohen, Toby's wife, threatened to revise my treatment plan. They insisted it never happened. It was crazy delusional talk getting out of hand." Shannon paused to gather her thoughts. "To me, this all meant one thing. I could be subjected to the same treatment as Vesta."

"Did you ever go off the ward to freely explore the campus?" Welker asked.

"Never without staff present. We sometimes were taken on walks. If we agreed to engage in occupational therapy, we could leave the ward. I was assigned a job to stuff toys in plastic bags where we would be paid a small amount for each toy. I quit. It was so boring. The best trips off the ward were to the patient library. I read most of their holdings," Shannon said.

"Had you ever been in the hydrotherapy building after it was converted to an aquarium?"

"Never except for our visit on that awful day."

"Why did you leave the patient group listening to the docent and go to Fred Hepp's old office?" Welker asked.

Shannon fidgeted and looked out the window. Her eyes closed and her face grew taut. Moments later, Shannon said, "It's not clear I can be sure where this will end up."

Her lawyer Pauling asked for a pause to have a private conversation with his client. Shannon and Pauling along with Sheldon retreated to the hallway. "If you feel this is too traumatic to discuss or self-incriminating, we will end it right here," Pauling said.

"It's more than that. There could be serious consequences anyway you cut it if I gave a truthful answer," Shannon said.

"Has someone posed a threat for your testimony?"

"Yes, my ex."

"In what way?" Pauling asked. Shannon gave details of her husband's philandering leading to a fight with her husband and committed to the hospital. She learned from Vesta whose sister worked at his firm how he had taken a life insurance policy out on Shannon. His former secretary and lover had set their eyes on the purchase of an expensive home in the Chicago suburbs, according to Vesta. "They needed a large settlement from the life policy on me to make the purchase."

"So how does any of this relate to you going to Fred Hepp's old office?" Pauling asked.

"Fred Hepp raped Vesta in that office. It was a brutal assault. I wanted to see for myself details Vesta told me about what was at the scene of the crime," Shannon said.

"That still does not explain the connection," Pauling challenged.

"I still have the scene in mind. I wanted to have it right as to where things were located that she described," Shannon said. "Look, I find it upsetting to go over this again. I told Vesta's story to Linda Best and look what happened. Vesta received brain surgery. I don't want to be next."

"The priority is protecting you from any unnecessary upset. Let's stop the procedure now if this is too upsetting," Pauling said. "My advice is to be truthful. We can procure court protection."

"I don't know who to trust at this point. Could we meet in private Mr. Pauling?"

"Sure."

Shannon and Pauling retreated to an enclave with a sink filled with coffee cups, a half-full coffee pot, apple fritters, and a copy machine. "I don't know where to go next," Shannon said. "I don't trust attorneys and judges. They put me in an asylum and threw away the key."

"So, you don't trust me," Pauling said.

"It's who you represent, to be honest. Can I be sure you have not worked a deal with the prosecutor who wants to nail me for murder?"

"You just have to take my word. None of that is true. Your case was referred to me by your social worker Fitzgerald. She claimed there was a major civil rights question involving a patient who was a key witness in a murder investigation," Pauling said. "The only communications with the prosecutor centered around the procedure we finally agreed on and the date."

"Can I trust you never talked with the administration?" Shannon asked. "To me, it looks fishy. Why all of a sudden can I tell my story to investigators?"

"No. I have had no contact with hospital administration. That's not to say we may want to look at their role in denying your civil rights. But for now, let's clear up the question of why you went to Hepp's office. Is there more you haven't told?"

"Could you be legit. I just don't know. If you could be trusted. That's the big question?"

"I take confidentiality with clients as a very serious matter."

"This could be a huge mistake." Shannon stared at the copy machine and put these options in some kind of order. "Vesta told me she had a letter from her sister spelling out the details of my ex's insurance scheme in the pocket of her dress. When Hippo forcibly removed her clothes, the letter fell to the floor. Vesta said after Hippo finished and pulled up his pants, he turned to the door and told Vesta to be quiet. She spotted the letter on the floor and managed to scoot it under the throw rug where she had been raped."

"Is there any reason not to disclose this?"

"If the letter is missing, who will believe me? A mental patient who has been hospitalized for years ranting that her ex is gonna kill her for insurance money? This comes across no different than Maggie Nilsson on our ward. She tells anyone who will listen her son is stealing her estate. Nobody believes her because she insists people are stealing her thoughts."

"This letter. Could it still be there?"

"I never got the chance to look. It's been two years. What if it's no longer there?"

"I can't say how it will turn out, but what is there to lose? We can argue after this much time Fred Hepp may have found and destroyed the letter."

"You don't know Dr. Koeppen. He has made it clear I'm not ready for release. As he says, I have poor 'insight,'" Shannon said. "A missing letter is proof I'm still delusional."

"Maybe, maybe not," Pauling said.

"I've gone over what to say today a million times. You should know I kept a journal that gives details of ward abuse. It is with my social worker, Carla. I very much want to expose the scandals. But to be honest, I'm afraid. Since I opened up to the psychologist, Zeke Cody, I sense the staff are wary of me. They know somehow, I revealed scandals to him. And now they know I have testified to authorities. If I could check Hippo's office there's evidence that could show I'm tellin' the truth. But if missing, I face permanent confinement and the ice pick surgery of my brain."

"I'm confident that it can be arranged. Let's talk about going forward. I propose we end it here today and request a continuance of the hearing if and when the letter is retrieved. Is that a deal?" Pauling asked.

"Okay."

The two returned to the hallway where guardian ad litem Sheldon and Fitzgerald were waiting. Pauling updated them as to continuing interrogation.

Sheldon turned to Shannon. "I want to bring you up to date on your status. You have been assigned a court-appointed attorney by the name of Gary Gladden. He has sent me a copy of the petition. I'm no judge, but the clinical assessments of Dr. Cody and Dr. Koeppen reached very different conclusions. Cody's report is your best hope. You are scheduled for a December court appearance. The judge, if consistent with past adjudications, will ask you a series of questions, most centered on whether you can care for yourself or are a danger to yourself or others. I recommend you drop all the suspicions about your ex given the radically different clinical assessments. As I see it, if you insist your ex is a threat, the court would agree with Dr. Koeppen's view. Your accusations that Fred Hepp had raped or mistreated patients are delusional."

"As her attorney, I see it as a civil rights question," Pauling said. "Frankly, this whole procedure today is a sham. To me, this is the type of case that is long overdue to expose the light of day. Yes, we need to advise

Shannon as to potential pitfalls, but not at the expense of denying her civil rights. This comes down to a question of Shannon's competence. It appears staff has used a spurious assortment of psychiatric assessments to silence patients such as Shannon making complaints of patient abuse. Consider that Shannon has been blocked from the disclosure of abuse to protect her right to privacy. Even more damaging, Shannon has spent years confined and muzzled by the whims of a manipulative husband and an enabling court. Given the long list of involuntary patients on the Cook County unit who for some have been here a decade or more, it is clear at least to me that Chicago judges in the past were on a mission. They were determined to keep the homeless and mentally ill off the streets. Just think about it. Patients on this unit were never scheduled for years to have a competency hearing."

"What are you recommending?" Shannon asked.

"The remedy is clear. Let me ask Goldberg for a recess and propose you be transferred to an undisclosed mental health treatment center. Next, we can clear up your competency question. How does that sound, Shannon?"

"I have to trust you at this point. Right now, that's hard to do and I can't be sure I am not being set up. How can I trust even you, Mr. Sheldon? You never visited me even once! And my so-called attorney who could not appear today. What's his name—Ah, something like 'Gladhand'—whoever—We've not met."

"With your consent, I'd like to take your case," Pauling said. "What do you think?"

"Are you married?" Shannon asked.

"Yes."

"What would you do if your wife during a serious down period in her life got into a big argument with you over who should carry out the trash or pick up after themselves?"

"That hits home. To be honest, you should ask my wife. Sometimes, she loses patience with me after numerous reminders to pick up my dirty socks and underwear. But before I over-react to her harsh criticism, she redirects me to look at my negligence for what it is and believe it or not count to ten before saying another word," Pauling said. "It works."

"Mr. Sheldon. After all these years, why did you bother to show up today?"

"You have to realize we all want you to have your day in court. But you must understand I have 500 individuals for my caseload. Some require extensive time involving large estates. I had to miss court dates to travel to Jacksonville to take your case," Sheldon said.

"Again, why did you bother to see me today?"

"Isn't it obvious? Without my petition for a hearing, your status does not change. A court order for involuntary treatment is still in effect. As to the timing, you could be called as a material witness in a criminal matter and yet your competency is still a question."

"Why are you avoiding the real reason?" Shannon asked. "Was my ex notified of the competency hearing?"

"Victims are notified," Sheldon said.

"Holy shit! You say he's a victim?"

"The police report is still on file. It's not good. They reported you struck him with an object causing a facial laceration. You locked yourself in the bathroom and refused to cooperate with the police when they requested you come out. After some time, you unlocked the bathroom door. Police placed you under arrest. When they asked you to turn around to be cuffed, they reported you struck out at them and you were hysterical," Sheldon said.

"I can see where this is headed. I have nothing more to say." Blood rushed to her cheeks and her ears. She sobbed, wiping the tears with her sweater sleeve. She turned towards the exit. Without warning, Shannon rushed from the office. Pauling caught up with Shannon and stepped in front of her.

"Take a deep breath. This is not the time to throw in the towel. On the matter of trust, I get it. Believe me, I have told you everything about my involvement. There's no deal on my part. If you decide to go forward in December, I would be happy to represent you. I'm convinced we can win that fight."

"It gets complicated. The reality is if I continue there's no reason. I only dig the hole deeper. You have to realize how much power the staff has to keep patients in line. It's not only the abuse. It's the diagnostic sword they use to slice away at who you are. It reduces you to a heap of detached memories."

"As I said before, we can have you transferred if you feel so threatened."

"Believe it or not, it's been so long. I'm not sure I'm ready to abandon my friends. They look up to me to help them get over their rough spots."

"Reconsider everything. The justice system is not perfect, but there are remedies. If we get all of the procedural questions before a judge, or a jury, we can win this. Let me ask for a continuance. You can think about going back to the scene. I recommend you take the plunge."

"Okay. I know I'm a damn fool for trusting you like I did with Cody. But when you tell me you've had moments when you were about to react with anger to your wife's harsh criticism over not picking up for yourself but listening to your wife and holding yourself in check, I want to believe you are an understanding husband. You can appreciate where I'm coming from."

"I take that to mean you are willing to halt the inquiries today and consider your options after returning to the ward."

"No. I want to continue the inquiry. I want to answer their question," Shannon said.

"Are you sure this is what you want to do?" Sheldon asked.

"I'm prepared to make a statement."

Shannon, along with, Pauling, Sheldon, and Fitzgerald returned to the temporary examination room.

"Miss Audrey, after advice, is prepared to answer your question about entering Fred Hepp's office," Pauling said.

"I realize what I am about to say could have lasting consequences. But Vesta Diaz can no longer be ignored for this terrible injustice." Shannon could not hide her tears. Pauling reached for a tissue. Shannon dabbed her eyes and blew her nose. "You see, Vesta was raped in that office and she left behind something that could prove she was assaulted. I don't know if it's still there. If it isn't you can believe what you want. All I ask is permission to visit the office and locate the evidence if it is still there. I will not disclose what I seek. It will become obvious if I find the evidence."

Pauling pulled the mike toward him. "I think at this point I need to speak for my client. We want to terminate inquiries at this point. To protect my client's interest, I suggest we arrange a date and time to visit the crime scene. My client at that time will reveal what she seeks in the victim's office."

"Given my charge is to protect the best interests of Miss Audrey, I concur. This inquiry is over." Social Worker Welker said.

Chapter 26

*Reckoning*

Turpin headed for Michael's office. "Hi, Detective. I need to run this by you."

"Let's settle this now once and for all. There's the back door to the alley," Michael said.

"Okay, okay. How 'bout 'Michael?'"

"Make it 'Sergeant Michael Dyson.'"

"Here's the deal. Let me run this by you. Blaze Hepp told Koeppen her husband had found out about their affair and intended to kill them both. Koeppen took Blaze's advice to make contact with a contract killer she knew from the old days. In short, the contract was bungled. Hepp survived the garroting attempt and blow to the head. The doctor was called in to finish him off."

"That's a possibility, but I jist' can't see this guy dirtying his hands. The other problem—Why put a head in a fish tank?"

"Coulda' been to divert attention to the likelihood a psychopath - that some patient had gone round the bend. Even you said that was your guess when we first got on this case."

"Who all did it was tryin' to send a message of some kind. We gotta' dig deeper with Koeppen. Someone coulda' got him ta' talk too much 'bout his war killin' and he was blackmailed," Michael said.

"I agree. Let's grill Koeppen. You are better prepared to cover his past. He may open up much better with you. In the meantime, I want to try round two with Blaze."

"Make sure you leave the door open."

"Got a better idea. You join me. Think we make a good team."

"That works for me. Like to see up close how Blaze reacts to da line of questioning 'bout the drugs and affair with Koeppen," Michael said.

Michael sketched out some notes he wanted to cover with Koeppen. Earlier he had made a call to the anti-defamation league and verified Koeppen had enlisted in a mountain division but there was no evidence of war crimes. Most on their list were notorious Nazis engaged in the infamous concentration camps. Less was known about local Nazi pogroms in occupied territories where partisans were under threat of death to conduct the mass killings at large burial sites.

Michael phoned Koeppen's office. After a couple of calls with the secretary indicating he was unavailable, Michael took another route. He dialed Dr. Gomez. "Could you help me make contact with Dr. Koeppen?"

Ten minutes after the call, Koeppen's secretary contacted Michael. She said, "Dr. Koeppen will agree to meet you on condition you verify you have been officially assigned to investigate the Hepp murder case."

As with the HR call to Dorothea Dix hospital, it was another instance of doubting his credibility in whitey's world. Michael stormed into Turpin's office. Turpin quickly cleared up Michael's status by having the chief put in a call to Koeppen.

As Michael approached Koeppen's office entrance,

Koeppen stood up and walked around his desk. He extended his hand.

"Appreciate y'all agreein' to answer a few questions," Michael said.

Koeppen said, "Good afternoon, Sergeant Michael Dyson. Where is Detective Turpin?"

"Detective Turpin is on 'nother assignment. Appreciate it if y'all could clear up some questions about the Hepp case that have come up recently."

Koeppen signaled for Michael to have a seat. "Glad to answer any questions you have. Speaking for our unit we all want this nightmare to end," Koeppen said.

"Let's start with Fred Hepp. Have any patients ever made complaints about Fred Hepp's physical or sexual abuse of patients over the last five years?" Michael asked.

"None that I can disclose. If there were complaints, rest assured any incidents would have been thoroughly investigated. If evidence of such abuse were corroborated, we would have terminated his employment."

"Basically yar' tellin' me, no witnesses came forth to back up the complaints."

"Don't distort what I just said. My staff and I have interviewed all potential victims and witnesses to any alleged incident or incidents and found since I have been here no complaints have been validated."

"All that fancy dodgin' does not square with a least one patient account. A patient complained to you of how her friend had been brutally raped by Fred Hepp. This patient has accused you of a coverup. None of this was ever reported to the police. Even worse, you have been accused of approvin' a brain surgery of the rape victim that resulted in turnin' her into a vegetable unable to testify."

"Even in the U.S., those charged with a crime are mandated the right to face their accuser in a criminal trial. Who is your source?"

"Let's not do this jive, man. You ain't foolin' nobody. Ya' damn well know who made the complaint."

"Just for the record, I don't. Patients often make complaints that are not based on fact but symptomatic of their chronic psychosis."

"So, y'all are sayin' in effect patients can't be relied upon to get at the truth of any complaint because they're crazy. What about your staff? If they back up a patient's version would y'all still make the same call?"

"Your question assumes I never give any credence to patient complaints." Koeppen paused and reached for his phone and pressed an intercom button. "Hello Mahalia, this is Dr. Koeppen. Could you drop by my office?"

"Is it urgent? 'Bout ready to do our meds," Mahalia Ross said.

"Yes, it is. We need to validate our procedures."

"Sure. See ya' soon as I checkoff patients."

"LPN Ross who is the ward coordinator for patient care will outline how we deal with patient complaints," Koeppen said.

"While waitin', let me go down 'nother fork in the road. What was your role servin' in the German army?"

"In less than ten minutes you have accused me of covering up a rape. Let me guess. Now you think I was a member of the Waffen-SS and exterminated Jews, homosexuals, gypsies, and suspected enemies of the Third Reich."

"I ain't accused y'all of anything. But since ya' brought it up, were you ever directly or indirectly involved in the killin' these groups you mentioned?"

"Of all people given your ancestors' history of slavery, how could you not be sensitized to stereotypes of any race or ethnicity? You, like so many Americans during the war, assumed all involved in the war effort were members of the Nazi party and marched in lockstep to Hitler's eugenics goal of purifying the Aryan race. Because I speak with an accent and was raised in German culture, you rely on a mental shortcut based on propaganda here in the U.S. I don't have to tell you how such shortcuts lead to profound injustice," Koeppen said.

"There's one big difference. Despite what you see as prejudice, my dad believed freedom was worth fightin' for during the war—freedom Germany eliminated from Jews and others like me."

"I want to emphasize there were a group of German intellectuals in Munich who like your father believed in freedom. We resisted Hitler's mad racism. I nor my friends ever joined the Nazi party."

"Didn't you get special treatment durin' the war to complete your medical education? And before you answer that, isn't it true you received special assignments while enlisted in the army?"

"I don't know what your sources are, but this sounds like Gestapo tactics used against my friends who were shot or hung for painting anti-Nazi messages on our university wall."

"What I'm drivin' at is simple. Is there somethin' you did durin' the war that could be seen as a war crime?"

"Even if that were true which it is not, do you think

anyone would confess to such a crime if they faced harsh punishment including the death penalty?"

"Not really. But someone who had evidence of your past involvement in mass killin' could make ya' a target for extortion. Somebody with medical trainin' was involved in the murder of Fred Hepp. Just askin' for the record, where were you on the October 30th and 31st, 1970?"

"I was scheduled with patients from 8:30 in the morning until late Friday, the night before Halloween. As I recall, I drove to my apartment, changed into a sweater and khakis, grabbed a quick bite, and went to a movie. On Saturday, I read a book and listened to my favorite opera, Mozart's '*The Magic Flute.*'"

"Two questions. What was the name of the movie and is there anyone who can back up how you spent those two days?"

"I suppose your next question is whether I have a tattoo under my left armpit?"

"Answer your own question. Do y'all have a blood type tattooed there as others in the SS?"

"This is ridiculous. I would ask for an attorney, but any fool could see you have seen too many propaganda films or reading too much Dashiell Hammett—a communist and anti-fascist novelist. You are not Sam Spade. No pun intended."

"You put up a good front all about fighting for freedom. Then ya' let your guard down. Jist' couldn't help trashin' me as a 'spade.' But I ain't gonna bite. Let's get back to the movie. Surely somebody like y'all who's never come in second to anyone as to your smarts cannot remember a movie you jist' saw and who was with you?"

"It was a forgettable American movie. Something

like a Doris Day picture full of trite dialogue that bored me. I left before it ended."

"So ya' can't remember the title of the movie and y'all can't come up with someone who can verify you were there?"

"Let me ask you, Sergeant Dyson. Why were you sent to interrogate me? Did I hit a nerve with Detective Turpin?"

"You ain't foolin' anybody with your tactics. Let's get back to your non-alibi and your relations with Fred Hepp and his wife, Blaze Hepp."

A knock on the door interrupted the exchange. Millie Funderburk, Koeppen's secretary, announced, "Mahalia Ross is here."

"Your timing is perfect Mahalia. Let me introduce you to Sergeant Michael Dyson. He's investigating the Hepp murder."

"We've already met. Hope ya' got some good news that this monster's been identified."

"Not really. Jist' wanna' say Mahalia Jackson is 'Queen Mahalia' to my Mama. Were you named after her?" Michael asked.

"Proud ta' say my Mama loved her gospels also and ya' got it right," Ross said. "Now what's this fuss 'bout procedures here?"

"Sergeant Dyson seems to think we cover up complaints of patient abuse. Would you mind reviewing our protocol as to investigating any alleged incidents?"

"Don't know where y'all comin' from, but ya' can read all the fine print handed down by a bunch a' lawyers and y'all will see our nurses are lookin' into these complaints followin' every step we agreed to when negotiating our union contract."

"How 'bout one patient that filed a complaint recently, a Shannon Audrey? Could we go over that investigation?"

"I get it. Somebody from the administration is tryin' to pin that on Dr. Koeppen—that he's coverin' up someone from this center who was somehow involved in the murder," Ross said. "If that's the rathole youse followin', y'all's a fool. I can't speak my mind 'bout this patient, but if you knew the facts it all is clear. This administration wants ta' put us on the streets."

"So, let me get this straight, Mahalia. You're tellin' me Shannon Audrey lied about Fred Hepp raping her best friend?"

"Let me answer that, Mahalia. There are records in our files of all investigations and every requirement was met as to reviewing sources. If abuse in any form was found to be evident, corrective measures have been implemented."

"I jest can't keep my mouth shut. If I get fired for tellin' the truth, then I'll survive. Sergeant Michael ya' got this all wrong if y'all think it's the doctor who is the killer. Ya' gotta see from the superintendent on down the line of command they tryin' to eliminate us for doin' our job to care for these poor souls. That's the real story 'bout this bullshit over abuse."

"Y'all sayin' the top dawgs are out to clean house. Would that mean eliminatin' Fred Hepp one way or 'nother?"

"I wouldn't put anything past these quacks. Their newbie kids on the wards have been hired to spy on us every day lookin' for trouble. They stirred this whole thing up over a sick patient who makes up all kinds of crazy complaints that never happened. And somethin' else - This patient you investigatin' is very violent and dangerous."

"Y'all should let us do our job if what you say is true," Michael said. "We need ta' check out all leads includin' anyone from the administration who coulda' been involved."

"Thank you, Mahalia, for your perspectives," Koeppen said. "I've got to see a patient now. If you will excuse me, Sergeant Dyson, I'll show you to the door."

"Before you leave, jist' one more question? Have you 'n Blaze Hepp ever hooked up, you know, straight out, did y'all get some booty?" Michael asked.

"Such a libelous question. If you were a good investigator, that question would be put to Superintendent Scott." Koeppen without waiting for an answer grabbed Mahalia's arm and exited the office.

Chapter 27

*Something Fishy*

Michael entered his makeshift office, kicked up his shoes on top of the desk, and loosened his tie. He stared at a dying houseplant. Maybe dumping the swill from his coffee cup into the flower pot had stressed out the plant. The leaves had turned brown and withered. Time to get his head straight on this case and not worry about a plant's stress level.

Michael pondered over the obvious unknowns such as the whereabouts of Fred Hepp after leaving the ward at the end of his swing shift. Whoever was involved with this murder must have known he would be there at the aquarium and had access to the entrance. Setting up a large fish tank filled with water suggested someone knew the storage of spare tanks and access to a water source. Dusting for prints in Hepp's office and the storage room came up empty. Likely they were wiped clean or the culprits were wearing gloves. No blood traces were found.

Turpin knocked on Michael's temporary office door. "Hi Michael. Checked with the FBI. They will not commit to going to the Justice Department for a search warrant on Blaze Hepp," Turpin said. "They needed more concrete evidence like a witness to corroborate siphoning drugs from the hospital and evidence that these meds were used to cut heroin and cocaine in a major drug trafficking scheme. But on the question of the fake doc, they took a much different tone on what they would do."

"Like y'all said earlier, boss, we better git ta' gittin' before the FBI gets involved," Michael said.

"Once again drop the 'boss' shit. I'm with ya' on movin' sooner than later. Checked with the prosecutor about gettin' an expedited arrest warrant for Teagarden chargin' him with fraud and forgery on top of federal charges," Turpin said.

"Roger as to nailin' Teagarden without delay," Michael said. "Think he's high on the list of suspects, but it does not add up. He had to have some help if he knocked off Hepp. Keep thinkin' we've overlooked some key evidence. Anxious to see what Audrey was lookin' for when she went to Hepp's office," Michael said. "I've been thinkin' we gotta' go back to the scene ta' get at who possibly had access to the aquarium. Maybe a key was copied. And one more thing. If someone took his head off and filled the tank with water, more, more, than likely the dawg or dawgs ran a hose to clean up the mess and fill the tank."

"No disagreement. Let's get on it. Maybe we need to dust for more prints and blood traces."

Turpin grabbed his gun and badge. "Let me make a quick call to the professor and that grad student and see if they can meet us at the aquarium. They might help us figure out who could have been there after midnight."

Turpin made a call to the professor. By chance, Wentz and Lazzo were headed to the aquarium. Turpin agreed to meet them in thirty minutes. On the way to the aquarium, Michael asked, "What if it all happened somewhere else other than the aquarium? Like where Hepp was coldcocked?"

"Think that's a possibility."

"And strangled—what's that word?"

"Garroted."

"Yeah, with what? A piano wire as the outfit does?"

"That's a gonna' be difficult to nail down unless we get a prime witness to break." Turpin pulled into the small parking lot. William Lazzo, the graduate student, and his supervisor, Stan Wentz, were chatting near the entrance.

"Thanks for meeting us. Just to be clear you two are the only ones who have regularly been inside the aquarium since marked as a crime scene. Is that correct?" Turpin asked.

"As far as I know. We have to schedule cleanings and feedings for each exhibit," Wentz said.

"Let's go into details if y'all don't mind. Who exactly has a key to the entrance and again to be clear the storage room to the extra water tanks?" Michael asked.

"I can't say about who here on the campus has keys other than campus security. As for the entrance, William and I have an entry key. In addition, I and William have the key to the storage room," Wentz answered.

"Where do you store cleaning stuff for the tanks?" Turpin asked.

"Such as scrub-brushes, mops, and hoses? That's all stored in the same room as the extra tanks."

"Let's take a look. Do you mind if I borrow your key?" Turpin asked.

Turpin and Michael were directed to the storage room. Turpin used his handkerchief to open the door. A light switch was located and flipped on. Two heavy-duty hoses were coiled on the shelf. Aquarium tanks of varying sizes were stacked on reinforced shelves. Buckets, a mop, and brushes along with cleaning agents were placed on the floor. A stack of white cloth towels was on a shelf nearby.

"Have either of you accessed this room since the murder was reported," Turpin asked.

"No," Wentz said.

"Where's y'all's cleaning area for the tanks?" Michael asked.

"It's over here, a converted shower room," Wentz said.

Wentz led the way and pointed at a large basin with a sink. "So, this is where we clean the tanks."

"How does that work?" Michael asked.

"The tank filtration systems have worked well. Most fecal and irretrievable food sources are eliminated. Our last cleaning of a display was over a week ago."

"What exactly does that involve?" Michael asked.

"Depending on the species, we remove the rock and fecal matter and check the filters. We only replace approximately twenty-five percent of the water. All of the cleaning equipment is on this large cart. Cleanings on average are done every two weeks."

"Are there any hoses other than those in storage that you use to rinse the floors and the sink?" Michael asked.

"There's a hose under the sink but we rarely use it," Wentz said.

"We need to have the hose checked for prints," Turpin said. "A couple more questions. Where is the facet hookup for the hose?"

"The facet is in the corner here." Wentz pointed to a small panel door where a facet was embedded inside the wall.

"Have you touched the door or the facet since the incident?" Turpin asked.

"No. Thought it best not to clean anything until the investigation is completed."

"How about you, William?"

"Nope. To be honest, I've got bad vibes about this place," the graduate student said. He brushed his hair back and stroked his head.

"Will need to check for traces of blood and fingerprints in this area," Turpin said.

"Jist' curious, Professor," Michael said. "Where da y'all keep your notes and stuff?"

"I was provided a small office near the victim's. I've got a file cabinet and desk. We have a corkboard where we post schedules for feeding and cleanings," Wentz said.

"And who has key access to your office?"

"I have the office key."

"Do you keep the office locked?" Michael asked.

"More or less. I lock it when leaving the building."

Michael turned to Lazzo. "You are doin' fish research, right?" Michael asked. "Where do you keep your stuff?"

"In the back of my van. Why do you ask?"

"Jist' establishin' who coulda' been here at the scene. Where were you from midnight to the time the head in the tank was discovered?"

"I was in my apartment watching television, 'Get Smart.'"

"Were ya' alone?"

"My private life is private."

"Let's try it this way. As I said before, we are

'tempting to establish exactly who coulda' been in this buildin' before Hepp was killed. If you ain't got nothin' to hide, jist let us know who can verify where y'all was at this time."

"I'd rather not. It's personal. My partner is not ready to come out."

"How does comin' out stop your partner from simply confirmin' you were in front of the tube?" Michael asked.

"He hasn't told his parents. They have been led to believe he's engaged to a very nice sweetheart he dated for some years during and after high school. I can't do that to him, expose our relationship to anyone."

"Give me his phone number. I can call him. All he has to do is answer a few questions. If he confirms what you say, that's police business. No reason to reveal his name to anyone includin' the press," Michael said.

"Let me talk with him. I think I can talk him into contacting you soon," Lazzo said.

"Make that tomorrow," Michael said. "Switchin' topics, tell me—Does your research involve guttin' fish?"

"Not exactly. I study reproductive organs."

"So, y'all do surgeries on fish, right?"

"Yes. I'm not sure why this is relevant?"

"Jist' curious what your research involves. Do you get any help with the surgeries?"

"Yes. Usually Dr. Wentz."

"Could ya' show me your surgical instruments?"

"They're in his office."

"If y'all don't mind, I'd like ta' take a look at 'em," Michael said.

Wentz approached his office door, unlocked it, and

entered. Turpin, Michael, and Lazzo followed. "Dr. Wentz, jest wonderin'. Are these similar to surgical instruments used on humans?" Michael asked.

"Yes, and we use a similar protocol for sterilization," Wentz said. He pulled a box atop a stainless-steel table and opened it. A variety of instruments were exposed including different size scalpels. An autoclave was nearby.

"Is it possible others may have known about the location of this kit and its contents?" Turpin asked.

"I doubt it. I've never discussed our research in any detail with any of the volunteers or visitors."

"Do you mind if we do a quick check on these instruments for any traces?" Turpin asked.

"No problem. I've got access to another set of instruments at my apartment."

"That's it for me. Do you have anything more Sergeant Dyson?" Turpin asked.

"Not now."

Chapter 28

*Witness Protection*
*Friday Morning*

Turpin and Michael met Prosecutor Goldberg along with Attorney Pauling and Shannon Audrey at the aquarium entrance.

"Shall we get started?" Goldberg asked.

"I'm ready." Shannon took a deep breath. "I hope I'm doing the right thing."

"This is an ongoing investigation. If you or your attorney feels what you are about to reveal is self-incriminating, the search for such evidence can be terminated," Goldberg said.

"To be honest, I don't think so. I have never had possession of the items I was told are in that office," Shannon said.

"It's your call. Do you want to consult with your attorney?" Goldberg asked.

"I've thought it over, and I still feel Vesta deserves justice whatever turns up."

Turpin led the group to Hepp's former office, He turned to Audrey and announced, "We will be filming your activity. Sergeant Dyson will be using a Super 8mm film camera to announce our location, the time, and parties present." After the introduction, he will film activities. Are there any questions?"

"No," Audrey said.

After Dyson finished identifying the occasion, those present, the time, and location, Turpin then pulled out a key and opened the door.

Shannon peered inside the door. The gruesome tank was missing. The smell of mold triggered dark memories of Hippo's violent temperament. The file cabinet was still there. Her heart raced when she spotted the large throw rug anchored by the legs of an institutional metal desk. Shannon walked to the southeastern corner of the desk. She fell to her knees and put her hand under the rug. Nothing could be felt. Shannon struggled to force her hand further past the desk leg holding the rug in place. Again, nothing was evident. She made a sweeping motion with her hand twice. On the third effort moving in the direction of the edge of the desk, the unmistakable sensation of a letter's edge was detected. Shannon grasped for a better grip and pulled the letter out. She read the address and return address.

Shannon opened the letter and silently read the contents. "It's all there. This shows I'm not crazy about my ex. It's clear he was scheming to collect life insurance money to pay for an expensive home." Shannon gave the letter to Pauling who read it. The attorney handed the letter to Goldberg and after reading it gave it to Detective Turpin.

"I'm not finished. There's one more item Vesta mentioned."

Shannon moved toward the office chair and rolled it away from the desk. She struggled to pull the center drawer all the way out. She dropped to a kneeling position and looked at the underside of the desk. The lighting was poor. She pushed her hand in front of the back of the middle drawer searching for what Vesta said was hidden. Shannon yelled, "There it is!"

Shannon tugged to detach a metal container. The magnets holding the container were powerful. With a strong pull, the container was dislodged. She moved a clasp far enough to open the container. "I found it," Shannon cried.

"I have no stomach to view these disgusting photos," Shannon said. The container of photos was passed to Pauling and Goldberg. Turpin and Michael huddled to view the lurid sexual photos. Their eyes remained glued to each photo. Shannon's eyes moistened as she recalled the awful rape Vesta described. "What a terrible price Vesta had paid," Shannon said. "Vesta had disclosed before Hepp assaulted her he pulled a metal box of photos from under his desk and scattered the photos on his desk masturbating while looking at the photos and then attacked her."

"There it is. Proof of what this beast did before he raped Vesta."

Chapter 29

*Negotiation*

On a Friday, three weeks before the slaying of Fred Hepp, Ty Crowley called Hepp to request a sit-down negotiation to resolve differences with the current mission of Cook County Center. Hepp said he had no idea what Crowley meant but as far as he was concerned everything was running smoothly. Crowley clarified that unless Hepp and other ward staff got on board with reform measures, there could be layoffs of ward staff.

"So, that's a threat on top of eliminatin' the hydrotherapy treatment. You got some kind of balls," Hepp said.

"I see we need to look at some options Fred," Crowley said. "Could we meet at an inconspicuous spot and iron out a few details as to how this can be settled?"

"To make it clear shit-head, there's no negotiatin'. I'll spell out what you will do. Meet me tonight at my old hydrotherapy office after I get off at midnight. I know you're fuckin' your secretary," Hepp said. "You can get all the pussy you want, but don't threaten me with layoffs if you want to keep things running smoothly as I said before." Hepp slammed the phone.

Crowley's fears raced as he hung up. How did Hepp find out? Significantly, how did Hepp come to believe he could dictate terms unilaterally given the solid backing Mahalia had with the union? Putting all that aside, Crowley wondered what bargaining chip would satisfy Hepp? It was hard to see any of this getting past Koeppen.

After midnight, Crowley slowly pulled into the dimly lit parking lot and turned off his lights. The small window in the middle of the entrance door of the hydrotherapy building was dark. He scanned the parking lot. There was no sign of Hepp. He approached the entrance and knocked. He waited moments and knocked louder. Suddenly, Crowley struggled for air as a large hand with overpowering force cut off his intake of air and blood to his brain. Crowley reached for the thumb and tried to break loose.

"Stay put you piece of shit and listen carefully. We are goin' into my office and you will sit down and go over what's in store for you. Do I have that right?"

Crowley grasping for air uttered a faint reply, "Okay, okay, Let's talk."

Hepp opened the door and led Crowley to his office with his large hand clasping his neck and throat. His office door was unlocked with his right hand and with his left hand still on Crowley's neck forced him to sit in a chair near his desk.

"I'm gonna let go with one condition. You will stay in the chair and listen, Okay?" Crowley nodded his head while at the same time trying to loosen the overpowering grip around his neck.

"Here's the deal, motherfucker. It's not all that complicated. First, you will fire your kiddy little shits takin' our jobs and you will have a memory loss any of this meeting ever happened," Hepp said.

"I don't see how that solves anything," Crowley

said.

"There's nothin' to solve dickhead. You and that piece of shit Scott are gonna put things back the way we do things here."

"I can't control how this plays out. You have overestimated my influence."

"Let's spell it out. Your golden boy, Toby Cohen, He's fuckin' my wife. Let me show you some pictures," Hepp said. Hepp pulled out his desk drawer and pulled out a metal box with prints and negatives. He found an envelope labeled "Hippie." He took out the first one showing Cohen penetrate Blaze from behind as she knelt on a bed.

"Why are you showing me this? This is between you and Toby."

"You really are a dumb fuck. When I showed him these pictures, the hippie told me a whole lot of shit about you and your fuckin' outfit."

"Here's another one." Hepp put the print in Crowley's face. It showed the pair engaging in mutual oral sex on one print. Hepp selected another print that exposed traces of semen on Blaze's chin. "Is your dick gettin' harder?"

"What's the point of this porn show?" Crowley asked.

Hepp grabbed him by the throat and yelled, "If you want to see another sunrise motherfucker you will get on your knees right now and beg me to accept your apology for referrin' to my wife as a porn star."

Crowley tried to nod in approval as the blood slowed to his brain. Hepp released him. Crowley quickly went to his knees and pled, "I absolutely was wrong to ever think that your wife was in any way engaged in a quid pro quo."

"God dammit! Say it in plain English."

"I'm truly sorry for suggesting in any way your wife is engaged in exhibiting sexual acts for money," Crowley said. "Please forgive me."

"Get up, you worthless pussy."

Crowley awkwardly stood up and reached for the handle of the chair to steady himself. Hepp forcibly shoved him back in the chair with one hand. He placed the photos on the desk and extended his large arms to each handle of Crowley's chair. Hepp moved forward such that his face was inches apart from Crowley.

"I want you to read my lips very carefully fucker. You will shut down any changes you've planned 'round here for any reason. Three weeks from now you will get approval for a new setup from your prick boss. I will be the new Cook County Center Director and Dr. Davis will be appointed clinical director of the hospital. Is there anything about that you don't understand shithead?"

"No…no… no… I only have one question. What about Cohen?"

"Cohen is fully cooperatin' just like I expect outta' you."

"And Dr. Koeppen?"

"You said one question, prick. Now here's some answers to questions you didn't ask. Your office playmate tokes and you supply her the weed. That's Toby for ya'. He just can't keep his mouth shut," Hepp said.

"That's total bullshit."

"Toby's just like a whore. If the price is right, he'll do or say anything. You gotta' be more careful about who you hire, do you know that?"

"I don't want to annoy you. You know, piss you off. But could I say simply this could be a win-win if the 'kids' as you put it are furloughed, you know fired? But Koeppen's a major problem. You must realize he would never agree to you being head of the Center," Crowley said.

"You are a very stupid fuck!"

"What am I missing?"

"Nothin' yet. Just realize if you don't shut down takin' our jobs away, somebody's gonna knock on your wife's door, Regina, right? And tell her all about your drug dealin' and you fuckin' your secretary. And guess what? You will have been missin' for days or maybe Regina or the kids," Hepp said.

"I get it. I do. But I'm not positioned to make all that happen. That's up to the superintendent."

"You still don't get it. I'm losin' patience with you," Hepp yelled. He grabbed Crowley by the throat and squeezed with such force Crowley's glasses fell off and he could not speak. Crowley again pulled at his hand as hard as he could which provoked Hepp to squeeze tighter. Crowley grew more and more lightheaded. As Crowley weakened and his body grew limp, Hepp released his hand.

Crowley slumped forward. Moments later, he rubbed his face. He took several deep breaths. Images were blurry. The brutish face was missing. "If it's okay, I'd like to locate my glasses."

"Sure, if you have a good memory of how you lost them. And tattoo this on your brain. You will also have a good memory of what happens in three weeks right here at the same time where your ass is parked," Hepp said. "Now, tell me pussy. What will you deliver in three weeks?" Hepp challenged.

"Assurances you are appointed as center director and Gomez is replaced with Davis," Crowley said with a weak voice.

"You know that box of rocks between your ears is workin'. You're in deep shit. Now get your wimp-ass outta' here and make it happen."

# Chapter 30

*Encounters*

His throat was in pain. Despite the lateness of the hour, Crowley headed for his office. He ruminated over what could be done. He pulled out a bottle of Bombay Sapphire gin hidden behind John Locke's "An Essay on Human Understanding." Hiding his booze behind this classic was a reminder at some point he needed to read primary sources he quoted at seminars and conferences. He poured a generous amount into a tumbler. He looked outside his large window to see headlights from the aquarium moving toward the exit.

Fred Hepp had to be handled in a manner that was not in his playbook. But how? The short timeline to put Hepp's name in as center coordinator could be a pro forma manipulation, but what about Koeppen?

With contacts in Springfield, just maybe information offered surreptitiously that the administration was out of control spending money on racehorses and rare fish could trigger major organizational changes Crowley thought. Legislators would express outrage and increase pressure to shut down the institution. Such a move would weirdly pre-empt both Scott and Hepp to cut back on reformist staff. Knowing Scott as he did, Crowley reasoned, Scott would purge staff at all levels to convince legislators he was taking the scandal seriously.

Hepp's threats could not be handled politically. Crowley feared the worst. Hepp must have had a sordid past. But what was it? Maybe he had connections to the mob world. The photos and his insistence that Davis becomes the next clinical director and that Hepp is director of the center must involve others. But who else was involved?

Crowley considered bringing in law enforcement, perhaps the FBI. But there was no concrete evidence of any federal crime committed or that Hepp was tied to organized crime? If Hepp got word he was in touch with law enforcement, his wife Regina and their two sons, Ari and Harmon, were at considerable risk. There was no doubt. Hepp was not bluffing.

Drastic circumstances required drastic remedies he thought. Crowley poured another gin. If he did nothing, everything that he had worked so hard to make happen would blow up—his marriage and his rewarding affair with Shelly, maintaining the reform, and highest on his list—a future academic career. He downed the gin choking on a rapid burn of alcohol.

Crowley reviewed all the preparations he had carved out to complete his degree at The New School for Social Work. This would vaporize. "Dammit, it had all gone so smoothly." He fondly recalled how the breadth and number of his published papers convinced Jerry Sparks, a full professor in the New School psychology department, to spearhead efforts to complete the deal. Sparks argued it was a game-changer for the reputation of the psychology department to offer Crowley an adjunct professor position while he completed a doctoral degree. The psychology department after heated debates voted to offer Crowley the position.

But as to offering Crowley a degree, the faculty took a hardline. Sparks proposed to give Crowley full credit for completing the required courses for the degree based on his publications and reputation in the field. One holdout was quite vocal in opposition. "A Ph.D. graduate from our program who cannot demonstrate even the most rudimentary knowledge of basic psychological principles to chairs and faculty of other departments discredits our department and the institution."

The gin did its job. The buzz with hints of a lemon-juniper-berry flavor pushed back some of the despair over Hepp. Ideas about organizing graduate seminars in New York held sway. Despite lacking the coursework requirements for the adjunct professor position, Crowley garnered several recommendations from published heavyweights in mental health reform to persuade his supporters in the department to overlook his shortcomings and offer a competitive salary to his present position. Best of all, Crowley concluded the teaching load would be limited to seminars on social contract theory and institutional reform. This could be a platform to contact like-minded scholars and acquire professional gravitas that could launch an expansive reform of treatment strategies nationwide.

So much was at stake. Crowley turned to the small orchid carefully nurtured on Shelly's desk. Shelly would have to go, but not until getting cover of a staff purge from the superintendent. The larger issue was Fred Hepp. Given his size and violent nature, there had to be a pre-emptive strike. But how and who? Hire a hitman? Where would such a killer be located? How could the very large cash payment be raised without exposing such a plot?

Crowley ruminated over what seemed the impossible. Avoiding the Vietnam war draft may have been a mistake after all. It was not in his nature to kill. He recalled his dad taking him on hunting trips. But on the topic of hunting, Crowley agreed with his mother. What was the point of bringing back a dead duck that was never consumed because of the buckshot?

Despite the lack of hunting interest, Crowley developed competitive skills in handgun marksmanship. He dreamed of making a shooting team that could lead to Olympic competition. He locked his special-built handguns in a security box in his bedroom to make sure his two sons or anyone else had access.

Crowley agonized he had never killed any living organism much beyond a mouse. But this was a special case. With Hepp, he had to be proactive. Crowley asked himself, "Could I go through with it? Or maybe I should disappear for good. Even a bullet to Hepp's brain might not stop this bemouth. If I found the nerve to shoot him and take him out, what would I do with the body? How could I mislead investigators?"

Another gin was poured. Crowley rehashed his options. What was the point of passively playing the role of a spectator watching the inexorable destruction of everything meaningful? Only those who get in the game to actualize their dreams whatever the outcome can ask 'what if' queries.' Killing Hepp in that context could be justified if clues of my involvement could all be eliminated.

Crowley gave way to the alcohol. He stretched out on the office modern couch with a stainless-steel frame and unforgiving cushions. The rising morning sunlight stirred him from his sleep. He looked out the window at the parking areas below. Staff were heading for the administration building. Crowley thought of his wife Regina. He dialed her.

"Hello, Regina. Need to let ya' know I hit it too hard last night. Slept it off in my office rather than risk a DUI."

"What the hell's going on Ty? You're in trouble. I can tell."

"It's the moving target toward our mission here. There's only so much I can do."

"Booze is no answer. We've been through this before and I won't go another round," Regina said.

"I hear you. Right now, I've got to put some plans in action. Will be home early tonight. Ciao."

Shelly Bower turned the office door handle. It was unlocked. She slowly opened the door to see Crowley at his desk unshaven and disheveled. "Good God! What happened? "Did you finally tell Regina about us and that you're leaving?"

"Not in so many words, but she threatened to end it if I repeat last night. I pushed my limits with booze last night and did not want to face Regina. Enough of that. Right now, I need to freshen up and make some rounds with our change agents. Now listen carefully Shelly. I'm serious. Your very existence on this planet depends on never revealing the source of what I'm about to instruct you to do. You gotta' swear you will not breathe a word to anyone, not even your cat!"

"What happened? Is it something you've done or about to do?"

"No details for now. I want you to go on an errand this morning and find a payphone. Call the following legislative assistants and read them the following,"

Crowley said.

*I have it on good authority that tax dollars spent on reform efforts involving racehorses and exotic fish are enriching friends of the administration at Jacksonville State Hospital. I will send you details at your legislative office. Goodbye.*

"Oh My God! You are somehow mixed up in a scandal."

"No. But don't ask any more questions. The less you know the more protected you will be. It's as simple as that," Crowley said. "Now, get on to the payphone. The sooner this message is delivered the better the outcome."

"What does this mean for us?"

"It all depends on the fallout. Make no mistake, if the pieces fall in place there will be a future academic career for both of us. For now, no more details. You need to get on with your calls."

Shelly gathered the note and the four names with phone numbers and ran down the old stairs back to her VW bug parked a block away.

Ty Crowley followed Shelly out the door headed for Zeke Cody's office. Crowley moved down the hall of the Cook County Center and caught up with Cody as he was about to enter his office.

"Hey, Zeke. Got a minute?"

"If you're askin' for anything, let's make a contract for just five minutes," Cody said with his perpetual smile.

"I need less time than that. We've got big issues to tackle. To be clear, our entire operation is likely to go down in flames if we don't act proactively to keep the bad guys from running off the sheriff."

"So, is this 'High Noon?' "

"Close." Crowley pushed his glasses back and stroked his thin blond hair to the side. "The locals are about to cave into a lawless gang that is about to take over this center."

"That must mean Koeppen or Hepp is ready to shoot up the works and take over."

"For a variety of reasons, I can't confirm specific villains or if a dude wearing a badge will save the town," Crowley said. "Villains are spreading rumors that friends of the administration are stuffing their wallets with dollars that were marked for reforms such as the racetrack and aquarium. That means you and I are implicated. If the administration goes down, so do we."

"Level with me Ty. You are somehow mixed up in a power move, right?"

"You've got it all wrong. Just be aware these rumors are bad news for all of us," Crowley said. "Our first move is to take out Koeppen as center coordinator."

"Assuming you're being candid, which I'm not sure I can tell at this point, going after staff, particularly Koeppen, will poison the well forever."

"You'll simply have to make a call. You know the script. Accept the status quo of regressing to the past, or negotiate new social contracts to make this happen."

"Yippee-ki-yay. I'm just an ol' cowpoke tryin' to protect the water well and you tell me to git locals ta' believe Koeppen is the bad guy who threatens to poison it."

"Your cowboy metaphor is weak. This is not 'us-them.' Rather, it is back to planting the right info to the right people to generate complaints about corruption at the Cook Center. The attack will be personal rather than categorical."

"Jesus Christ.—You do have an oral fixation for muddying the waters. Can you ever say in plain language what you're up to?" Cody turned to the office window to enjoy the sun rays. "Maybe the solution to this mess you say exists is for you to fire Koeppen as a sexist for promoting the phallus claim or…'phallusy'…that, that women's problems all center around penis envy."

"I'm in no mood for your humor, Zeke. I'll leave it to you to figure out your role. I need to make my next move. Enjoy the morning."

Crowley quickened his pace to the superintendent's office.

"Good morning, Ty," greeted Belinda Fast. "Would you like a cup of coffee? Craig Sweeney's on the phone. He's expecting you."

"Great! Had an uncomfortable night. Need to consider a new mattress or sleeping partner," Crowley said.

"Hope you're only joking. Regina is such a delight," the secretary said.

"Everything comes down to the last settlement in social negotiations. Regina and I will be fine in the end."

"Good to see you, Ty. What brings on this sudden visit?" Sweeney asked.

"Let's go to the conference room and close the door."

"Fine. I'll get a legal pad," Sweeney said.

"Forget it. This involves a very confidential conversation that never happened."

"If you insist. Be apprised of certain revelations that are unlawful or violate the mission of the hospital, you realize I am duty-bound."

"Right now, you better consider your ass rather than

being a boy scout." Crowley led Sweeney to the conference room and opened the door. After Sweeney was seated, Crowley closed the latch lock of the door.

"This is for your ears only. If you repeat our conversation to anyone, there will be serious consequences."

"What consequences? I'm a warrior when it comes to politics. Believe me, I've handled threats and I've not only survived but thrived," Sweeney said.

"Hear me out. We've got a scandal that is about to take us all under. There are unnamed individuals floating the rumor to legislators of funds for our reform efforts such as the aquarium and the racehorses are being inappropriately squandered to personal friends of the administration. As you are well aware, conservative legislators are pressing for budget cuts to the bone. There are rumblings they could shut down our institution."

"The breadth of this alleged funding scandal is manageable if we get ahead of it and be completely transparent," Sweeney said.

"Don't punk out me out and reveal any of this to Scott. You are right. We get proactive. Tell your Springfield contacts the current administration agrees that budget audits are needed. And add the frosting. The administration will review the current budget and ensure all projected recruitment of staff will follow traditional job descriptions. Furthermore, reformers recently hired will be furloughed to meet budgetary goals of the legislature," Crowley said. "This is a game-saver negotiation if we can hold the wolves at the gates until we complete other efficiency moves involving administrative reform."

"I can't do that. I'm not stupid. What or better yet

who's leveraging you?"

"No need to get into details. Just react, listen, and make it sound spontaneous. To repeat, you will say you've heard rumors of thefts and the hospital is moving swiftly to extract the guilty parties for misappropriating funds. I will handle spelling out names and dates of those involved."

"You seem to forget I am the assistant superintendent and still have clout in Springfield. I could tell you to go to hell. And in the final analysis, whatever the legislature does I will be a survivor."

"Why do I have to repeat myself? I am not bluffing. If you are not on board, I will make sure the legislators hear you are mixed up in quid pro quo deals with the Seven Lively Arts projects. You have to understand we are in this together. It's all about survival. Exposing this corruption investigation before others is our best strategy."

"I'll think it over."

"Gotta go now. Just to be clear, I have my network in the legislature. If you go off-script, you should make your final goodbyes to any future in the Illinois government."

Crowley got up and left Sweeney not waiting for a reaction. He skipped steps on the old wooden staircase and headed for Koeppen's office. He reviewed on the way how he was about to handle Koeppen. It would not be easy, but this was a necessity. It would be difficult to convince Koeppen that Hepp was plotting to upend Koeppen as director of the center. Hepp implied he had Koeppen controlled in some manner. Somehow, Koeppen had to be convinced the administration would back him if he decided to terminate the scourge under him.

"Good morning Mr. Crowley. What a pleasure to see administrators like you involved with hospital business at this hour of the morning," Koeppen said.

"And you of course operate like a clock. Your behavior is so predictable. Just like historical precedents such as the German professor Wilhelm Wundt, I would guess you arrived at exactly 7:30 this morning to resume where you left off at precisely 4:15 yesterday afternoon," Crowley said.

"I have other matters to attend to rather than sitting here and dealing with your overblown stereotypes," Koeppen said.

"You under-estimate your role here. You command respect on several levels. Your credentials and staff loyalty have not gone unnoticed by the administration."

"My, my Mr. Crowley. Your compensation is showing. Must be painful not having a professional degree."

"I did not come here to have a verbal fencing match. In a very narrow window of time—we either pull together in the same direction or we both face extinction. Take that literally and figuratively."

"What crisis have you dreamed up to save your ass?" Koeppen asked.

"I have every reason to believe you are being extorted in some manner. There is at least one source we both know who is leveraging you. And number two, removing this individual will solve problems for you and the administration."

"Why would I trust you at any level. You have spent your entire tenure bent on my removal," Koeppen said.

"Given your record to fend off potential threats to

your authority, I'm flummoxed that you did see this one coming. Your staff have played you."

"You are playing a chess game of bluff."

"Oh, there's a threat, and you are targeted. Very simple. If you continue without a strategy to ward off this threat, you are doomed any way you look at it. Your career will be over, and in the extreme your life," Crowley said.

"Is this an amateur blackmailing attempt? What big secret do you possess? That I slept with a prostitute in New York City on a spree in 1968?"

"Let's get to the threat you face. Fred Hepp is extorting you. I'm not interested in the details of what Hepp has on you. But I am very aware of his potential for violence if he doesn't get his way. Currently, he is demanding to take your place as director of the Cook Center. He will resort to violence if you show any signs of reneging on any agreements you have made with him. Hepp is well connected. The smart move is to make him think everything is falling in place."

"Where is your evidence?"

"I've already told you. He is demanding the administration appoint him to take a new position as Director of Cook County Center or he will expose whatever he has on you. That means you will be reduced to a staff psychiatrist or canned. If we play this smart, let's put the pieces in place to make him think he will be appointed as director of the Center. Here's the deal. The administration will send him application forms. The job description shall be such that he will be led to believe he has been singled out for the position."

"You are making a lot of assumptions. In no way would I ever malign the reputation of Dr. Gomez by promoting such a scheme," Koeppen said.

"What's your game plan if I'm right?" Crowley asked. "I'll answer that. The shit will hit the fan in very short order. That is a certainty. Your concern is how will you be positioned when it all goes down. We can cooperate to get rid of Hepp, or you can deny everything and go down when the truth comes out," Crowley said.

"Take your conspiracies with you. I'll manage Fred Hepp."

"I seriously doubt that," Crowley said. "Be in touch later this week."

Chapter 31

*Showdown*

Target practice was scheduled at a shooting gun shop. Crowley recognized his weakness. If he had Hepp in his sight, would he pull the trigger? A headshot would be critical. Wounding this bull would be a disaster. He squeezed off two rounds of his specially built target-shooting revolver imagining the bullet penetrating just above the eyebrows.

Killing Hepp would be easier if the psychologist Albert Bandura's theory was right. Crowley recalled Bandura offering evidence at a conference that American soldiers faced with aggression anxiety over killing so many Viet Cong resorted to despeciation—making use of racial slurs like 'Gooks' that characterized enemies as nonhumans. Maybe Jacobson's systematic desensitization technique could be altered such that he would envision an image of Hepp transformed into a grizzly about to attack him and condition himself to relax about making an actual kill shot.

That evening, Crowley entered the front door of their family rambler home seeking his wife.

"What in the hell have you done this time, Ty?" Regina asked.

"We are up against more than the old guard. It's complicated. I still don't have the answers. But I'm gonna find out this week whether we survive as a model for reform."

"Fuck the reform. What about us?"

"I'm committed to getting this right. In the short-term, I want you and the kids to return to Kansas to your folks' farm and stay there until this clears up."

"Is this same melody—Second verse Ty? Back in Kansas. you got careless one evening and one of the docs making rounds caught you banging a nurse in the nursing station," Regina said. "Then you begged for forgiveness. Said it was the booze and a sexually aggressive nurse. You told me then you had grown weary of fighting the medical establishment and said it was time for a new setting. Jacksonville was our fresh start so you told me back then."

"This time it's beyond getting past a very brief moment of body chemistry. There are bad actors not to be toyed with. I fear for you and the kids. Leave tomorrow. It's that bad."

"So, who is it this time—an attractive young secretary?"

"Don't pull out the fucking jealousy playbook. Somehow, I've gotta get through the next two weeks. Having you get super-paranoid at this moment will make it impossible to get this mess cleared up."

"Don't worry. The kids and I will be outta' here by tomorrow. Lawyer up. And plan on the couch tonight or better yet sack up with your secretary."

"I need a shower and some sleep. I don't have the patience to sort out your wild speculations tonight."

Regina exited from the front room toward their sons' bedrooms. Crowley could hear the muffled voices of Regina with Ari and Harmon. It was clear. Regina was getting the kids ready for the move and their breakup. A move to Kansas Crowley envisioned was a good solution for the short or long term.

Crowley considered his options—sleeping on the couch or spending the night with Shelly. Crowley moved to the master bedroom and randomly pulled out clothing and toiletries and threw them in a duffle bag. He returned to the front room. At least he should offer some kind of goodbye to his sons before departing. He knocked on the door of Harmon's bedroom.

Regina opened the door. "Go do what you have to do Ty. It's over. There's never been enough room in your grandiose scheme of things for the kids and me."

"That's something we can take up next week when things are settled."

"There's nothing to settle Ty other than custody and a generous account to pay for my education—a degree in psychiatric nursing," Regina said.

"If that's your petty way of rebuking everything I've stood for, have at it," Crowley said. "Right now, I want to say goodbye to Ari and Harmon." Crowley awkwardly hugged each son. "We'll hook up next week I promise," Crowley said. Harmon the twelve-year-old said, "Goodbye Ty. Don't rush to Kansas. We will manage without you."

Crowley exited and joined Shelly at her apartment. "I am so happy you made the move," Shelly said. "Now we can leave this dinosaur facility and whatever has you so upset and get on with our life."

"It's not that simple Shelly. I need more time to think about a particular dinosaur and going forward."

The next morning Crowley dropped into Scott's

office unannounced. "I'll keep it brief. We face a scandal involving one of our actualizers, Toby Cohen. Fred Hepp has discovered Cohen is fucking his wife Blaze and is threatening to make this public. Also, Hepp has threatened to spread rumors about administrators lining their pockets with our 'Seven Lively Arts' funds if we don't appoint him as director of the Cook center," Crowley said.

"Give Fred Hepp a megaphone. Who gives a shit if staff hook up—even if both are married?"

"Hepp has grandiose aims to contact legislators about alleged misappropriation of funds. He wants to take out this administration."

"That's on you. You assured me Hepp had bought into some of our reforms after getting near a settlement of the lawsuit. There's no question he's malignant," Scott said. "But this is all on you to correct it any way you can or else."

"What do you suggest?"

"I'll leave it to you as to how he's removed—just take him out," Scott said.

Chapter 32

*Debts*

Wednesday before the scheduled Halloween rendezvous with Hepp, Crowley called Dr. Davis. "I'm calling asking for your help. For some reason, Fred Hepp has demanded you be appointed clinical director replacing Dr. Gomez. What's this all about?"

"Beats me. I have the greatest respect for Dr. Gomez," Davis said.

"I've agreed to meet Hepp after his midnight shift on the 31st to discuss his demand. It would be helpful to everyone involved if you could make this meeting and sort out what Hepp is demanding."

"Look, I have no idea why this Fred Hepp would make such a demand meeting at midnight. Give me a break!"

"Let me spell it out. Hepp hinted at having links with crime bosses and something about extorting Dr. Koeppen." Crowley added, "I'm telling you this because Fred Hepp told me he believes you ratted him out to Dr. Gomez about these rumors."

"That's ridiculous. I know nothing about Fred Hepp, crime syndicates, or Dr. Koeppen's relationship with any of his staff."

"I surmised as much. So, that's why, though extraordinary, if you could show up, we could get this cleared up in short order."

"Not sure I need to get involved."

"I can't imagine any of this to be true given your excellent credentials and work record," Crowley said. "The best way to fight this corruption is to have a competent and resourceful professional like you to step up and confront Hepp. The administration would be favorably impressed if you served as an arbiter and witness to Hepp's demands." Crowley added, "Just a suggestion. A brighter future awaits you if the superintendent has confidence that you are not mixed up in any of this."

"I'll think it over."

Crowley hung up feeling confident Davis may have been convinced. If not, plan B.

****

*Halloween*

Crowley looked at his watch. It was a half-hour before Halloween midnight hour. This would give him time to get positioned in a grove of trees out of view and rehearse his moves. He had driven Shelly's VW bug and parked in a spot near a wooded area a block from the aquarium. He concentrated on the entrance to the aquarium.

Regina and the kids had arrived in Kansas. This made it possible to locate his father's deer hunting rifle in the crawl space of his garage attic and avoid having anyone witness he had such a weapon. His dad insisted he take ownership before his death. Regina or their sons were never told about the weapon given the family's staunch anti-gun stand.

Crowley scanned the parking lot. No sign of Hepp yet. The rifle gave him some relief from the intense anxiety awaiting the confrontation. During the week, he tried target shooting with the rifle. Crowley located a remote bluff area in Ray Norbut State Fish and Wildlife reserve which was a favorite for whitetail deer hunters. His experience with handgun target shooting paid off with the deer rifle. He set up targets at 100 yards. With a minimum of shots, he proved to be deadly accurate with small targets about the size of Hepp's head.

The plan was to only resort to sniper action if his disinformation failed to produce results. The game was on. Where was Hepp?

Crowley used his spotting scope to detect any movement near or at the entrance to the aquarium. If Hepp and Davis showed up at the same time Crowley reasoned, this would confirm the two were involved in the extortion business. If Hepp showed up and later Davis, Crowley decided he would enter also. He was wired with a recorder and carrying his target pistol.

If only Hepp showed up, Crowley geared himself to go through with the execution. Crowley remained tense. If there was the opportunity, it could be a split-second decision. If he made a kill with a direct hit to the head, police might see this at first blush as a professional assassination. Such a notion could be reinforced by ward rumors that Fred Hepp had a history with mob figures. Toby Cohen and Blaze Hepp could be leveraged to leak these rumors to avoid any exposure of the erotic photos of the pair.

Out of the darkness, there was movement. A young male appeared in the parking lot headed for the aquarium. The face could not be seen clearly. Crowley removed his glasses and adjusted the scope. "My God, that's William Lazzo, the grad student who's doing fish research," Crowley whispered to himself. Lazzo skipped up the steps to the entrance and pulled out his keys to unlock the door.

This complicated the situation. Crowley pulled his down coat up around his ears. He checked his watch. It was five minutes past midnight. Where was Hepp? He watched the second hand on his watch pass minute by minute. There was movement. It was Hepp circling the parking lot on foot. What was he looking for? Then he moved toward the aquarium door and entered.

It was too risky to follow Hepp into the aquarium. Crowley calibrated his options. If Lazzo exited earlier than Hepp, the sniper attempt was on. If they both came out roughly the same time, everything was off.

Crowley grew cold. A half-hour had passed and no one had exited. More minutes passed by as Crowley anguished over what might be happening. Did they strike up a conversation about the rare fish? Could Lazzo be involved with Hepp—maybe in the extortion business?

It was one in the morning. The chill penetrated his body. Minutes ticked silently. At 1:15 a.m., the entrance door opened and the doorstop engaged. A hand truck loaded with a large bundle was wheeled out the door. Crowley spotted Lazzo scan the area. He pushed the loaded hand truck across the parking lot toward a VW bus parked on a side street to the aquarium. Crowley carefully moved to a better view behind a large tree. He could make out Lazzo opening the side door and pushing the hand truck forward. With considerable effort, the load was shoved into the van. The door was shut. Lazzo righted the hand truck and pushed it with a near jog back to the aquarium entrance.

Minutes later, Lazzo exited the building scanning

again for any activity. He walked hurriedly toward the van. The engine started after three attempts. Lazzo directed the bus toward the campus exit with headlights turned off.

Crowley gathered the hunting rifle and headed for Shelly's VW bug. No activity in the area was apparent. He directed the bug to his family home. Crowley stashed the rifle back in the garage attic. He quickly pulled off his coat, shirt, and trousers. In minutes, he was asleep. Deep sleep dominated. The phone rang. It was eleven in the morning. Repeated rings did not rouse him. After the fifth attempt, Crowley turned over in bed and answered.

"Hello. Could you call later. I'm half-asleep."

"This is Shelly. Wake up, Ty. Just got a call from Scott's secretary, Belinda Fast. Scott's wondering why in the hell you are not answering the phone. There's been a murder at the hospital."

"Had a rough night with the booze. What's up?"

"It's really sick. A patient discovered a decapitated head in a fish tank."

"Where and who was murdered?"

"It was in an office in the aquarium and the victim was Fred Hepp. It is so eerie on Halloween. Who would commit such an act on this day?"

"I have no idea. As if I didn't have enough on my plate now. I suppose Scott wants me to get out front of this incident and spin a tale such that the Center is not seen as complicit such as lacking adequate security."

"I don't know what Scott wants. But I do want to know why you did not return my car. You said you were going out to the deli to get us something to eat. What happened?"

"I had to pick up some of my drafts of uncompleted

papers. I got into one on 'Contractual Paradigms and Attribution Theory.' I did some editing while downing too many drinks. I crashed at the desk. Woke up around three in the morning and went to bed," Crowley said.

"You could've called."

"Right. But this paper could be our ticket out of here."

Chapter 33

*Pieces of the Puzzle*
*November 7, Saturday Morning*

Turpin and Michael agreed to have morning breakfast at the Star Café early before the Saturday crowd arrived. Both ordered ham and eggs with buttermilk pancakes and a carafe of coffee. "Those photos have changed my thinkin' 'bout this case," Michael said.

"Me too. I still think the prime suspect could be this fake doc—Teagarden. But we have to add the possibility either Koeppen or the hippie Cohen would have the motive to wipe out Fred Hepp to eliminate those photos from ever being made public. I'm still wonderin' about Blaze. Was she a bystander or the praying mantis?" Turpin asked.

"Glad ta' see y'all is seein' things more clearly. By the way, I kinda' figured out your secret source. Audrey cleared that up for me. It was Zeke Cody, right?" Michael asked.

"Now that it's out, you got it right. I trust Cody unlike you, not so much. Do you still think after all we have uncovered about the drug business and extortion that somehow the administration could have been involved?" Turpin asked.

"Somethin' 'bout our first interview with Scott and

the rapid change of heart 'bout Audrey testifyin'. Someone in the administration knew of those photos, at least the one's with Koeppen."

"I don't get the connection."

"Remember, this Cody told y'all that Fred Hepp had made a deal with Koeppen to stop any complaints against him from being leaked. Cody never indicated his source. I went along with you believin' Audrey was the source. And it turns out, Audrey was aware of the photos and led us to them. However, let's go back. Remember Dr. Gomez when asked 'bout the hookup between Koeppen and Blaze Hepp said 'no comment.' Who ratted the affair to Gomez? Coulda' been someone from the administration—like this Crowley dude Blaze fingered."

"I don't see how this Crowley or anyone else could've known of the photos. The only one who knew 'bout them was Audrey."

"Jest a hunch, but how 'bout Crowley? Maybe Hepp threatened Crowley to disclose the photos of Koeppen bangin' his wife to higher ups if he did not close the deal on the law suit?" Michael asked. "It's clear the big dawgs wanted Koeppen out. And they also wanted Hepp out, but he was protected by the union and Koeppen. It's possible Scott pushed for Audrey's testimony to allow investigators to expose what Cody had heard from patients. And, this Ty Crowley was the dude to make it happen."

"What are you driving at?"

"Strictly a hunch, but if Crowley was the point person to make everything happen. He could be our guy," Michael said.

"I still don't get it."

"Yesterday, I got to thinkin' none of suspects fit

what we know. Who had access to the aquarium, the tanks, and maybe a hose to clean up the mess if that's where Hepp lost his head? I went back to the aquarium and looked to see where cars were parked during the day. Someone who parked there that night could have stood out to campus security makin' rounds. I checked with Campus Security Guard Fred Thompson who was on duty that night if he had noticed any out-of-state cars or any other unusual car that stood out that night," Michael said. "Thompson said none that he could recall."

Michael took a sip of coffee. "Maybe it was luck, but I noticed this VW bug with flower decals on the windows parked across the street where Thompson and I were standing in the parking lot. I asked Thompson about the VW bug. He said that belonged to one of the secretaries. When I pressed him, he thought it was Ty Crowley's secretary. And here's the clincher. I asked him if the car was regularly parked in that spot routinely. He nodded yes. 'How 'bout the night of the murder?' When he took out his pocketknife to clean his nails, he turned his head to a parking spot a block from the administration building. Then he looked at me and he said 'Yes. I remember wonderin' why her car was parked there so late at night?'"

"Maybe you are on to something."

"Again, refresh your memory. Blaze said 'Ask Crowley.' It's clear to me Crowley and Fred Hepp were involved in some kinda deal," Michael said.

"Why was his secretary's car parked near the aquarium the night of the murder?"

"My take is this. The car was there because for some god-only-knows reason Crowley set up a meetin' with Hepp after his shift to settle matters—like the lawsuit and Koeppen. He borrowed his secretary's car to avoid detection that he was at the hospital the night he met with Hepp."

Michael placed his over-easy eggs between the flapjacks and poured a raspberry syrup over the stack. "I think we need to see what Crowley has to say about the night."

"Before you down those pancakes?"

"Not that hungry. Think we gettin' close to the goal line. Let's bust up the middle with the center fakin' a hike to the quarterback and takin' it in."

"Like fakin' Crowley that we've got testimony that his secretary was not at his office that night but her car was?" Turpin asked.

"You my man!"

Michael rang the doorbell a couple of times. Crowley opened the door after the third attempt. His eyes were red and cheeks flushed. His tie was loosened and bottomed-down-collared shirt rumpled. His pants were unzipped and his shoes removed.

"I'm Sergeant Dyson and this is Detective Turpin. Y'all mind if we ask a few questions - that is if you okay? Looks like y'all have been into the hair of the dawg that bit ya'."

"Nothing but a hard night of editing a manuscript. What brings you two here on a weekend?" Crowley asked.

"We have reason to believe yawl was makin' some kinda deal with Fred Hepp before he was murdered," Michael said.

"That's my job to negotiate with stakeholders such that their social contracts with the agency align with our mission," Crowley said.

"If I git your jive, y'all were tryin' to figure out a way to git Fred Hepp to shit or get off the pot."

"That implies I was somehow involved in some kind of nefarious move. That's not my MO."

"Let's get to the bottom of what we know so far," Turpin said. "We know you were meeting with Hepp to settle matters the administration had directed you to handle."

"I don't deny I met with Fred Hepp. That's my role here."

"Would one of those meetings been the night of the murder?" Michael asked.

"God you two don't have clue. Why on earth would I meet with a ward attendant after their midnight shift was over?"

"So, y'all was aware of Hepp's work schedule. In fact, you knew that Hepp was not headed back to his home but actually to the aquarium, right?" Michael asked.

"I don't know where all this conjecture is going, but I think it best we do not go any further without an attorney," Crowley said.

"Your secretary is Shelly Bower, right? Doesn't she drive one of them beetles…one with some flowers slapped on the windows?" Michael asked.

"You'll have to ask her."

"Her beetle was there at the aquarium the night of the murder, but Shelly was not in your office," Michael said.

"Sometimes I take her home and she leaves her car there."

"That's weak Crowley. Why not tell us what

happened. The VW bug was there because you didn't want anyone to know you were on campus that night. Let me go further. You met with Hepp and confronted him that you were aware of his drug business. You threatened him. Either he shut down the lawsuit against the administration and get behind efforts to sack Koeppen, or you would inform authorities. Hepp got very angry and as he came at you. You picked up a heavy object and hit his head with such force he was bleedin' out his nostrils. You grabbed a rope or small cable and finished him off by strangling him," Turpin said.

"Such a fantasy. Where's the body?"

"You would know. Why not tell us?" Turpin asked.

"Is this all you've got?"

"Right now, you are a prime suspect," Turpin said. "We are fairly sure you met with Hepp at the aquarium. Blaze Hepp has implied you had at least one previous contact with Fred that did not go well for you. –And, Shelly Bower's version of what happened to her car the night of the murder could prove interesting. We think we have a case you had the motive and opportunity to slay Hepp."

"Let's review where we are," Crowley said. "You two have been misled from the beginning. You attributed nefarious schemes originating with the administration designed to take down those ideologically opposed to our reform efforts. No one in administration would ever endorse options leading to murder or any other assaultive remedy. However, I can't speak for any given staff member who may have felt so threatened by the victim they took out Hepp on their own."

"Is this a way of sayin' you at least considered takin' out Fred Hepp?" Michael asked.

"No. But I was convinced we could make a deal," Crowley said.

"And what might that be?" Turpin asked.

"If I tell you the whole story, will you agree to protect the innocent once this is revealed?"

"That depends. If you or others are criminally involved, all bets are off," Turpin said.

"No one in this administration, I can say unequivocally, is in any way involved in the murder of Fred Hepp," Crowley said.

"Y'all just said in fancy words you know a lot more. What else is missin'?" Michael asked.

"It's an extraordinary story. I'll tell all if this can be handled confidentially."

"Again, that depends. For example, explaining where were you the night of the murder…and did you meet Fred Hepp in the aquarium," Turpin said.

"I was not in the aquarium the night of the murder. If that is where we start, I can tell you what I do know."

"Okay, let's hear your version," Turpin said.

"First, Shelly Bower has nothing to do with anything I'm about to tell you. I did borrow her car to pick up food at a deli the night before the murder and did not return it until the morning Hepp was found in the fish tank. Hepp had insisted on the midnight meeting with me to reassure him the administration had confirmed his appointment as the new director of the Cook Center. Hepp two weeks earlier violently attacked me when I confronted him about his suspected criminal activity. We had heard that he was a suspect in drug theft. He nearly strangled me to death when I threatened to expose this evidence if he did not drop the lawsuit. I only survived that night by agreeing to not ever rat him out. Otherwise, he made it clear he would kill me or members of my family. To make good on my silence, he insisted we meet two weeks later at the aquarium after his midnight shift ended. I had to secure administrative proof he would be appointed as the new center director," Crowley said.

"So, you planned a preemptive strike given lives were on the line—yours and your family," Turpin said.

"That's not what happened. Let me finish—I surveilled the aquarium before midnight to check out Hepp's arrival. While checking out the entrance, I did observe someone entering the aquarium I did not recognize at first. Then it dawned on me it was the graduate student, Lazzo."

"How could you be so sure with the poor lighting?" Michael asked.

"Streetlights to the parking lot exposed the area. As for Lazzo, it was his beard and height. He's about six-four and also, I recognized his vehicle. I'll get to that shortly. After Lazzo went to the aquarium, I continued to look for Hepp. About ten minutes later Hepp entered the building. I was not certain why Lazzo showed up and whether it was safe to go into the building. I had heard rumors Fred Hepp had connections with Chicago crime bosses and I feared somehow, I was being set up. You have no idea how violent Fred Hepp was in our previous meeting," Crowley said.

"How 'bout identifyin' Lazzo's rig?" Michael asked.

"I'll get to that in a moment. I kept my eyes on the entrance for at least another hour. It was about one-thirty in the morning the entrance door opened and I observed Lazzo exit with a hand truck carrying a very large load wrapped in a tarp. Lazzo looked around and then headed for a VW bus. He opened the side door and with some effort shoved the bundle into the bus. He then returned the hand truck and locked the building. I spotted his headlights headed for the exit."

"That makes an interesting story, but somethin' missing. What motive would Lazzo have to kill Hepp unless maybe you made a deal with Lazzo to take care of Hepp given he was such a threat to you?" Turpin asked.

"I barely know Lazzo. I have dealt with Wentz. I'm quite pleased with the deal we made with his university."

"Did you manage to get Hepp appointed as the new director?" Turpin asked.

"No. It was all a ruse."

"So, you're tellin' us you were gonna go into the aquarium after Hepp arrived knowin' y'all were gonna get your ass kicked or worse for not nailin' down his new position?" Michael asked.

"I'm not that naïve. I brought along a target revolver in case Hepp attacked me, strictly for self-defense."

"Or to take Hepp out. Everything you said about Lazzo actually could apply to you," Turpin said. "Let's see what happens when we bring both of you in."

"Of course, I need to consult an attorney if this is an arrest."

"Let's make it simple. If Lazzo tells us he has a witness that he was elsewhere, your ass is grass. If y'all ain't givin' us a hose job, I think you better bust your balls to get down to the station and get this cleared up. Otherwise, we will see you as a prime suspect. If Hepp's connected, y'all know the end of that story," Michael said.

"I don't know what happened between Lazzo and Hepp. There's little doubt Hepp was killed and Lazzo took the body somewhere. I'm taking a calculated risk, but if you officers respect the innocent, I plead that you honor my request for confidentiality after you find out what happened," Crowley said.

"We'll see how this plays out. Get your jacket. It's pretty chilly out there," Turpin said.

On the way to the police station, Michael called dispatch and asked for Lazzo's address. The apartment was within a mile of the station. "Let's swing by and see if Lazzo's bus is nearby," Dyson said.

A VW bus was parked near the address. "Is that the bus you saw the night of the murder?" Turpin asked.

"Yes. I remember the sliding door and the dent on the front door. It was too dark to see the color of the bus…but it was a lighter tone…maybe the orange-tan color of this one."

"There's one way to nail this down," Michael said. "Now stop and let me out. Make a call to Lazzo tellin' him we would like him to come in for questionin'. I'll take cover nearby the bus and wait. If he panics and makes a dash for the bus, I'll be there to greet him."

After dropping off Michael at the end of the block, Turpin patched in a call to Lazzo.

"Hello," Lazzo answered. "Who's calling please?"

"This is Detective Turpin. Would you mind coming to the police station? We would like to ask a couple of questions about your research."

"I'm just headed out to collect fish samples. Could we handle this Monday?" Lazzo asked.

"Not really. We have a person of interest that claims you were in the area of the aquarium the night of the murder," Turpin said.

"I've already told you I was watching television that

night and went to bed," Lazzo said.

"Why don't you come down to the station," Turpin said. "It won't take long to get this sorted out."

"I can't do that now. Those samples are important. Goodbye." Lazzo ran out of his apartment and headed for his bus.

Michael stepped forward from the side of an apartment building and confronted Lazzo. "Hey, now where might y'all be headed?"

Lazzo stopped and turned toward Dyson. "Is this a police state like some third-world country?"

"Maybe on the subject of civil rights, but not in this deal. You can cooperate and come in peacefully or I may have ta' kick some ass. How's it gonna be?" Michael asked.

"Let's get it over," Lazzo said.

****

Lazzo was directed to the interrogation room. "Let me read you Ty Crowley's signed statement," Turpin said. Crowley's flowery statement sprinkled with legalese established where he was hidden during the night of the murder and what he had observed.

"Look, this is a case of mistaken identity. Crowley's either has very poor vision or is trying to pin a murder on me," Lazzo said.

"Except you hauled ass right to your bus when my pardner asked you to come in. Why would you make a beeline like that if y'all is innocent?" Michael asked.

"I panicked—just like a lotta people do when they think the police have something on you when it's absolutely untrue," Lazzo said. "You gotta believe me. It was late and the lighting was poor. Someone who had my features like a beard and had a VW bus coulda' carried out an execution."

"How would y'all know anything 'bout lighting that night?" Michael asked. "I'll answer that one. You were scannin' the parkin' lot and beyond to check nobody had seen ya'."

"There were other nights I worked late on my research and sometimes it was hard to find my car due to the poor lighting."

"Glad y'all brought up your research. We've invited your professor here to find out what's left for y'all to do to get that piece of paper," Michael said. "Wait just a moment."

Turpin entered the interrogation room with Professor Wentz. "Hello William. I can't imagine what this is all about?" Wentz asked.

"It's mistaken identity. Dr. Wentz tell them how I often work late at night."

"Yes, William often burns the midnight oil working on his research and reading a wide range of topics related to fish."

"We established earlier that your graduate student William uses surgical instruments in his research, correct?" Turpin asked.

"Yes."

"We checked for blood traces and found none. Wasn't it your routine and William's to sterilize the instruments before placing them in special containers?"

"Yes, that's standard procedure."

"Could I have a private moment with ya' professor?" Michael asked.

"Sure."

Michael and Wentz stepped out into the hallway.

"Jist' wonderin'. Would Lazzo have any reason to

break into your office?"

"No. That's where we keep our dissection and sterilization tools."

"But you told us previously you keep it locked. Why?" Michael asked.

"Frankly, I didn't want anybody in my office that was not linked to research."

"Did Lazzo have a key to your office?"

"No. He had access when I was there if he needed research tools," Wentz said.

"Could you tell me if you're his boss? Like our setup—If the chief thinks you're a good cop, you get a step up the ladder?"

"It's not exactly like that, but close. Doctoral students have three hurdles beyond passing their coursework requirements. One hurdle is completing a research project. A second hurdle is to pass comprehensive qualifying exams in areas considered basic to the field of emphasis. In my specialty, a student would need to know the basic biology of all living organisms in addition to specialized concentration on the study of fish," Wentz said. "And the third hurdle is to successfully defend their thesis results to faculty."

Do y'all have anything to do with gradin' Lazzo?" Michael asked.

"Yes, but it's more complicated than simply assigning a grade."

"I'm not sure I understand. What 'bout passin' those basic exams? How does that work?" Michael asked.

"In our graduate program, we as faculty all submit essay questions for students who have completed their course of study. These are broad questions that cover major core areas such as asking a candidate to defend or critique the theory of evolution as applied to fish,"

"Do you submit some of these questions on his basic exams?" Michael asked.

"Of course."

"Do y'all have those questions in a file somewhere?"

"Yes. They're in rough draft form in my file cabinet in the aquarium."

"Would you mind returnin' back to the interrogation room?" Michael asked.

"Happy to."


"Jest checked with the professor and he gave me a rundown on what it takes to get that piece of paper so folks can call you 'Doctor.' Now one of those hurdles is, if I get this right, passin' a final exam that covers your field, is that right?"

"Yes."

"So, sometimes do grad students fail those exams?" Michael asked.

"That's possible."

"Would that apply to you?"

"Of course. But I'm confident that won't happen," Lazzo said.

"I don't like what you are implying. William is one of our bright researchers who would not need to get an edge. He's a top student as determined by his undergraduate and graduate performance and scores on the Graduate Record Exam," Wentz said.

"I appreciate what you are sayin' but let's hear from William. Why are you so confident y'all will pass those exams?" Michael asked.

"It's simple. A lot of study."

"And if y'all fail, what would you do?"

"Never thought about it."

"I have no idea where a fish guy who failed to qualify as a doc would end up. Maybe workin' at a bait shop. My point is your goal I suspect is to have a career like the professor. Anything short of that would be hard to deal with, right?" Michael asked.

"That's my goal which everyone would agree is no different from other grad students."

"That's right, William, except y'all took it one more step. You were after an insurance policy. Let's try this out. You burned the midnight oil the night of murder for one reason. You were after Professor's questions for that final exam. You know, the qualifying exams, right?" Michael asked.

"I did not need to cheat. I'm confident of my knowledge of the field."

"That's right Sergeant Dyson. William has excelled in all his coursework. He's very creative in constructing research problems that potentially will advance our knowledge of fish reproduction," Wentz said.

"While you had no reason to cheat from what the professor jist' said about you, you could not take any chances. You realized any position as a professor or researcher was unlikely at least with the big dawgs if you failed. You figured no one would be around after midnight. You borrowed the Professor's keys, copied them, and broke into his office to see if you could locate the questions in his files. The shocker—Fred Hepp caught you and you panicked. You picked up a heavy object and hit him in the head," Michael said.

"Where's your evidence for any of this?"

"Crowley testified you entered the aquarium just

past midnight and he says Hepp entered the building minutes later. An hour later, Crowley identified you leaving the aquarium with a hand truck transportin' a large load. You had access to the fish tanks and were familiar with the tank cleanin' area. Wonder what we'll find if we impound your bus? And what about where y'all gettin' your fish out of the river. If we dragged the area for a body, what might we find?" Michael asked.

"None of this means anything. This was a gruesome murder. Anybody who did this is sick. It's clear either some kind of psychopathic killer like in the news or some kind of person who had a vendetta is responsible. How do I fit any of those profiles?"

"Who said you did?" Michael asked. "I think this is how y'all wanted others to think—It was a psycho or hit job. But I think in the final analysis, it was a snap judgment. You could see everything you'd worked for goin' down the drain when Hepp appeared."

"It's all mistaken identity. Check Ty Crowley's vision. Those coke-bottle lenses suggest he could have easily been mistaken as to who entered and exited the building."

"Let's check that out. We can invite Ty Crowley in to see what he has to say 'bout identifyin' you," Michael said. A few minutes later, Ty Crowley entered the interrogation room accompanied by Turpin.

"We'all asked you here Crowley to clear up jist' how you identified William Lazzo entering the aquarium. How far were y'all from the entry to the buildin'? And if it was over a hundred yards, how well with your glasses could you identify William Lazzo?" Michael asked.

"It was near a tree some distance from the door that

I identified William. His beard and facial characteristics are easy to distinguish. As for my vision, I'm somewhere around 20/25 vision," Crowley said.

"'Bout how far were you from the entrance as compared to a football field?" Michael asked.

"Maybe the length of a football field, maybe longer."

"Now you told us you had a handgun with you that night. Lazzo claims you are makin' up this whole thing to cover up what you did. If y'all took the trouble to stake out the aquarium at that distance, I don't get it. If you had the shit beat outta' ya' in your previous meetin' with Hepp, it makes no sense you would git around Hepp at any distance with no witnesses or protection other than the handgun. So, at that distance I wonder, did y'all have somethin' that would take down Hepp at a distance, say a long-range rifle?" Michael asked.

"I realize this case comes down to proof of positive identification. Yes, I was hidden and I had my dad's rifle. It was strictly self-defense. There was no question Hepp was determined to kill me one way or another if I didn't show him his demands had been met," Crowley said.

"Did this rifle have a scope?" Michael asked.

"I did have a long rifle with a scope there that night. I want to emphasize again it was for self-defense. The best way to deal with Hepp was in the parking lot at a distance. When William arrived, that changed everything. I anticipated once William left, I could more clearly figure out what to do. If Hepp realized after Lazzo had left that I was a no-show or anyone else, I expected him to exit heading to the parking lot. This is when I planned to confront him at a distance with a rifle in hand." Crowley said. "I wanted to make it clear to

Hepp I was willing to take him out by legal means or with a rifle if he made any more threats to me or my family."

"Did you use the scope to monitor the aquarium entrance?" Turpin asked.

"As to vision that night, I could see clearly through the scope of the rifle it was William Lazzo who entered the building and exited with the hand truck," Crowley said. "I think you will find I've won awards for target shooting using a special handgun. My vision and steadiness are exceptional for such competition. I realize what I'm about to reveal may incriminate me, but it is in the best interests of all parties that this case is closed."

"So, let me get this right," Turpin said. "You had the rifle for only self-defense—a rifle with a scope over a hundred yards away?"

"No point in misleading you. I considered taking Hepp out. But the fact of the matter is I did not. No one has reported hearing any gunshot because it never happened. Hepp's body left the aquarium bundled with some kind of tarp and rope. I'll leave it to William to reveal what he used for a murder weapon and why Hepp's head ended up in a fish tank," Crowley said.

"There's nothing to explain. You don't have to go to the movies like 'Psycho' to deduce the killer is a psychopath who has a screw loose. Ask about Crowley's past," Lazzo said.

"That's what you wanted everybody to think," Michael said. "The question should be directed at you. It's time for y'all to tell us who your partner is. This could save your ass if they back up your story you were watchin' TV the night of the murder."

"I've explained I can't do that. Especially now that

this is all gonna be reported in the press at some point."

"I don't get it. You're willin' to take a murder rap to protect someone who could be your ace in the hole, an alibi witness?" Michael asked.

"He doesn't deserve any scandal. He is the most loving, loyal, and sensitive human on the planet."

"Someone in the neighborhood musta' seen you two together," Michael said.

"Yes. Like when we got careless holding hands at the grocery store and this guy who was the manager told us to leave. He made it clear he wanted no fags touching anything in the store. So, you're probably right. You would have identified him at some point. His name is Kevin Koch. He's an untenured prof at MacMurray College. He's the love of my life. I would do anything for him. We dreamed of relocating to a larger city with a university. I needed to matriculate with no hiccups so we could live our lives in obscurity," Lazzo said.

"So, ya' reasoned that you needed that edge," Michael said.

"I'm tired of this whole process. It's unlikely you're gonna stop until I tell you what you want to hear." Lazzo rubbed his eyes and teared up. "Please, please—do one thing if you want the whole story. Never disclose Kevin's identity."

Chapter 34

*Aftermath*

A knock on the door stirred footsteps. The apartment door was opened. "Hello, I'm Detective Turpin and this is Sergeant Dyson. Does a William Lazzo share this apartment with you?"

"Why do you ask?"

"William Lazzo has confessed to the murder of Fred Hepp who was decapitated. Just want to clear up a couple of questions. Early in the investigation, William Lazzo indicated he was watchin' TV the night of the murder. He refused to reveal your identity as an alibi witness. For the record, did William Lazzo spend the evening and night of October 30th and 31st here as he first claimed?" Turpin asked.

"I don't want to fall prey to a trap. However, I answer this question, it does not bode well for William or anyone else," Koch said.

"To be clear, y'all's lover wants to keep it buried that you are shackin' up with him. Best to be truthful at this point," Michael said.

"God, I feel awful. I can't believe William confessed to murder—I mean it's not him. He's not a violent person, so slow to anger. I don't want to jeopardize him any further," Koch said.

"You were here when William received a phone call

yesterday, right?" Turpin asked.

"Yes."

"So, did William tell you who was on the phone? And did William explain where he was headed when he hung up?" Turpin asked.

"No to both questions. But to be honest, I thought something was wrong," Koch said.

"Did y'all talk 'bout the future?" Michael asked.

"Yes. We both planned to apply for an academic assignment in a larger city that would be more receptive to our lifestyle. William was aiming for a research position and I was hoping for an appointment in an English department with a specialization in modern American literature. This all came down to William completing his degree."

"So that piece of paper was all 'bout getting' outta here?" Michael asked.

"Right. And in a way, I feel responsible. William watched too much TV. I nagged him he had to get his priorities straight if we were ever to get out of Jacksonville. He loved his research but he was not into serious study for his qualifying exams," Koch said.

"Let's get a straight answer. Did you watch TV with William the night of the murder?" Michael asked.

"To answer your question honestly, William disappeared that evening and came in really late, like four in the morning. I feared the worse. He was cheating on me."

"Or how 'bout another version? Both of y'all talked before he left 'bout gettin' in Professor Wentz's files to make sure he passed?" Michael asked.

"Of course not. I'm tough on any of my students at MacMurray caught cheating," Koch said. He added,

"Can I visit William? I need to be with him now."

"Here's the deal. He doesn't want your identity revealed. That's impossible if you visit him in the holding cell," Turpin said.

"Coming out is the least of my concerns now. These are the times when love overpowers ridicule or worse," said Koch.

\*\*\*\*

*June 1971*

A jury of twelve, six women in their thirties and six men with post-graduate degrees found William Lazzo guilty of second-degree murder. Prosecutor Goldberg had charged the defendant with first-degree murder. The prosecutor argued in closing the defendant in cold-blooded fashion struck the victim with a golf club owned by Professor Wentz knocking him unconscious. When observing the victim was still breathing, he located a nylon rope to strangle him to death. He then decapitated the victim and placed his head in a fish tank. This was all done to mislead investigators to believe the murder was committed by a psychopathic killer from the hospital. His motive was clear, Prosecutor Goldberg emphasized. "Fred Hepp shocked the defendant when catching him rifling through the professor's files searching for exam questions. William Lazzo at that moment concluded all his dreams of an academic research career would evaporate if Fred Hepp was not eliminated."

The jury was hung for two days. The jury foreman initially was the lone holdout. He  requested jury members re-visit Ty Crowley's testimony. "The fact that Crowley had positioned himself in a sniper position the night of the murder showed to me his terror of Fred Hepp. If Lazzo does not show up, we could be sitting in the jury room trying Ty Crowley," the foreman said. "My point is we still do not know one way or another whether Hepp lunged at Lazzo as the defense argued on closing. It is not out of the question when Lazzo grabbed the professor's golf club, Hepp did a bull-rush toward Lazzo."

A woman juror with a background in treating autism agreed with the foreman. The thirty-five-year-old therapist said, "It seemed to me it was a stupid snap decision a lotta' God-fearing people make when so threatened they don't engage brain. It's like flippin' out when some guy on a four-lane highway cuts in front of you nearly takin' you and your family out." Other jurors offered strong opposition arguing such a heinous crime of strangling the victim after a lethal blow to the head indicated malice aforethought and deserved the maximum penalty. Some argued this was a case where the death penalty should have been an option.

As the hours passed, the foreman who in his private life had practiced dentistry for eighteen years requested that jurors ask the judge the legal definitions of first- and second-degree murder. Jurors agreed to submit the questions. In response, the judge cited legal definitions emphasizing the difference was based on whether the evidence proved the defendant had formed malicious intent prior to the murder. On that question, jurors debated for three hours as to whether Lazzo had formed intent in a split second to kill the victim when grabbing the golf club? Was strangling the victim later a coverup to make sure the victim never recovered to identify the defendant?

The foreman pressed for a verdict of second-degree murder given there was no testimony Lazzo had any reason to take out the victim, unlike Crowley. "There was no evidence Lazzo had any prior contacts with Fred Hepp or even knew who he was," the foreman said. The last hold-out who argued for the death penalty swung to the foreman's position that Lazzo had likely acted on impulse in self-defense.

*June 1972*

The state legislature and governor agreed that the Jacksonville State Hospital, aka "Center of Human Actualization," did not adequately serve the mentally ill and developmentally disabled. A year earlier, Sam Scott was sacked and most reformers resigned. The historic hospital was transformed to serve only the developmentally disabled.

Blaze Hepp was assigned to a witness protection status after revealing the names of key drug traffickers including mob bosses. Teagarden was taken into custody by the FBI. Initially, New Jersey prosecutors and the Department of Justice struck a deal with Teagarden to talk about his crime boss connections. Federal investigators found some leads helpful, but others were dead-ends. While being held in a federal facility in New Jersey, Teagarden was brutally stabbed and killed while taking a shower.

Dr. Gomez and his family moved to Miami-Dade County. Santiago and Virginia took possession of a home in a Latino neighborhood—many neighbors having immigrated from Colombia. He was appointed Director of a modern mental health facility located nearby.

Zeke Cody relocated to California and took on another reform promoting an alternative degree program to train clinical psychologists. Cody and other reformers recruited faculty to offer a new degree, the Doctorate of Psychology (Psy.D.). A distance learning center was created with a mission to substitute breadth of field courses required in Ph.D. programs with a major emphasis on clinical practicums. The new degree enabled mental health workers in a variety of settings to qualify as candidates for licensure to practice, teach, and in some settings engage in research.

Sam Scott took a position at a midwestern university and died shortly after his arrival. He suffered a massive brain aneurysm while driving to a conference in New York. Ty Crowley and Shelly Bower relocated to Manhattan. Crowley was hired as an adjunct professor for The New School of Social Work. Faculty resistance to his appointment grew. Critics claimed there was a conflict of interest where faculty in the department evaluate the performance of a cohort such as the case with Crowley seeking a terminal degree. Ultimately, Crowley was dismissed from his adjunct position. His drinking increased. Shelly returned to Illinois. Crowley's despair overshadowed everything including his drive to punditry. Within a year, Crowley died of exposure in an alley after binge drinking for two days.

Carla Fitzgerald remained in her position as a social worker long enough to ensure Shannon Audrey had her day in court and her rights restored. Her husband Charley Fitzgerald was offered a tenure-track position at Northern Arizona University. Mahalia Ross remained at the Cook Center. Dr. Koeppen was charged with rape. The press coverage over the salacious scandal with Blaze Hepp and exposure to possible links to the SS led to his disappearance. Investigation of possible war crimes continued.

Audrey's rights were restored. Shannon organized a grassroots organization in Chicago advocating the abolishment of involuntary commitment laws that denied patients the right to periodic reviews. Advocates suggested Audrey write her story of commitment and submit it to newspaper editors. Publications of her story gained national attention. Shannon was offered an ombudsman position for the mentally ill detained in Cook County jail. Her tireless advocacy much later led to a career with the National Alliance for the Mentally Ill. Essays were collated and published in a memoir that drew rave reviews. Her stories of the ordeals of the treatment of the mentally ill such as Vesta Diaz gave the public a critical perspective on the urgency of reform.

And as a final prologue, when the news broke that the Hepp case had been solved, the Jacksonville police union rewarded Turpin and Dyson with a party of well-wishers. There were several toasts and high-fives. The next morning, Chief Brady called Michael to his office. "I'm promoting you to detective. You've earned it." Michael looked up at the flickering fluorescent light and then made eye contact with Brady. "We need to talk."

## A word about the author...

Tale based on serving as a research director at an asylum, Jacksonville, Illinois during the 1960s. Later as a professor of psychology, I concentrated on studies of aggression and violence in student and clinical populations including mentally-ill offenders.

Thank you for purchasing
this publication of The Wild Rose Press, Inc.

For questions or more information
contact us at
info@thewildrosepress.com.

The Wild Rose Press, Inc.
www.thewildrosepress.com

www.ingramcontent.com/pod-product-compliance
Lightning Source LLC
Chambersburg PA
CBHW051139030726
47504CB00004B/949